THE INHERITANCE

THE INHERITANCE

A JOHANNA HUDSON MYSTERY

R. FRANKLIN JAMES

CAVEL
PRESS

Kenmore, WA

CAMEL PRESS

A Camel Press book published by Epicenter Press

Epicenter Press
6524 NE 181st St.
Suite 2
Kenmore, WA 98028

For more information go to:
www.Camelpress.com
www.Coffeetownpress.com
www.Epicenterpress.com
www.rfranklinjames.com

Cover design by Scott Book
Interior design by Melissa Vail Coffman

The Inheritance
Copyright © 2021 by R. Franklin James

ISBN: 978-1-60381-737-0 (Trade Paper)
ISBN: 978-1-60381-741-7 (eBook)

Printed in the United States of America

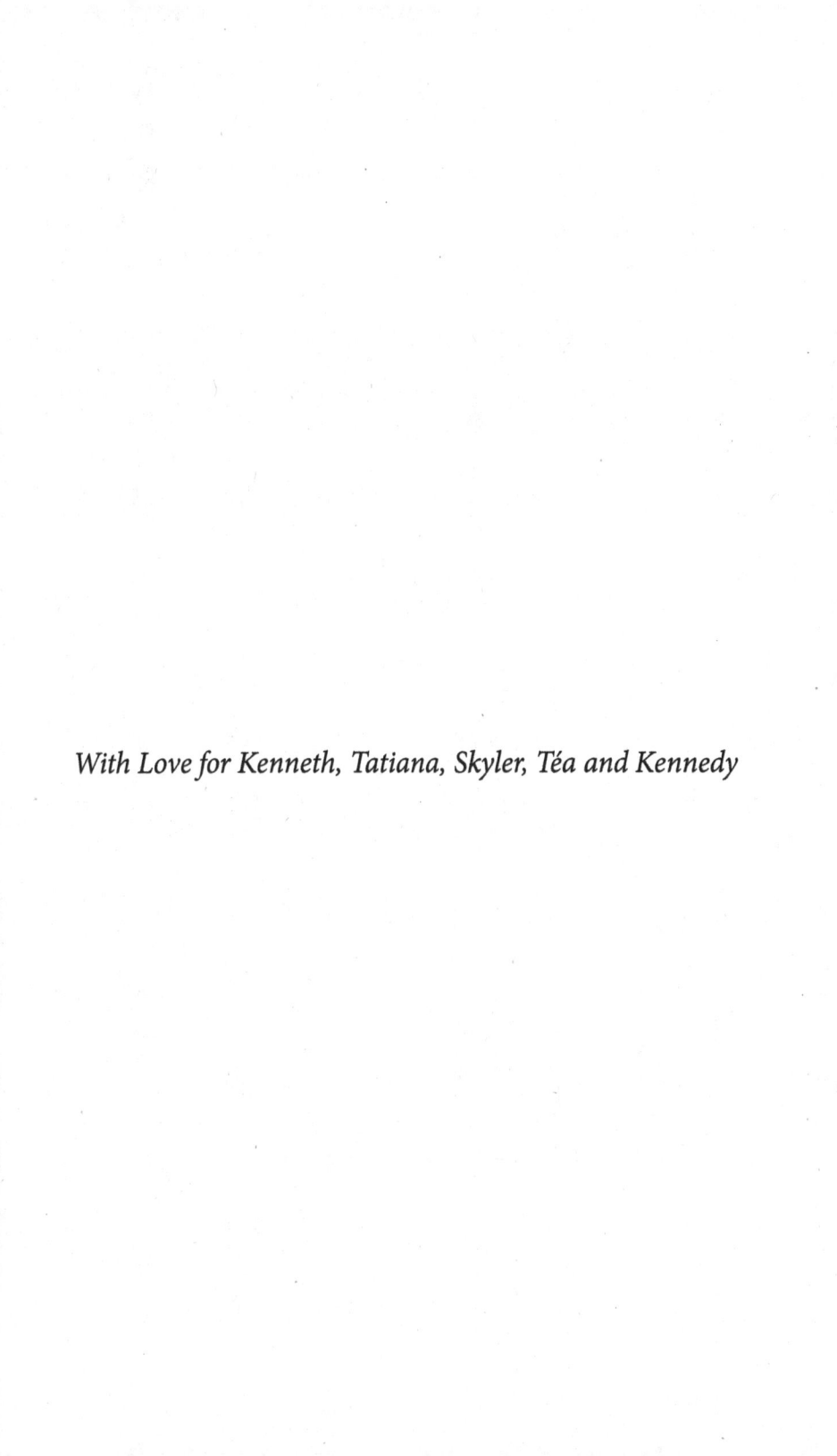

With Love for Kenneth, Tatiana, Skyler, Téa and Kennedy

ACKNOWLEDGMENTS

THERE ARE SO MANY WHO LIFT ME UP and become the wind beneath my wings.

First and foremost I want to acknowledge Jennifer McCord editor, publisher and all-around supporter. Heartfelt thanks to everyone at Epicenter/Camel Press.

A big thank you to my critique group: Kathy Assay, Pat Foulk, Cindy Sample and Karen Phillips. Over the years, they have offered their expertise and traveled this road with me.

Then there are those who continue to inspire me to do better: Carol Oliveira, Barbara Lawrence, Patsy Williams, Penny Manson, Freddie Condos, Geri Nibbs, Joyce Pope, and Yolanda Vega.

CHAPTER ONE

"ONE THING CLIENTS DON'T CONSIDER is that genealogy outcomes can be disappointingly unpredictable," Johanna Hudson said into the office speaker phone. She closed the thick file she'd been holding with a slap like a period at the end of a sentence. "That's what I'm going to tell our client, that there's no reason to prolong providing the results. I have no other leads." She leaned back in her chair. "Brandon Reed was upset when I even broached the idea his family didn't come over on the Mayflower. Now that it's been confirmed, he's not going to be happy, but there is nothing anyone can do about it."

On the other end of the call was Ava Lowell, her business partner and friend, who was currently at the local public library on another research matter. Johanna glanced out the office window. If she leaned over in her chair she could see the San Francisco Bay Bridge in the space between two adjacent office buildings.

"Jo, I can't talk louder, I'm in the book stacks," Ava said in a loud whisper. "Can't you wait a few more days, please? I don't think we can afford to disappoint one of our biggest customers. Reed has a huge network of friends. He gave me an introduction to the Pattons, and I used him as a reference to get the Thorntons."

"I admit Geraldine Patton will be an interesting family tree to pursue, and the Thorntons were very happy with their charts," Johanna said. "In fact, I think we're going to sign another family thanks to Bill Thornton."

To Johanna, Ava's plea to hold back bordered on withholding information the client had paid for. Brandon Reed was thirty-four years old with aspirations of an aristocratic life. He'd shared that once his lineage was verified, he was prepared to propose to his long-time sweetheart. He wanted to impress her parents with his pedigree. To assist with Johanna's research, he'd presented her with carefully-preserved letters. Yellowed with age, they alluded to other letters from distant family members along his maternal line about a long-ago voyage. But after four months of intense searching, the value in the letters, though immensely interesting, was limited to insights into the history of the period. As a consequence, it appeared the only ship the unmarried, pregnant, and indentured Maria Obermayer, Brandon's seventh great-grandmother, boarded in the late 1700s was from France, not London.

"He should be fine. There is still good history and a worthy story," Johanna said. "Maria Obermayer was a cousin of Therese Obermayer."

"Yeah, so?"

Johanna clicked open a file on her laptop and scanned the table of family tree members. "Therese Obermayer was the mistress and eventual wife, of Johann Beethoven, brother of Ludwig."

There was a brief silence. "Well, I suppose there's something to be said for celebrity by association," Ava muttered. "I don't know, Jo, it's pretty slim."

"It's all I've got. It will help to balance out the fact that on his paternal line, his third great-grandfather was hung as a bank robber."

Ava laughed, and Johanna could hear her hurried mumbled apology to nearby library patrons.

JOHANNA HAD ALWAYS FELT HUDSON AND LOWELL, Legacy Consultants, sounded grander than the small nondescript office they leased in Milton Glen Business Park, high in the east bay hills overlooking the San Francisco Bay Area. Located adjacent to the city of Hayward, the town of Milton Glen was unincorporated, and relied on Maricopa County services. But what it lacked in government oversight, it made up in its small town setting. From time to time, the office had visitors, but to the greatest extent possible, they arranged to see potential clients in their clients' homes or offices.

This Monday, after clicking off with Ava, she added final comments to the Brandon Reed report.

No more stalling.

Johanna hoped her findings wouldn't be the reason he didn't marry the love of his life. At first, she put the report in a manila folder for mailing. Then, sighing with a shrug, she put the folder in her tote. It would go down easier if she presented it in person.

She waited for Reed's response to her text that she wanted to deliver the results.

Meantime, she checked phone messages and picked up the pieces of mail that had been pushed through the slot in the door. It was all advertisements, except for a notice from the American Society of Genealogists and a handwritten envelope with no return address. She frowned at the envelope; there was no postage. Her name was spelled with one 'n' and the address stopped at the street name, with no numbers or town.

Hand delivered? She opened the envelope and lifted out a piece of lined paper with a note scribbled in blue felt tip pen:

Ms. Hudson, I don't have a lot of money, but I need your help. I'm being cheated and Trini said you can help me. If okay, let Trini know and she will make arrangements. Eloise Manley.

Trini?

Johanna had to think a moment before she remembered the woman who cleaned their office in the evening. She knew her as Trinidad, probably named after her island of birth. Trinidad always brought a smile to Johanna's face. Her colorful clothing and wavy dark hair wrapped in a variety of joyful coordinated scarves, contradicted the woman's dour personality. When the property manager introduced her to Ava and Johanna, Trinidad had clutched a pendant around her neck and peered at them. Ava later commented she might have been calling up a curse.

"A curse?" Johanna had chuckled. "A warning maybe, but I do get the feeling she doesn't do windows."

She checked the time. Brandon had texted he was available to meet. Trinidad wouldn't be coming on duty for another three hours. She could present her report to Brandon Reed and be back in time to meet the cleaner.

Johanna ran her fingers through her dark brown curls and after a quick glance in her pocket mirror renewed her mascara and blush. With doe-brown eyes, she wasn't pretty but "attractive" was a label she could live with. Her favorite mauve tunic and black leggings showed off her slim frame. Gold earrings completed the picture. Packing up her briefcase, she tucked Eloise Manley's note in her purse and headed out the door.

THE REED HOME WAS PERCHED HIGH in the Berkeley hills over the Caldecott Tunnel. Johanna caught her breath as she took in the expanse of the four trans-bay bridges. The most magnificent, the Golden Gate gleamed bright against the deep blue of the sea. She never tired of the sight.

Stepping with care among the embedded clusters of ground cover and shrubs, she counted eighteen steps up to the first landing. After thirty steps, and another landing, she was more than a little winded. At last, reaching an elaborate stained glass double-door set into polished redwood siding, she pushed the doorbell.

"Johanna, you should have called me from your car," Reed's voice came through a small speaker situated below a disguised camera over the transom. "I'll be right there."

Moments later, the door opened. Brandon Reed would not be called handsome but his affable personality was evidenced in a welcoming smile. His gray slacks held a sharp crease and his black V-neck sweater revealed an attractive glimpse of dark chest hair, and his eyes appeared to hold a cunning that put Johanna on guard.

"I forgot this is your first time here," he said, stepping aside to let her in. "These homes must have been designed by mountain goat owners. My parents had to put in a custom elevator around that cluster of tall shrubs next to the driveway."

Johanna, still winded, smiled, mentally vowing to renew her gym membership. "No worries. I'm glad you were able to see me on short notice."

"Hey, you've got my future in your hands. I can make time." He pointed toward what appeared to be a den off the entry. "We can meet in here. I'm housesitting until my parents return from Europe."

They took seats opposite each other in front of a deep fireplace covered in large river stones. Johanna looked around the spacious room. The huge bay window overlooked the tops of trees out onto San Francisco Bay. The morning fog layer hung like frosting between the gray waters and slivers of blue sky hovering over the Golden Gate. She had to tear her eyes away to focus on the purpose of her visit.

"Brandon," she said. "Let's go over our findings. Feel free to interrupt at any time if you have questions." Johanna opened her file and pulled out a folded page which, when opened, covered the coffee table. "This is your family tree."

It took under an hour to review the details of the Reed ancestors. Johanna took pains to fill-in with probable stories behind the names as they moved through the years. Brandon followed along with her presentation and perused the boxes of family members displayed over generations. She glided over the bank robber on his father's side without his questioning. It wasn't until she indicated the last box at the top of the page and finished her report that he spoke.

"What are you saying?"

Johanna stiffened, noticing the strained shift in his tone. "I know you were counting on hearing you had ancestors on the Mayflower, but we weren't able to confirm that story," she said. "We did locate a female on your mother's line who sailed on one of the earliest ships to New France, or what we know today as Canada."

Brandon stood and began pacing. "My mom said her family could be traced back to the earliest arrivals of the pilgrims in Plymouth," he protested. "I made it a big deal and told my fiancée's family I was getting documentation. I can't tell them my ancestor was a single mother, and a servant at that. You can't even assure me Josephine ever got married."

"No, I can't, but Brandon—"

"Wait, I know." He ran his hand over his head and started pacing again. "You said her cousin was having an affair with Beethoven's brother. Maybe Maria's baby belonged to Ludwig Beethoven."

"Whoa." Johanna held up her hand. "First of all, Maria Obermayer had her baby *before* Johann ever knew her cousin, Therese—a year before. I already checked. It is unlikely she was acquainted with Ludwig." She took a moment to think about her next words, and then continued, "You have no reason to be ashamed. Your ancestors can be traced to people who populated and built North America."

"Yeah, right. You don't understand. My fiancée is a thoroughbred. Her mother is a member of the DAR."

Johanna raised her eyebrows. A Daughter of the American Revolution was not a membership to sneeze at, but there wasn't a lot Brandon could do about his background now.

"Brandon, I—"

"Your work is confidential, right? I mean, you can't tell anyone what you found, right?"

"Well, no, we promise complete confidentiality," she said. "However, what I found was in public records. Except for the letters you gave me, anyone who was determined could find out the same."

He shook his head. "Nope, those letters are what got you started. Without those letters a person would hit a block wall after a few generations." He scowled. His eyes moved from side to side as if reading a book.

"This could still work," he muttered.

It was at this point Johanna didn't want to know how this "could still work." She gathered her briefcase and purse.

"Why don't you read through our report at your leisure?" she said, standing. "Take some time to go over your family tree, and don't hesitate to contact me if you have any questions. Now, where's that elevator?"

He looked up from his thoughts.

"What? Oh, over here," Brandon said, guiding her to a narrow door not far from the front one. "Thank you for all your hard work. Invoice me, and I'll send you my final payment."

Back in her car, Johanna went over the meeting in her head. Considering Brandon Reed's obvious disappointment, things had gone well. She put aside the likelihood he was ready to embellish his ancestors' lineage despite her disclaimers.

She glanced at the time. There was less than an hour to get back to work and the conversation with Trinidad.

WHEN JOHANNA ARRIVED AT THE OFFICE, Ava was the only one there. Trinidad was late. Johanna quickly took her partner through her meeting with Brandon Reed.

"He stopped listening to me," she concluded, opening her briefcase to remove papers. "I definitely got the feeling our client was contemplating editing our results."

"You can't please everybody," Ava said, shaking her head. "Did you tell him not to use our name as producers of his revised family chart?"

Johanna nodded. She looked on from her cubicle as Ava readied her briefcase to meet with a potential client. Their business was slowly, but steadily, growing. It had started with a loan from Johanna's grandmother, and Ava's cashed-out annuity. After living off parental grants for the first year, word of mouth referrals were now starting to pay off. They weren't in the black yet, and there were no real profits, but they were covering overhead and both took a very small salary—every so often.

Ava Lowell was in her forties but looked thirty. Like Johanna she'd been born and raised in the Bay Area, but unlike her colleague, Ava had married out of high school, divorced twenty-three years later and then entered college to study anthropology. Sandy brown hair, deep blue eyes and just shy of six feet, she carried herself with confidence.

"Anthropology is rewarding," she'd once told Johanna. "Besides I think I have a phobia of the present. In the present, I always feel I have to justify myself."

Johanna replaced the Reed paperwork in the closed file drawer.

"You ready for your trip?"

Her partner ran her fingers down a list of "to-do" items typed on a sheet of paper. "I better be." She looked up at Johanna. "By the way, from the Manley note you showed me, you could be facing an interesting challenge. It didn't sound like our typical client."

"I think you're right. But I'm not traveling on our client's dime halfway around the world. That's not typical either."

"Agreed. The Watson's chart could be real exciting," Ava said. "It's an old Gilroy family with ties to Australia. And I've always wanted to go to Sydney."

"Sydney is a little far for me," Johanna said. "I'll stay here to cover the home base. Did you prepare the Watsons for the possibility their origins may include a prison colony?"

"That's just it, he's banking on it. He and his wife are hoping we can find that their great, great, great-grandparents served prison time in New South Wales, before it was Sydney. He's trying to get a documentary funded and thinks it might help his platform."

In the years since starting the business, Johanna had already heard varied and unbelievable reasons for persons wanting to explore their heritage—from simple curiosity to qualifying for an ancestor's college scholarship, to clearing a paternity question. Their periodic live workshops at the community library had provided a major source of clients who wanted their ancestors revealed. Although, it was their referral clients, like Brandon Reed, who brought them the higher paying, if not more complex, cases.

Ava cleaned her black-framed eyeglasses with a tissue and looked at the clock. "Well, I think I've stalled as long as I dare to hear Trinidad's story, but I've got to go do last minute errands," she said. "Remember everything Trinidad says, and we'll talk over coffee tomorrow."

She dashed out the door.

In the silence that followed, Johanna could hear the faint sound of a vacuum in one of the other offices. Good, her curiosity about Trinidad was making her crazy. She went back to the papers on her desk. Forty-five minutes later, Trinidad tapped on the glass door and poked her head in.

"It okay I clean?"

Johanna waved her in. "Yes, come in. There's something I want to talk with you about." She pointed to a chair next to hers.

Trinidad's eyes widened; it was evident she was unsure about sitting on the job. She looked over her shoulder and then back at Johanna. With a nervous smile, she took a seat. Johanna handed her the note she'd received.

Trinidad barely looked down at the paper before handing it back. "I wrote note for Eloise. She told me what to say."

Johanna leaned back into her chair. "You want to tell me what it's about?"

Trinidad was not a large woman. With small sharp features and the longest eyelashes Johanna could ever wish for, Trinidad could pass for any age. Never shy with the color spectrum, she wore a lime green floral blouse, yellow pants and had woven a lime green and yellow scarf into her hair. Her skin was the color of milk chocolate, and the combination made Johanna think of the islands.

"You wait to end to ask questions," the cleaner directed. "Eloise is my neighbor, she live by herself. She has a boyfriend, but he come and go, and that is her business. She younger than me and a good woman. She good and kind." She moistened her lips. "About two weeks ago, a man came to her door asking for Eloise Sutton. I was not there. Eloise was scared. Sutton was her name before she lived in a foster home. She took the name Manley from the family who raised her."

"Why would she be scared?"

The question slipped out, and Johanna did not miss Trinidad's look of reproach.

"I will tell you my way. No more questions until end."

"Sorry, of course."

"This man said he was looking to give Eloise Sutton her inheritance. Her mother's mother wanted to find her. He say she not close to Eloise's mother but wanted to know if Eloise was her granddaughter. Eloise father didn't know he had a daughter." Trinidad took a bottle of water out of her deep pocket and sipped. "Anyway, Eloise already tell me her mother didn't want anything from her father that why she never told him about Eloise."

Johanna didn't try to suppress a deep "ah."

"Yes, I know, I do same," Trinidad said. "But Ellie is suspicious. She wants to know what's in it for her grandmother, who she never know for years. And, most important, this man, how he find her?"

She reached down once more, picked up her bottle of water and took a long swallow.

Johanna gave Trinidad credit for the sense of drama and remained silent. Trinidad gave her an approving nod.

"I cut story short," she said, straightening her shoulders. "The man said if she was the Eloise Sutton he was looking for, she could be entitled to share of her father's estate—millions of dollars of estate. If he is her father, he is dying and his lawyers are looking for all his heirs. But the man still didn't tell her how he found her, and he wanted her to sign paper that gave her grandmother and him per . . . partage of money she might get."

"A percentage," Johanna corrected with a murmur.

"Yes, yes, percentage," Trinidad said. "The paper say he wanted percentage, but Eloise not like him and told him she not know Eloise Sutton. Of course, she wanted money but not to work with *him*. Anyway he was furious she didn't jump at chance. He balled up his fists. She told me she thought he was going to hit her." She wrinkled her nose in distaste. "Then he said—he said he would be back to see if she changed her mind."

Her words hung between them. Trinidad leaned back in her seat and nodded for Johanna to ask her questions.

"What does she want me to do?" Johanna said, reaching behind her for a note pad and pen. "Sounds like she needs a private detective, or maybe a lawyer."

"I tell Ellie you find people. That you can find her father's and his people. She won't need the man."

"Ah, I don't know. I can try to help her. She would have to give me any details she knows about her father." Johanna scribbled a note. "On the other hand, I could start with her maternal grandmother. But you said she's stayed distant. Is she nearby?"

Trinidad shrugged. "I don't know. The man has information about grandmother. He didn't give her name. Ellie not know her grandmother. Like I said, she never see her since her mother died when she was five."

Johanna frowned. That answered her question about Eloise being raised in a foster home.

"How and when did her mother die?" she questioned.

"In prison." Trinidad said. "She died while serving time for killing her husband."

CHAPTER TWO

JOHANNA'S STARTED IN DISBELIEF. "WAIT A minute, let me get things straight." She wrinkled her forehead. "Eloise went into a foster home when she was five, because her mother was sent to prison for murdering her father. But you said he just died or may be dying. What's with that?"

"Her mother killed her husband, not Ellie's father." Trinidad's arms crossed her chest. "I figure this out myself when I try to help Eloise. She stay with foster family all her life, but they never adopt her. Even though she use their name. When she was growing up, they told her about her mother in prison. Her mother died of tuberculosis when Ellie was twelve, and people said she could go to funeral. She did. But Ellie never see her mother's face. She not remember what she looks like. It's very sad."

Johanna took notice of the concerned expression on Trinidad's features. The woman looked away and cleared her throat.

"So, she'd had an affair with Eloise's birth father?" Johanna prodded.

Trinidad nodded. "I make story short again. I figure it out. The Manleys told Ellie that her mother's husband was a bad man." Trinidad gestured as if wiping her hands. "Her real father didn't know about Eloise. Maybe he knew about her mother's death, I don't know. But now this man come, and I tell Ellie her grandmother must think there is money to be had, or maybe she wants to get to know her granddaughter before she crosses over. Either way, I see you and other one look for things. I see you pick up little pieces to find families. I tell Ellie, you can help her and get paid later."

Johanna would have laughed if she wasn't so taken off guard. Deferred payment aside, this project wasn't going to be as simple as it seemed at first, but it had captured her curiosity.

"I can try. When can I talk with Eloise?" she asked. "Where does she live?"

Trinidad scowled. "All you do is ask questions. Do you ever have any answers?"

"Sometimes," Johanna pushed back. "But you came to me. If I'm going to help Eloise, I'm going to have a lot more questions. So. . . ."

"All right, is true." Trinidad nodded in agreement. "Ellie live in trailer park in Castro Valley, the Whispering Oaks off Redwood Road. I live three spaces down and across from her. She work part-time at studio in Hayward during the day so I help her sometimes before I go to work."

The word "work" must have caught her attention. She looked over her shoulder at the clock on the wall and stood.

"I got to go back to cleaning. I talk too long."

Johanna stood.

"Trinidad, tell Eloise I will meet with her," she said. "If you want to be there too, we can get together on Saturday if it helps your work schedule."

"Thank you very much. I tell her and talk back to you."

Johanna said with a forced straight face, "Good."

IT WAS ALMOST SEVEN O'CLOCK IN THE EVENING when Johanna put away the last dish from dinner. The silence in her townhouse greeted her like an unwanted guest. She looked out the patio doors into the small private yard that held a shade tree and a bed of impatiens. Years ago she would have had music blasting from the sound system. She loved Spanish classical guitar. But that was before . . . . Now, she hated music and the memories that came with it.

She shook her head.

She wasn't going down that road, because down that road "there be dragons."

The phone in her purse buzzed.

"I was hoping you'd be home," her mother said. "I want you to come with me to MOMA Tuesday evening. I got tickets to see the Whistler exhibit."

Johanna was glad her mother couldn't see the expression of rejection on her face. "Mom, I can't take the time to go into San Francisco tomorrow. I'm working with a new client, and I need to do some research before our meeting on Saturday."

Elizabeth Girard was silent for a moment.

"How much of what you just said is a lie?"

Johanna chuckled. "About twenty percent, but I do have someone I hope to sign as a client."

"You used to love go to the Museum of Modern Art," her mother chided, her voice gathering steam. "You cannot bury yourself in that sterile house of yours. You're just thirty-one. It's been over a year and—"

"How long should it take, Mother?" Johanna snapped. "Am I off schedule? My house is sterile because by the time I removed everything that caused me pain and . . . and remembrance, there . . . there was nothing left. The house was empty, and I was empty."

"I know, sweetheart, but you've got to try. You've—"

"I do try." Johanna's voice broke. "I do try. But I hear voices." I stop . . . but my mind doesn't: I hear my little three-year old Amber playing with her daddy. I hear Joel telling me he's going to take her to the store. And then I hear a voice over the phone saying to come to the hospital, and then the doctor's voice is telling me Joel is dead. And . . . and then if I thought I still had a glimmer of hope, my angel daughter hangs on by a slender thread for three days until the thread breaks, as she holds my hand, and I hear her little voice say: 'Mommy'—and then she's gone." She took a breath. "That's just it, Mom, I am trying. All I do is try."

She broke into tears.

"I'm coming over," her mother said.

"No," Johanna almost shouted. "I need to deal with this my way." She sighed and then lowered her voice, "I'm okay, or, I'm going to be okay. Maybe not this evening, but I'll be okay."

"If you're sure."

"I'm sure."

CHAPTER THREE

THE CRY MUST HAVE DONE HER some good. Johanna slept without dreaming, and the wake-up alarm of escalating chimes didn't jar her. She was ready to start the day, and, as she had for the past year, she shoved the memories into a corner of her mind and locked the door.

For once, she would get into the office before Ava and put on the coffee.

However, when she arrived, she could smell the fragrant blend from the door. Ava, a mug in one hand, was using the other to hold the phone as she conversed with someone in Spanish. Ava also spoke French, German and Russian. Her skill with languages was a research boon. When Johanna had questioned why so many, Ava replied it was a knack she had, and that it came in handy.

They had met three years earlier at a fundraiser reception soon after Johanna had signed the office lease. They hit it off from the beginning. After a long lunch and an early dinner, Ava offered to bring her unique skills to form a partnership, and they decided to give it a try.

"I'm genetically nosy," Ava confessed. "This will give me a chance to use my anthropology degree without getting dirty. Genealogy digging is perfect for me."

They became friends later.

For Johanna, their bond was sealed when Ava sat next to her in the hospital for almost two days, saying nothing: no platitudes, no words of wisdom, no banal conversation. Ava's silent presence gave Johanna strength to keep the despair and desolation at bay. When the end came, Ava had embraced the sobbing Johanna and driven her home.

They had not spoken of the experience since. There was no need.

Ava Lowell was a yoga aficionado and health foodie. This morning, she shook her head reprovingly when her partner took a glazed donut out of a baggie.

"Glazed donuts? Really, Jo, don't you notice how your energy crashes an hour later?" Ava admonished. "Your body needs real fuel, not vague fumes."

"Ah, huh. And, I feel terrible about it, too," Johanna quipped, taking a bite while pouring a cup of coffee. "Did you pick up the mail?"

"I put it on your desk," Ava said. "By the way, there's a letter from a law firm."

In an attempt to decorate, they had used two tall bookcases and over-stuffed chairs, gifts left behind from the attorneys who had moved out, to form an L-shaped sitting space near the door. There was enough room in the rear for two moderate-sized cubicles. Under their sole window, Ava had insisted on a small refrigerator to hold water and fresh whatever.

Johanna took a letter opener and raked across the top of the envelope.

"Oh, no," she groaned, as she scanned through the pages.

"What's the matter?" Ava turned her chair to face her partner.

"We're being sued."

"Are you kidding?" Ava called out. "For what?"

Johanna handed over the cover sheet and continued to read the remaining pages.

"Fraud." It was Ava's turn to frown. "You've got to be kidding."

"And, accessory after the fact, according to the complaint, as a result of the findings from our ancestor research. It says the Ackermans invested a considerable sum of money in an annuity we knew to be a scam."

She handed pages to Ava.

"The Ackermans, that's Howard and Diane. I thought they were such a nice couple. They own a furniture store in Pleasanton." Ava continued to read. "What have we got to do with their annuity?"

"The lawsuit asserts that the Ackermans used the background infor-mation we provided to invest in an annuity established for investors who could verify their ancestors originated from a now-defunct province in central Europe. This annuity was a shell, and it folded after the scam-mers got the Ackermans' money. The suit says we didn't exert care in validating our research that their ancestors lived in a legitimate region." Johanna handed the remaining pages across to Ava. "I think we're going to need an attorney."

"I don't know any, do you?"

Johanna shrugged. "What about the ones we got our office space from? They seemed nice."

"At least, they know us," Ava agreed.

"It's a place to start," Johanna said, collecting the pages and returning them to the envelope.

AVA PULLED OUT THE ACKERMAN FILE and started going through the papers while Johanna located the business card for Dean Cameron, Attorney at Law and made the call.

"First of all, call me Dean," he said. "And, if I'm going to help you, I'm going to need to see the complaint—it's those papers you're holding—as soon as possible. In California, you have to respond within thirty days."

She took down his new address.

"So you think you can help?" Johanna asked. "Neither of us has ever been sued before."

"It can be daunting, but it only gets messy when you ignore things," Dean said. "If you like, I can see you both this afternoon. You can bring the papers with you. Our new office is in downtown Oakland."

Johanna gestured the question to Ava, who nodded in the affirmative.

"Scan over the complaint," he said. "Your first hour is free consultation, and I can do some preliminary checking before you get here."

Johanna assured him they would be there at four o'clock.

She clicked off and faced Ava who was closing a file. "What did you find out?"

"The Ackermans' charts were straightforward," Ava replied. "I handled the contract last spring. I remember I was excited. It was one of the oldest lines I'd ever researched. Diane's line went back to the end of 17th Century, and I traced Howard back to mid-19th Century Scotland."

"Anything unusual?"

Ava gave her a look. "You mean besides the fact I found her ancestors in the 1600s? No, I thought that was pretty good." Ava flipped through the pages. "I need to go through this in detail, but for certain there was no mention by me, or them, about an annuity." She flipped to the back of the file. "And they got our couples discount."

Johanna scooted her chair into Ava's cubicle, pulling out the brochure. "The name of the annuity was The Elan Star Annuity. They offered additional interest percentage points for individuals who could show their lineage."

Ava shook her head. "Doesn't sound familiar at all."

"You ladies open for business?" Trinidad set a vacuum down next to a bookcase. "I say hello, but you talk to yourselves."

Johanna smiled. "Hello, Trinidad, yes, we are open for business." She stood and walked out to the front of the room. "Were you able to make a meeting with Eloise?"

Today Trinidad wore a rainbow-colored scarf and matching t-shirt.

"Yes, you can come this evening. I take off work." She blew out a long breath and smiled. "Simone will cover for me."

"Oh, Trinidad," Johanna said with regret. "I thought it would be on Saturday. I can't meet Eloise this evening. We already have another appointment. What about tomorrow?"

The woman rolled her eyes. "Wait here, I go ask Simone. She in next building."

"Do we have a new client?" Ava asked standing next to Johanna and watching Trinidad make her way across the lawn to an office building at the end of the parking lot.

"Maybe."

Johanna recounted the background on Eloise Manley.

While they waited for Trinidad to return, the two compiled a folder of duplicated items for the meeting with Dean Cameron. When they were finished, it was thick with papers. The Ackermans were excellent record keepers, which, at the time, had made the research job easier.

"She's on her way back," Johanna said, looking out the window.

Trinidad entered the room with a wide grin on her face.

"Okay, we can go tomorrow, Wednesday," she said. "I call Ellie to say yes."

CAMERON AND CLARK, ATTORNEYS AT LAW, had moved up in the world. Located in a downtown Oakland high-rise on the twelfth-floor, their new office had an expansive view of the Marin peninsula. Johanna and Ava sat across from one another in front of an austere looking receptionist who would not take her eyes off of them.

"Hurry," Ava quipped in a loud whisper. "Slip the candy dish in your purse."

The receptionist stiffened, and Johanna choked back a laugh.

"Ava, Johanna, good to see you again."

Dean Cameron strode toward them with an outstretched hand. After, pleasantries were exchanged, he led them to a modest-sized conference room with a view of Oakland's Chinatown. Cameron was one of those persons who lived up to, what-you-see-is–what-you-get. Average height and build, with thick black hair and moustache, he was straightforward and personable. He came across as both trustworthy and compassionate.

"How's the office working out?" he asked.

"We like it," Johanna replied. "It suits us."

"Good. Have a seat," he said, and let's get started. "Thanks for sending over the complaint. It gave me a running start to understand where the plaintiffs are coming from."

"And where's that?" Johanna urged, wanting to hear their fate.

Dean cleared his throat. "Howard and Diane Ackerman say, based on information and research you provided indicating they had ancestors with roots in old Europe, they submitted financial documents to qualify for a high interest earning annuity from an insurance company in the United States. They discovered last month the annuity was essentially a fraudulent scheme, and the court issued an arrest warrant for the directors, who have since disappeared. The only people the Ackermans' attorney could find were you two."

"Us," said Ava, shaking her head. "We don't tell our clients what to do with their charts."

"Did you know they were going to buy this annuity as a result of your research?" Cameron asked.

"I might have," Johanna admitted. "Howard made vague references to me *after* Ava had done the research. He called to get the remaining balance on their invoice. But, as a matter of course, unless they tell us during conversation, we never ask what our clients plan to do with their charts."

"Are either of you familiar with Elan Star Annuity, or any of its employees?"

"No," Johanna and Ava replied together.

He looked amused. "All right, then. Let's fight this." He picked up a page. "They're claiming you are accessories after the fact, which requires at least one of three elements: you, in some third-party fashion, participated in the crime; you knowingly concealed the criminals who did commit the crime; and, or, you helped the criminals escape prosecution."

Johanna waved his statement away. "That's easy. None apply." She puckered her forehead. "How much do they want?"

"A million dollars."

"Are they crazy?" Ava called out. "Is that how much they invested?"

Cameron shook his head. "No, according to the complaint they invested their life savings of five hundred thousand dollars, the other five is for mental anguish and stress." He put his pen down. "Look, this is just an opening salvo. They want a settlement. I'm sure their attorney knows there is no way you're going to admit to, let alone pay for the Ackermans' poor judgement."

"We can't pay," Johanna said. "We can't pay any amount. What do we do now?"

"If you want me to represent you, I'll respond to this right away with a complete and total denial of alleged facts and rejection of the suit." Cameron leaned forward. "I know their attorney; he's not a bad guy. I think he realizes the foolhardiness of his clients' financial decision and wants to show them they can do something."

"That doesn't help us," Johanna said. "Make sure we ask for legal costs. That is, if you want us to pay you." She grinned.

"I'll remember that," he said deadpan and then smiled. "This case has very shaky legs, but the Ackermans should have thought of that before they filed a lawsuit." He put his pad of paper on top of their file. "I'll take it from here."

CHAPTER FOUR

ELOISE MANLEY'S AIRSTREAM HAD ONCE BEEN BRIGHT RED, but now in the morning sunlight, the peeling paint revealed patches of the base metal and dull plastic. As if in defiance of its exterior, however, window boxes overflowed with pink and red geraniums, and their singular heady fragrance reminded Johanna of summers spent as a child with her family at Clear Lake.

Trinidad put her hand on the doorknob, blocking Johanna's advancement. "I go first and tell her you're here."

Amused, Johanna stood to the side.

Trinidad tapped on the door as she walked in and shut it behind her. Moments passed and then she motioned for Johanna to follow.

Later, when she related her visit to Ava, Johanna admitted she hadn't known what she expected to see, but it wasn't the bright and airy open-space front rooms. Laminate bamboo floors, almost snow white walls and pale blue kitchen cabinets made one think of a beach house. The counters were deep and curved, to give separation between living and cooking spaces. A sliding door closed off the rooms to the rear of the coach. From the smell of things, a pot of spaghetti was on the stove.

"Ellie," Trinidad announced, "this is Johanna Hudson I tell you about. She come to help you."

Eloise sat at the far end of a pale-blue leatherette sofa facing the front door. Her strawberry blond hair was pulled back into a long thick braid. Her skin was the clearest Johanna had ever seen and complemented by hazel green eyes and a dimple in her chin. She was exquisitely beautiful by any standard, and that's when Johanna realized she was blind.

"Hello, I—" She held out her hand then dropped it.

"Hello, Johanna. Trinidad didn't tell you I was sightless, did she?" Eloise turned toward Trinidad who was sitting in a small chair. "I don't know why she's so reluctant. It's not like a person isn't going to find out."

Johanna smiled, and then recognized she couldn't be seen. "It doesn't matter. Can I call you Eloise?"

"Yes, of course," Eloise said. "I want to assure you I see a lot more than people think I do, just not with my eyes. I was born sighted, but a bad case of measles when I was nine took my vision. My foster parents were simple people. They thought it was an ordinary childhood disease playing itself out. By the time the disease ran its course, I was blind."

Trinidad waved her arm to dismiss any misgivings. "You strong woman. I don't tell about eyes because . . . because people need to see you."

Eloise lips broke into a wide smile.

"Trini, you can tell such tales." She turned to Johanna. "She was afraid you wouldn't want to help me—too much trouble."

"How long have you lived here?" Johanna asked.

"You mean 'here' in this dump?" Eloise replied, her voice sharp.

Johanna tilted her head. "I mean 'here' in Castro Valley."

"Oh, I'm sorry." Eloise sighed, contrite. "I didn't mean to snap. It's just . . . it's just that things would be so much easier with money."

Trinidad and Johanna exchanged looks.

"That is truth," Trinidad said.

"Let me get us something to drink before you hear my tale of woe," Eloise said.

She stood and moved with ease around the small kitchen. Johanna raised her eyebrows with admiration for the woman as she opened the door of a narrow, but full height refrigerator tucked in a wall niche and pulled out a pitcher.

"Iced tea?" Eloise asked, already reaching for a glass.

"Nothing for me, thank you," Johanna replied.

Trinidad went to Eloise's side. "We're fine, Ellie. Tell us your story. This lady has things to do." She patted her hand. "Start with the Manleys."

Eloise nodded and sat back down. "The Manleys were my foster family." She closed her eyes as if picturing them. "Like I said, I lost my sight when I was ten. The Manleys had taken me in when I was eight. My childhood was almost ordinary except I had to visit my mother in prison.

Trini said she told you about . . . well, even so, I pretended the Manleys were my parents. The Manleys explained to me my mother was incarcerated because she had to be punished. When she was finished being punished she would come and get me. That's why they didn't adopt me."

Trinidad clicked her tongue at this.

"No, Trini, it was okay. The Manleys were very good to me." She took a deep breath. Her voice was strong but soothing at the same time. "I was eight when I saw my mother for the last time. I didn't know she was dying. But I think she knew. She told me I had 'people,' and she had written things down for me and put it and papers in a box. She said the Manleys would give the box to me when the time was right. Only, I guess it never was, because the Manleys were killed in a car accident when I was seventeen. They left a little money for me, but they weren't rich to begin with." She puckered her forehead. "I . . . I was a very angry teenager, and I got mixed up with drugs. I . . . I spent all the money they left me, and then I had nothing. I lived on the streets for about six months."

Trinidad stared at Johanna to see her response, but Johanna was doing her best not to react one way or another.

"At a homeless shelter downtown, I met a woman named Frances Lynch who helped me see my life for what it was, and finally, through the drug haze, I fought to turn my life around. I have a pretty good voice, and I got a job coordinating and sometimes recording books in Braille into audio books for the blind."

"Eloise," Johanna said. "How can I help you? What do you want me to do?"

Eloise's eyes glistened with tears. "While I was on the street, I got pregnant. That's when I got clean. I had to. I had a little girl, and I named her Ruby. Her father was totally out of the picture. Frances helped me put her up for adoption; there was no way I could raise a child—I couldn't raise me. I made them keep her name. Whoever adopted her had to leave her name alone. Then I signed the papers." She turned to Johanna, a trail of silent tears slipping down her cheeks. "I never saw her, didn't want to."

She took a deep breath and, pulling a tissue out of a nearby box, dabbed at her eyes. She straightened her shoulders. "Understand, I still don't want to meet her; and I don't want her to see me. I have nothing to offer her." Her voice stronger, she continued, "But after that man came by, I'm thinking, the one thing I could give her is an inheritance from her grandfather."

"You want me to research your family background so you can find your father?" Johanna offered.

"Yes, the man said if I could prove I was Eloise Sutton, my grand-mother would make all the connections and take care of any legal costs." She shook her head. "But I'm not stupid. They'll use me to get all the money for themselves. I figure, the more I know about my background the less they can trick me."

At that, she seemed to have run out of steam. Eloise sank into the seat cushions like a deflated balloon and sighed. She reached for an envelope sitting on a small shelf above her head and handed it to Johanna. "Here's my birth certificate. It gives my mother's name and address. My father is shown as unknown, but I think different. Trini says you can find family members and build family histories. I want you to build mine. I want to know who my father is."

"So she can get money for Ruby," Trini interjected.

Eloise, blind as she was, gestured with her hands as if to say "enough." Trinidad crossed her arms over her chest.

Johanna accepted the envelope and took out a paper. It was a worn copy of a birth certificate.

Jeanette Sutton was nineteen years old when Eloise was born. The box was checked for married and then crossed out. A name had been written under father and then dabbed with what looked like white cor-rection fluid. The address listed was in Daly City. From the date of birth shown, as of next month, Eloise would be twenty-six.

"Was Sutton your mother's maiden name, or married name?" Johanna asked.

"I think maiden," Eloise said. "I don't think she would give me the name of her husband."

"It's a start. I can follow the trail and see where this birth certificate takes me," Johanna said, slipping the page back into the envelope. "But it may not be far enough to lead to your father. Do you have any other information about your mother? It has been over fifteen years, and the address may not provide much help. Did the man give you your grand-mother's name?"

Eloise shook her head. "No, he didn't say."

"What was his name?" Johanna had pen to paper. "Did he leave a card?"

"No, he didn't leave a card, but he said his name was James Bryce."

Trinidad gave a slight cough to catch Johanna's attention, and then signified an air outline of a box with her fingers.

Johanna nodded. "Eloise, what was in the box your mother left you?"

"Not much. I'll give it to you when you leave. There are baby clothes, a couple of greeting cards, pictures of Lake Tahoe, my mother's high school yearbook, and an envelope with five, ten-dollar bills," Eloise added. "I spent the money."

Johanna asked, "Why did your mother think the contents would tell you about your people?"

Trinidad cleared her throat. "Nobody ask me, but I think Manley people took things," she offered. "I think they take her mother's letter. Maybe there was more money and maybe more papers."

"Trinidad," Eloise cautioned. She turned to face Johanna. "There was nothing that indicated anything was missing." She ran her hand over her forehead. "I think about it a lot. Even when I was on the street, I would always try to hide the box. Like I said, I spent the money and kept the rest hidden, but maybe . . . maybe," Her voice drifted.

For a moment, no one spoke.

Johanna took a deep breath. "I am willing to try and fill in your family tree, but I can't promise you I will discover your father, or that he will have an estate of any value." She hesitated. "Did you consider if your father is wealthy, he will probably want a DNA test to verify his paternity?"

"I know." Eloise smiled. "I'm counting on it."

CHAPTER FIVE

"**D**ON'T GET INTO TROUBLE WHILE I'M GONE," Ava warned, putting on her sunglasses.

"Who me?" Johanna smiled. "I think I can handle five days without your oversight while you dig around Australia. It will take me that long to wrap up a couple of clients and start work on Eloise Manley's file."

Ava looked doubtful, as she stuffed papers into a folder. "You realize, of course, this entire Manley matter is on the fringe of what we do."

Johanna shrugged. "I know, but I want to help. She doesn't have money for a lawyer or a private detective, and I'm only offering to research her family. But with our report, she'll have something to take to an attorney to pursue her case."

Two hours later, with Ava gone, Johanna, wearing plastic gloves, lifted the top of Eloise's dilapidated plastic container. It had a dank and sour smell. Eloise's hiding places when she lived on the street were likely in less-than-pleasant locations. The baby clothes on top consisted of a pale pink satin bonnet with dirtied ribbon ties and a faded yellow cotton dress with tiny scattered daises. The dress was wrinkled, as if it had been rolled into a ball. One little baby sock was stuck by a food stain to the back of the dress. Johanna placed it all aside in a pile.

Next, a birthday card with a large cake on its front had: "Happy 21st Birthday" scrawled across the top. The card must have belonged to Eloise's mother, Jeanette. Johanna opened it.

"I am so sorry. Hopefully next year won't be any worse. Love B."

Well, that must have brought her cheer.

She opened the next card. It was in a dusty-beige envelope with a return address in Milpitas, outside Silicon Valley. It had Sutton written on its front. She lifted the flap, but there was no card, just a single page of heavy stock.

It was an announcement of a memorial for Denise Marie Sutton on May 15, 2002. The card was blank on the other side. She took out a pad of paper and wrote the address of the funeral parlor in Colma. It was almost eighteen years ago, but she had to start somewhere.

Next, she lifted out the photos that had begun to fade.

The creased picture of Lake Tahoe was of a large house on Carnelian Bay taken from the lake. Johanna recognized the length of beach. She and Joel had rented a house there with another couple for three summers. She smiled to herself, and then winced with the memory of loss.

Smoothing out the folds in the picture, Johanna strained to make out the couple in swimsuits smiling in a playful pose. They appeared to be adults in their 20s or 30s. There was no date stamp on the photo.

The next photo had a diagonal blotch across the front. It was of a young boy standing next to the carved bear along the highway where it entered Kings Beach, at the north end of Lake Tahoe. He was smiling and didn't appear to mind having his picture taken. Johanna put the photo close to her eyes. Under the yellowish blemish, the outline of a date was evident but too blurred to decipher. She would have to take it to a restoration professional.

Next, she came to a high school yearbook. It was dirty, and pages had started to pull away from the book spine, but the covers were held together with a thick rubber band. She knew of St. Bernard's High School; it was still around. It was an all-girls school near El Cerrito, not far from where the San Raphael Bridge crossed into Vallejo. The year was 1988. Johanna flipped through pages and stopped when she reached the name of Jeanette Sutton. She glided her finger to the squared photo of Eloise's mother.

Jeanette Sutton was as beautiful as her daughter. The yearbook photos were in glossy color and even though the book showed the wear and tear of past neglect, Jeanette's beauty stood out. Thick blond hair and sea-green eyes framed a generous smile with a hint of "I told you so." Eloise could have been her twin. Other than her name, there was no other notation. Johanna started at the beginning and studied each of the class pictures of sports, homeroom, library, and language study. She turned to a picture of Jeanette and a classmate bending over a microscope. Standing alongside her colleagues, Jeanette portrayed a look of concentration. Although staged, it left the impression of a studious pupil.

Johanna continued to flip through pages. Jeanette Sutton and Eugene Dawes were queen and king of the senior ball. The couple could have signed modeling contracts right after graduation. Their "court" was also notably attractive, but in the succeeding photos Jeanette's smile, when present, appeared forced. In one shot, she was almost grim as she waved to the camera. Even so, there were many autographs squeezed onto the insides of the front and back covers.

Johanna closed the yearbook and reached for a bottle of water. She had promised Eloise and, by default, Trinidad, to get back to them by the end of the week with an update on her likelihood of finding Eloise's father. Johanna wasn't discouraged. There were a lot of threads that could lead to an outcome, but what outcome she wasn't sure. According to Eloise, she did not have a lot of time if she were to make a claim to the inheritance.

She placed the items in a new plastic case and then on the bottom shelf in the office supply room.

The landline phone chimed, and Johanna rushed to answer. It was Dean.

"I need you and Ava to make sure I have all your work papers on the Ackerman chart," he pressed. "The folder you gave me had all the final documents, but I'd like to see the actual work papers. Will that be a problem?"

"I'll drop them off tomorrow."

"Ah, tomorrow will be fine, but make it in the afternoon. I have court in the morning."

It took less than an hour for Johanna to gather and copy Ava's research pages on the Ackermans. Ava had already made a set. She bundled and placed the information in a large folder.

That done, she spent the rest of the morning searching databases for any mention of Eloise Manley's mother, Jeanette Sutton. The problem was there were hundreds of Jeanette Suttons. Without Jeanette's married name she was at a loss, and the address in Daly City didn't provide any new information. For now, her search had turned up nothing. She called Eloise when she was sure there were no other leads.

"Eloise, do you have any other papers at all from your foster parents?" Johanna asked, propping the phone against her ear and shoulder, as she waited for an online response to her public record inquiry. "Maybe, the social services application or processing documents submitted by your foster parents?"

"I don't think so," Eloise said. "That was a long time ago, and like I said, I took a life detour and lived on the streets for a while. I . . . I have very little of my past life, except for what's in the box."

Johanna clicked her pen in thought.

"Okay, what about their names, maybe—"

"Wait, I have a Bible that belonged to my birth mother," Eloise exclaimed. "The Manleys, my foster parents, kept it. The house they rented was sold after they died, and one of the neighbors helped me with getting the house clean, so I could get the deposit back. She kept the Bible safe. Like I said, I took the money they left me, and ran with it. But the neighbor was a church lady, and one day she found me in a shelter. By then, I was ready to turn my life around. She told me about this motor home park, and gave me back the Bible. At first, I told her I didn't want it," Eloise said. "But, she insisted and I tried to take good care of it. Living in a mobile home, I can't store a lot of keepsakes, but even my touch could tell it is a beautiful book."

Johanna punched the air with her fist. "A Bible can be a great source of information."

"How?" Eloise asked.

"There's a chance someone in your birth family used it to record family marriages and deaths," Johanna said. "It's a source for more possible leads." Johanna checked her pad of notes. "It's a long shot, but I would feel a lot better if I checked every possibility. If you want to make your claim as soon as possible, it could fill in some gaps. I can come by now and pick it up."

"Now?" Eloise's voice held hesitation. "If, you come right now, no problem. I was meeting with . . . ah, someone." She hesitated, and then, "Yeah, sure, come now."

"If you like, I can drop you off at your meeting place?"

"What? No, that's all right. They're coming here. I'll give them a call and let them know I'm running a little late."

"Thank you." Johanna had already picked up her purse and keys. "I'm on my way. With traffic, I should be there within the hour."

Traffic. There was no specific commute time anymore. Bay Area highways seemed forever jammed and, just to make it interesting, ever-present roadwork practically guaranteed accidents. It was over an hour before Johanna pulled up in front of Eloise's coach.

She stared.

The metal front door swung back and forth with the wind gusts.

Johanna approached the trailer with caution, looking around her as she did so. Eloise's motor home was toward the end of a long row and the nearest trailer was about forty feet away. Mid-afternoon and there was no one was outside, although she could hear a distant TV and the rush of cars from the nearby highway.

"Eloise?" she called out from the entry. "It's Johanna."

Johanna stepped into the cabin, closing the door behind her.

"Eloise?"

The silence was complete. The living area was in order, no dishes in the sink, no clothing slung over the seating. The vague smell of a vanilla candle hung in the air.

A sheet of dirty wrinkled paper on the table caught her eyes. Eloise must have found the authorization form for Ruby's adoption. She leaned over and noted the names and addresses.

The door to the bedroom was closed. She halted outside.

"Eloise?" Johanna tapped. "It's Johanna, are you okay?"

There was no answer.

She took a deep breath, turned the knob, and pushed against the door, but it wouldn't budge. She pushed harder, and the small inches-wide opening created was just enough for her to see over a small dresser that had fallen. Beyond that, on the bed was a bloodied body with a rush of blonde hair covering in part the lifeless sea green eyes of Eloise Manley.

Johanna heard herself scream.

CHAPTER SIX

S HE BACKED AWAY FROM THE DOOR and taking out her phone, punched 9-1-1.

"Don't touch anything, and wait outside for the police," the operator directed. "They're on their way."

With a deep exhale, she walked out into the sunshine and sat in her car. She scribbled down the names from the wrinkled paper on the table, and then stopped.

Silly habit, she no longer had a client.

The mobile park was as quiet as when she first came. Trinidad would be at work, and perhaps the other residents were as well.

Still, where was everyone else in the park?

As soon as she expressed the thought, two police cars pulled adjacent to the trailer, one blocking her vehicle. Then, like answering a buzzer, people started to emerge from their homes, murmuring in loose clusters around Eloise's trailer.

She got out of her car.

"Mrs. Hudson? Officer Temple, you called 9-1-1?"

She nodded to the young uniformed man. Over the next minutes she described her discovery. Temple motioned with his head for the two officers in the second car to enter Eloise's trailer. They drew their guns.

"No, officer," Johanna raised her hand in protest. "There was no one else in there."

"You don't know that, Mrs. Hudson. You told me you couldn't enter the room. Someone could be hiding." Temple looked over the small crowd of residents now silent. He turned back to Johanna, his voice softening.

"It's a suspicious death until we know the cause. We take precautions."

"Of course," Johanna murmured.

A third police car pulled next to the trailer, and a tall dark-haired man wearing a tan sports coat and jeans approached them.

Temple straightened. "Detective Dominic Quinn, this is Johanna Hudson. She discovered the body and made the call."

The two officers who had entered the trailer earlier now emerged, guns holstered, followed by a harried-looking paramedic Temple walked over to them and listened as they reported their findings.

"Detective," the paramedic walked up to them and said. "We looked in through the bedroom window at the back. A piece of furniture had overturned and blocked the door. Since we didn't want to affect the crime scene, the officers took the door off. It appears as if she struggled to get out. We have a deceased white, female, in her 20s or 30s, stabbed in the chest."

"Okay, let's call in forensics. Temple, you and the officers, start interviewing the other residents of the park," Quinn ordered. Then he turned to face Johanna. "Mrs. Hudson, I'd like to ask you a few questions. We can talk over there," he said, pointing to a bench under a leafy weeping willow.

Johanna was numb, and she allowed him to lead her away. She sat down as Quinn waved at one of the officers, signaling he wanted a bottle of water.

"Now, take your time and tell me what happened," he said.

Dazed, Johanna looked at him and nodded. She spoke slowly and stared out onto the parking lot of scurrying people. Several minutes later, after taking a long swallow of water, she finished her recap. Her eyes now focused.

"A Bible?" Quinn looked up from his small notebook with a frown. "What do you do again?"

Johanna cleared her throat. "I'm a genealogist. I help people discover their ancestors and build their family tree."

Johanna was amazed at the number of personnel dressed in white overalls descending on the Manley trailer. Quinn followed her gaze.

"It's the forensic team," he said in response to her unasked question. "What were you doing for Eloise Manley?"

"She wanted me to build her family tree, so she could find her father." Johanna hoped her matter of fact tone ended any further questions about this topic.

"So you make house calls?"

Johanna took a loud breath. "Detective, this is the second time I have ever met . . . ah . . . visited Eloise Manley. She seemed to be a very nice person. I had no reason to kill her," she said. "I visited her at her home out of courtesy, since she's blind."

Quinn looked up from his notetaking. "Blind." He closed his pad and put away his pen. "We didn't know. Look, Mrs. Hudson, you can go. We'll be getting back in touch with you. Right now I have to let our forensic team know about the victim's disability."

"Detective there's one more thing," she stood. "Eloise asked for my help because she was approached by a man who wanted to verify her identity. He said if things worked out, she could receive a substantial inheritance, and that he was representing her maternal grandmother who was trying to locate her—for a share." Johanna wrinkled her brow. "Eloise told him she would think about it. That's why she contacted me, because she thought I might be able to find her family without having to pay."

"What's his name?"

"He didn't tell her."

Quin scribbled a note. "Like I said, we'll need to talk to you some more, but for now you can leave."

He gave a quick nod and walked hastily toward the cluster of forensic workers. It was clear his news of Eloise's condition reenergized the group. Two of the staff broke off from the others and returned to the trailer.

BACK IN HER OFFICE, JOHANNA SENT A TEXT TO AVA.

Eloise Manley murdered. I found the body. I'm okay, just sad.

Ava wouldn't see it until the next day US time, and Johanna could imagine the choice words that would leave her partner's lips.

It had been a long day. Johanna spent the rest of it listening to voicemail messages. Dean Cameron was one of them.

"I discovered other suits regarding the annuity Ackerman was involved in. All were suing the insurance company. He is the only one suing his researchers. This case shouldn't be a problem. I'll get back to you on Monday."

Johanna smiled. But, as quick as the smile appeared on her lips, it went away, and the image of Eloise Manley's body came to mind.

She packed up her belongings and headed for home.

Rummaging through her purse for her car key, Johanna didn't notice the man sitting on the bench in the parking lot walkway until she was almost on him.

"Mrs. Hudson?"

She swallowed a gasp and looked up. "Yes?" She squinted in the encroaching dusk. "Mr. Ackerman, is that you?"

He stood. "I didn't mean to startle you, but it's important we talk."

Howard Ackerman was of average height, but he carried himself tall. Military erect, salt and pepper graying sideburns, his thin lips and steel blue eyes bespoke a man who let little get past him.

And yet.

"Why don't we go inside to our office?" Johanna offered.

"No," he snapped. Then, seeing her surprise, he gave her a sheepish smile. "I mean, ah . . . here is fine." He sat back down and patted the bench.

It wasn't fine for Johanna.

"Mr. Ackerman, I've had a rough day." She crossed her arms. "You are suing us, and we shouldn't be talking at all without our attorneys. Moreover, I'm not going to talk about your claim in the dark, and on a cold bench with my warm office a few feet away."

"I need to explain. It's complicated," he said. "When Ava finished our chart—she couldn't have been more thorough. My wife and I were very pleased. But then—"

"Please stop." Johanna motioned for him to cease. "Like I said, we shouldn't be talking about your claim. Our attorney is –"

"Look, if you would give me a few minutes of your time, we can save a lot of money by not using attorneys. If you hear me out, I'd be willing to drop the suit."

THEY SAT IN A SMALL CAFÉ about three blocks from the Hudson & Lowell office. Howard Ackerman had caught Johanna's attention with his remark about dropping the lawsuit. Time out for coffee seemed time well spent.

"Mr. Ackerman, I still don't understand why you're suing Hudson & Lowell," she said her fingers encircling the hot cup of decaf.

Ackerman looked down at his tightly clasped hands. "The money I invested was all we had," His voice choked. "I did all the research. Elan had a proven track record for the past fifteen years, and the list of investors was quite impressive. It seemed . . . it seemed to me that there was very little risk. How many people can claim ancestry back to one of the oldest families in Europe? You saw our documents. There was no doubt we qualified. We were amongst royalty, and dignitaries, and . . . and . . . ."

His voice trailed into the air.

"But, Elan was not . . . viable?" she said.

Ackerman shook his head.

"Well, Mr. Ackerman, while I appreciate your candor in telling me your story, there is no way Hudson & Lowell is going to pay for your mistake."

"Oh, but you will." He raised his head and looked into her eyes. "You have insurance, don't you, director's insurance, or maybe errors and omissions?"

"Maybe so, but maybe not, for a number of reasons, including my rates going up—if our carrier doesn't drop us all-together. And then there is the fact we didn't make any errors—your lawsuit is a total fabrication."

"This was all the retirement money we had." His thin lips formed what looked like the slit of a smile. "You'll admit to making a mistake." Ackerman dabbed at his mouth with a napkin. "You will tell your lawyer to settle. We will reduce our demand. We will come to an agreement that five hundred thousand is fair. You'll file a claim with your insurance company. We'll get our money, and we'll all walk away none the worse."

Johanna would never say she had a temper, except when pushed to the very edge of her tolerance ledge, as she was now.

He had no intention of dropping his lawsuit.

"Look, Mr. Ackerman," she seethed. "I have not had a good day. So I want you to understand there is no need in continuing this conversation. Unfortunately, going forward, we must communicate through our lawyers."

"I think not." Again, he gave her an enigmatic smile. "You will do as I ask to protect your reputation."

She reached for her purse and jacket. "No, I will not," she said, standing. "The reputation of Hudson and Lowell would be ruined if we walked away from the truth and went along with your lies."

He rose from the bench.

"Not your company's reputation—yours." He leaned in, his stale breath reaching her nostrils. "My investment recommendation came from your thieving dead husband."

CHAPTER SEVEN

ACKERMAN'S WORDS WERE LIKE A FIST TO HER CHEST.
She and Joel had been married for two years before Amber came
along. Theirs had been a good marriage. She'd met him at a friend of a friend's
wedding reception. He worked with a bank as a commercial loan broker for
a large real estate group, and since it was a topic she knew nothing about, she
tried to learn as much as she could. Over the years, he supported them in a
comfortable lifestyle, while her job as a fact-checker for a popular blog had
supplied the vacation funds. Then, as she continued to build the Legacy business, they were able to put more aside. Now, six years later, here was Howard
Ackerman alleging she didn't know her husband at all.

She looked around the restaurant.

"How dare you!"

He didn't respond. Instead he retrieved an envelope from inside his
coat pocket. "Look familiar?"

She snatched it from his hand and took out a sheet of folded paper.
Her breath caught when she saw the letterhead, and her eyes went immediately to the signature line.

It was Joel's.

The letter indicated an unspecified agreement with Ackerman had
been reached, and Joel would be the contact. Johanna put her hand to
her forehead. The café had almost emptied. The glare from the overhead lights blurred the words on the paper. She felt as if she were losing
her balance.

"Could we go to back to my office? I can't . . . I can't," she murmured,
looking around at the tables. She grabbed her coat and purse.

"Ah, sure, I guess I didn't know . . . I mean, I thought you knew." Ackerman spoke in a rush as he gathered his things and hurried behind her.

She didn't wait to hear Ackerman say more. She brushed past him and half-ran out the door. Johanna crossed the street and went straight inside her office building.

There were still a few office diehards working late, illumination glowed under doorways along the hall. She flipped on her own office lights. Ackerman was close behind. She waited for him to enter and then shut door.

"Okay," she said, facing him with her back against the exit. "What is this all about?"

"I told you," Ackerman said, taking a seat and putting on a show of bluster. "Thanks to your husband, we lost our savings. That's why it's right you should make up for part of it." He moved to the edge of his chair and outstretched his hands. "Look, your insurance will cover this. Just file a claim, and we go away."

"Now, you're trying to blackmail me?"

"Of course, not." Ackerman stood, but stepped back when he saw her expression. "I'm sorry. Let's start over. Let's sit down?" He gestured to her cubicle. "I'm sure he didn't think you would ever find out."

A chill went through Johanna's chest. The air seemed to be getting thinner, and she realized she wanted nothing more than to see this man gone.

"No, I'm not going to sit down, and neither are you." She opened the door. "I don't believe you. Now, get out. In the future, I will only talk to you through our attorney."

Ackerman nodded his head. "Too bad you can't ask your husband." He reached into his pocket and pulled out a card. "In case you change your mind before irreparable harm is done."

When she refused to take the card, he set it on the chair and left.

Johanna slammed the door behind him. Shaking, she slid to the floor with her arms over her knees. She could feel her heart's rapid beat, but no tears came. Joel had more integrity than any person she ever knew, and she saw no reason to believe anything Ackerman said.

Still, what had Joel been up to?

AT HOME, JOHANNA, WITH A GLASS of wine in hand, sat in the dark of her living room in front of an unlit fireplace. Eloise's murder and now

Ackerman's accusations were a lot to process. How did he know Joel?
How did he know Joel was dead?

She had to get these answers first, so she'd know whose game board
she was playing on.

She wasn't hungry for dinner. She had to get rid of the feeling Joel had
a secret he kept from her. If he had it was because he wanted to protect
her. Her thoughts returned to the year before.

After the funerals, it was many weeks before she could pack things
away. Amber's toys and clothes were given to charity. Joel's clothes, CDs
and golf clubs went to a men's recovery center. His papers, however, were
dumped into boxes. She had never looked at them, she couldn't. Except
for their joint files, she'd moved the boxes and several large plastic containers into the downstairs storage cabinet and locked it.

She went to the basement and opened the cabinet door. She pulled
out one of the clear totes.

Joel had a secret. She repeated the words in her head over and over.
She straightened her shoulders. *What was he hiding from her?* Joel was
a pack rat. From the looks of the contents, he had never met a piece of
paper he could throw away. She pulled up files of his work notes. Joel
had worked for Oak City Development when they met. He said they
recruited him out of Redwoods College and placed him in their management training program. He'd just closed one of his largest commercial
deals when he proposed to her. She put these files aside in a box she
marked for later review.

Setting up a long table, she decided to sort the remaining boxes of
notes and documents by year. The papers went back six years, and they'd
been married five years. Joel had even kept the scribbled reminder to
pick up her wedding ring.

She choked back tears, brushing aside the few that slipped through,
and dabbed at her nose with a tissue. Here were family photos of their
wedding, Amber's birth in the hospital and each of her birthdays. There
were reservation confirmations for vacations and trips to see his sister
in New Mexico. From bank statements, she noticed he had purchased
bonds for Amber's college. She remembered he had tried to explain what
he was doing, but she had deferred to his financial acumen. She should
cash the bonds.

Digging deeper and deeper into the totes filling the cabinet, she
browsed through folders of unrelated papers, letters and brochures. It

was madness. Why hadn't she organized them from the beginning?

When Johanna finished, the trash can was overflowing. She sat down in a folding chair staring into the space of darkness outside the range of the overhead light bulb. Tomorrow she would go through each stack by year and, with luck, discover something that made sense.

She wouldn't let anyone, particularly the Ackermans, tarnish Joel's name. Cameron seemed fair, but she wasn't ready to talk about accusations against Joel until she knew more. She knew enough of the law to know that as a lawyer, he would have to report criminal activity of a separate crime to the police.

She rose to return to the kitchen.

Her cell phone trilled.

"Miss Johanna, I call you with news." The urgency in Trinidad's voice was evident. "Ellie is dead. She is murdered."

"I know, Trinidad," she said. "I found her body."

There was loud silence on the other end.

"Trinidad, are you okay?" Johanna asked. "I know you two were close."

The woman cleared her throat. "Yes, we were close," she said, her voice slowed in sorrow. "To see her like that was . . . must be bad."

"It was. It was very sad. I was looking forward to helping her out. I was there to get her Bible."

"But, Miss Johanna, I have the Bible. Ellie gave me family Bible to hold for her. She gave me long time ago. You can still help."

"It's a little late," Johanna said, rubbing her eyebrows. "I no longer have a client."

"But you do," Trinidad insisted. "You have Ruby."

"Ruby?" Johanna questioned in surprise. "But she's a child, and I can't contract with her. Besides, it will be difficult to uncover any connections to Eloise's biological . . . her real father without her here to guide me."

"I can guide you," Trinidad said rushing her words. "Ellie tell me everything. I be your client. I bring you Bible and . . . and other papers. I know the names . . . I know—"

"Trinidad, it's okay. I believe you," Johanna soothed. "Look, why don't you come to the office before you start your shift tomorrow? It's late now, and it's been a really rough day. Tomorrow, we can talk for a little while and see where we can go from here."

"Yes." Trinidad took a deep exhale. "I . . . I promised Ellie I would help her. She helped me when I had no friends, no family, *no one*," Her voice choked. "She help me find a job, she help me get home. She said woman helped her when she was in the street, and she said she wanted to help me the same way," she said. "Ruby mean everything to her. Finding money for Ruby is how I pay Ellie back."

Johanna heard the unsaid words behind the ones spoken.

"Okay, Trinidad, I'll see what I can do."

It was minutes after the phone conversation, before Johanna stopped staring at the wall and returned her gaze to the room of chaos in front of her. Her earlier meeting with Ackerman had drained her, but her conversation with Trinidad had energized her. She had work to do.

CHAPTER EIGHT

WHEN AVA CALLED THE NEXT DAY to check-in, at first, Johanna didn't mention her run-in with Ackerman. Instead she described Eloise Manley's death and Trinidad's plea for their assistance.

"I can tell you're going to take her on," Ava said. "I don't blame you, I would, too. I'll be home in a couple of days. We can go over things then."

"Good," Johanna responded. "Ah, one last thing, the lawsuit has taken a twist."

"In our favor?"

"It's hard to say," Johanna said. "I'll know more by the time you return home."

"What does Dean say?"

At first, Johanna had considered contacting their attorney, but almost immediately, she rejected the idea. This was personal, and until she knew what Joel was involved in, she was not inclined to discuss him with any more people than she had to.

"I haven't spoken with him yet," she said. "I will once you and I go over circumstances."

"Circumstances," Ava repeated. "Hmm, curious word. Remember, don't get into trouble until I get back."

"Got it."

"MISS JOHANNA," TRINIDAD CALLED FROM THE DOORWAY. "It okay I meet now?"

Johanna waved her in. She'd been searching online for the birth records of a client who was curious about his ancestors. It was a simple matter, which was why she'd chosen to delve into it now. It distracted from the weightier issues on her mind. As soon as she finished the search, she would go back to examining Joel's files.

"Trinidad, yes, I was expecting you. Come in."

Carrying a large plastic tote bag, she entered with a hesitance, took the chair offered and avoided looking Johanna in the eyes. This afternoon, Trinidad looked almost somber in a sky blue and lime tunic with matching head scarf.

"Can I get you some tea or coffee, maybe water?" Johanna offered.

"No, no, please."

Johanna had to think a moment about the response, before she sat down behind her desk.

"Trinidad, what's the matter? You've been here before."

The woman raised her head looking woeful. "True, but not as customer," she said. "I no . . . I no want to make mistake."

Johanna smiled. "You can't make a mistake. From now on, I work for you."

She patted the woman's hand, and Trinidad gave her a nervous grin.

"You work for me?"

Johanna nodded.

"Good," Trinidad said, reaching into her bag. "I have many things to show you. I bring everything Ellie gave me." She paused. "I . . . I miss her. Saying her name makes me sad."

"I understand."

Trinidad straightened her shoulders and brought out a large worn Bible and several greeting cards with personal messages.

"These things are hers. She gave them to me . . . well, most of them. When the man came from her grandmother, I saw him looking around—trying to look for papers. But Ellie caught him, and told him to leave."

Johanna frowned. "Did you—"

At that moment, there was a firm knock on the office door and someone entered. Johanna rose, but before she could come from around her desk, a female police officer and the detective she'd met on the day Eloise was killed, approached Trinidad.

"Miss Trinidad Owens?" he said. "My name is Detective Dominic Quinn with the Maricopa County Sheriff. We would like you to come with us to the station and answer questions about the murder of Eloise Manley."

CHAPTER NINE

TRINIDAD LOOKED LIKE A TRAPPED BIRD. She stood, and walked back and forth in the little space, as if looking for a way out.

Her eyes pleaded with Johanna's. "Do I have to go?" she said.

Johanna opened her mouth to respond, but Quinn spoke first.

"We would think you'd want to help us find your friend's killer," he said. "Is there a reason why you wouldn't want to talk to us?"

"She should call her lawyer," Johanna interjected, with a tremor in her voice. "She . . . she . . . English is her second language."

Trinidad stopped pacing and visibly forced herself to breathe regularly.

"I have work tonight. There's no one to cover me. I lose job if I go with you." She crossed her arms over her chest. "I come tomorrow and answer questions."

It was clear her response did not please Quinn, but he gave a brief nod and handed his card to Trinidad.

"Make it ten o'clock," he said, and then turning to Johanna. "We should have final autopsy results back by then."

Johanna said nothing but followed them to the door, closing it with a click.

"Miss Johanna, what this mean?" Trinidad said, sinking into her seat.

"Unfortunately, I think it means you're going to need a lawyer. You shouldn't talk to the police without one."

Trinidad's slim show of confidence slipped away. "A lawyer . . . but I not have money for lawyer." She leaned forward in the chair. "I no can go to talk. What I can do?"

Johanna's mind raced. Other than television, she'd had some exposure to police procedures, and two law enforcement persons showing up at the door could not be a good thing. "I know a lawyer, but I'm not sure he'll be able to help you."

"No, no lawyer. They mean trouble," Trinidad protested. "You come, if you please. You listen and tell me when not to talk back."

"But I'm not a lawyer. I don't know when you shouldn't talk back."

"In my village, lawyers are bad as police." Trinidad wrinkled her forehead in thought, and then patted the back of Johanna's hand. "Then, come to listen. Come as friend."

Johanna watched out the window as her new friend made her way through the parking lot to start her workday. She picked up her phone.

After a few minutes of explanation, she concluded, "So, Dean, what should she do?"

"You're right about one thing. She needs a lawyer, a criminal lawyer. I won't be able to help you."

"Do you know of anyone?" Johanna asked. "Trinidad doesn't like lawyers much. She'll need a referral."

"Let me get right back to you."

"Oh, one other thing," Johanna said. "She doesn't have any money. It will have to be pro bono."

"Then I won't be right back," he answered. "She should get a public defender."

"But even I know you can't get a public defender until you've been charged. She wants someone to advise her while she's being questioned."

Someone must have come into his office. He placed his hand over the phone. Then he cleared his throat. "Johanna, with this short notice, my advice is for you to go with her and use your common sense. If I go, it will look as if she has adequate representation, and she would not. Meantime, I'll try to track down an attorney who can help her. I'm sorry, but I have to leave for a client meeting."

It was getting late, and Johanna wanted to go home to continue the search through Joel's papers. She glanced at the Bible Trinidad had left with her. With another glance to the clock on the wall, she turned on the copy machine. As she'd hoped for, the back pages of the Bible held pictures and a partial ancestor tree filled with names in thin, spidery handwriting. After making copies and a folder, it all went into a file drawer.

Johanna felt she was bouncing between two window ledges—Joel and Eloise. This was all she could accomplish today for Eloise Manley, who was already taking up her tomorrow morning.

Tonight belonged to Joel.

SHE TOLD HERSELF SHE WOULD SEARCH THROUGH one year's documents, and then go to bed. The year of their wedding was the smallest stack, and it was over a foot high. It consisted mostly of Joel's work correspondence, and a few letters of introduction. There were several recognition certificates from the Chamber of Commerce and a large plaque for a financial industry top sales award.

She picked up their wedding guest book—she'd wondered where it had gone to. Theirs had not been a large wedding, and the guests' names only filled five pages. She flipped through the pages, a hint of a smile playing on her lips. Her mother had sprayed the pages with the essence of roses, and the faint fragrance wafted up.

Other than the guest book, she put everything aside for disposal. There was nothing indicating any contact or reference to Howard or Diane Ackerman.

Johanna turned off the light. Ackerman was lying.

How could she prove it?

CHAPTER TEN

JOHANNA WISHED TRINIDAD WOULD STOP FIDGETING. It made her look like she had something to hide.

Because it was the weekend, the waiting room was almost empty. Only two other people were present, sitting in opposite corners of the room peering at their I Phones.

"Why you think they take so long?" Trinidad whispered.

"It's been less than ten minutes," Johanna said, looking at the time. "You should take this as a good sign. It means they're not concerned about you."

"Really?" Trinidad smiled. "I try to dress best." Today she was dressed in a sky blue two-piece suit, a jacket and skirt, set off with two-inch bright red heels.

Johanna started to nod, when a grim looking Detective Quinn came through a pair of double doors and headed straight for them.

Or maybe not.

"Miss Owens," he said. "Come with me please."

Johanna stepped back.

Trinidad stood still and said. "I not come without Johanna."

"I'm sorry, but Ms. Hudson is also a witness in the case. We need to speak with you alone." Quinn took a deep sigh.

"I not come without Johanna, she here as my friend." Trinidad's arms crossed her chest.

Johanna moistened her lips and interjected. "Or, Detective, if I can't sit in as a friend, we can come back with her attorney."

Quinn tilted his head as he looked from one to the other. "All right, come ahead."

He didn't wait to hear their response, turning he strode to a door midway down a hallway. The windowless room was cold in temperature and in décor. Except for the large grey metal table with four chairs in the center of the room, it was bare.

Johanna and Trinidad sat beside each other, facing Quinn. He put the file folder he'd been carrying on top of the table. As if by signal, an older woman with blonde-gray hair entered and sat next to him.

"Good Morning, I'm Detective Linn."

She'd been carrying a small machine, which she now turned on. Giving the date and the names of all present, she gestured to Trinidad.

"Please give your full name."

Trinidad had lost whatever bluster she had and spoke in a mild voice, "My name is Trinidad Pamela Owens." She didn't look up from her hands in her lap.

"Are you familiar with Eloise Manley?" Linn questioned.

"I know her, yes."

"Can you tell us where you were on the day of March 24th?"

Trinidad looked puzzled. Johanna looked at the two detectives and leaned over. "That's the day Eloise was killed."

"Yes, I at home, and then I leave."

Quinn leaned forward in his chair. "Did you see Eloise Manley that day?"

Trinidad looked back down at her hands. "Yes."

"You'll have to speak up, Miss Owens, for the machine," Linn said. "Can you tell us what the motives were for your visit with Miss Manley?"

Trinidad turned to Johanna. "What is 'motives'?"

Johanna glanced at the detectives and faced Trinidad. "They want to know *why* you went to see Eloise on the ... her last day."

Trinidad's cheeks blushed red. "I tell her to stop seeing boyfriend. Ellie tell me to mind my business. We talk back."

"Were you angry?" Quinn asked.

Johanna stiffened. The tone in his voice was a little too nonchalant.

Trinidad caught it, too. "Not angry to kill. I love Eloise like sister. I ... I ...." Her voice broke off. Her eyes started to tear.

"Was she alive when you left?" Linn asked.

Trinidad, nodded then looked at the machine and said, "yes," but her voice was so low, they made her repeat it.

"Miss Owens, can you explain why your fingerprints were discovered on the doorknob of Miss Manley's bedroom?" Quinn prodded.

Johanna's heart went out to the downtrodden face of the woman next to her. "Detectives, she's there all the time. My prints should be there, too."

"We identified your prints, Mrs. Hudson." Linn crossed her arms. "But unlike Ms. Owens, your prints weren't in blood."

Johanna gasped and covered her mouth. She leaned over to look at Trinidad, but the woman's head was still down staring at her hands.

"Ms. Owens," Linn continued. "We know you were in the mobile home for some time during or after the death of Eloise Manley. We know you were overheard arguing with the deceased, loud enough to be heard inside the home of the nearest neighbor. We know this wasn't the first time the two of you argued. Do you still say Eloise Manley was alive when you left her?"

Trinidad said nothing.

Quinn and Linn exchanged looks.

He put away his pen. "Trinidad Owens, I am arresting you for the murder of Eloise Manley. Anything you say may be used against you in a court of law. You have the right to consult an attorney before speaking to the police and to have an attorney present during questioning now or in the future. If you cannot afford an attorney, one will be appointed for you before any questioning, if you wish."

Trinidad blanched and turned to Johanna. "I didn't kill her." She stood when the officers took positions on either side of her. "Keep looking for Ellie's father. Get money for Ruby."

Linn took a pair of handcuffs from her pants pocket. Putting Trinidad's hands behind her back, Linn snapped on the cuffs.

"But, Trinidad, what about you?" Johanna said. "I'll get you an attorney who will help you. Don't talk to anyone."

Trinidad nodded, and Linn led her out the doorway and into the hallway.

"Promise me, Miss Johanna. Promise me, you won't stop until you get money for Ruby."

Johanna raised her voice after them.

"I promise."

"When can I see her?" Johanna asked, turning to Quinn.

Quinn had remained to collect the machine and looked up at her question.

"It will take us a while to process Miss Owens," he said. "I suggest you check back this afternoon." He put the recorder under his arm and moved to pass.

"Wait," she said. "From this interview, are you saying the only motive you have is a rare argument? That's not going to hold up."

"Not so rare." He peered at her. "There's more."

"So you're holding her until you can come up with a stronger motive," Johanna persisted. "When is the arraignment? Can she get bail? She's not a flight risk."

"We would beg to differ," he said. "You seem to be fairly familiar with the legal process."

Johanna's face flushed. "Yes . . . well, my father was a policeman. He was killed in the line of duty when I was seventeen, and I have a brother who is a computer forensic specialist for the Denver PD."

Quinn nodded and then, as if having second thoughts, gestured for Johanna to return to the interview room. When she entered, he closed the door.

"Sorry about your Dad," he said, rubbing his thick mustache. "We're going to request the arraignment be held at the earliest opportunity. This is an election year for our DA, and that's never been good for cases in the pipeline. We think we have a solid case. I can't divulge any of the particulars, but I will tell you this, you need to get your friend an attorney as soon as you can."

CHAPTER ELEVEN

RECEIVING A TEXT THAT HE WAS AVAILABLE to meet, Johanna went straight to Dean Cameron's office after leaving Trinidad.

"Turns out my partner, Nolan Clark, started out in criminal law before practicing family law," Dean said, leaning over his desk. "It took some doing, but I talked him into taking Trinidad's case."

"Thanks for meeting with me on a Saturday," Johanna said. "I appreciate your partner's willingness to take this case. Out of curiosity, why did he leave criminal practice?" she asked. "If he took convincing, is he any good?"

"Nolan said he had burned out. A death penalty case took a lot out of him. Right now, he's with his family at a soccer game. Shall I tell him you're ready to meet with him?"

"Yes, yes, I'd like to speak with him as soon as I can."

Johanna left the legal office with the understanding Clark would call her when he returned.

"He'll want to talk to you this weekend," Dean said.

IT WAS ALMOST MID-AFTERNOON. The past week had pulled her away from the business, and Johanna needed to put in some quiet hours in the office before the day was gone. But today was not going to be that day.

There were two messages from Ava saying she was staying over in Australia for three more days. She was proud to announce she'd picked up a new client. Unfortunately, she would be incommunicado for a day due to poor cell coverage. Could Johanna send a new client contract and a profile sheet to her hotel?

Johanna smiled to herself as she scanned the forms to her partner. Their business was picking up. At this rate, they could finish the year in the black . . . assuming the lawsuit went away.

She glanced up at the wall clock. She should be able to go through the mail, and still have time to go to the jail and visit with Trinidad.

Minutes later she was almost finished when her phone rang.

"Mrs. Hudson, my name is Nolan Clark. I understand you have a friend who needs a lawyer." His voice was deep and clipped. "What can you tell me?"

Johanna gave him an overview, but when she started to go into detail, he interrupted her.

"That's fine," he said. "I think it would be best if I met you at the jail. You could introduce me, and we could visit with Miss Owens together. However, at some point I will have to ask you to leave—attorney client, you understand."

WHEN JOHANNA ARRIVED AT THE JAIL, Clark was already there, involved in an avid conversation with the security guard. When he saw her, he ended the talk and walked over. He was tall, of mixed heritage with an olive-toned complexion and sandy brown hair. Although he had an average build and face—when he smiled he was transformed into an appealing handsome man with more than his share of charm.

They exchanged pleasantries.

"Mrs. Hudson, we have a little wait," he said, directing her to a pair of chairs at the side of the waiting room. "They're still processing Ms. Owens. They want to make sure of her citizenship status."

"Call me, Johanna," she said, letting him guide her by the elbow.

"Feel free to call me, Nolan." He handed her a business card. "Dean Cameron told me your story. In full disclosure, I have to tell you it has been a few years since I've argued a criminal case. But Dean gave me the particulars of your friend's involvement, and I think I can help her."

"Thank you, I am so relieved," she said. "Trinidad is a character, but she loved Eloise like a sister. She never could have killed her."

Clark nodded and took out a pad and pen.

"I can't tell you how many times I've heard that said," he replied. He looked up and must have caught Johanna's dejected expression because he quickly added, "But let's hear your friend's story. How did you two meet?"

Johanna described her contacts with Trinidad and her limited encounters with the dead woman.

"So, you never entered the room with Manley's body? You didn't see any indication of another's presence?"

She grimaced. "No, not at all. I couldn't get in the room. I only saw her from a crack in the door opening."

Clark glanced at his phone for the time. They'd been waiting about thirty minutes.

"We should wrap up our conversation. They'll be finished with her soon," he said. "Is there anything else you think I should know? Or you need to know?"

"Yes," Johanna said. "There's the man who came to see Eloise, he could have a motive. I don't know his name, but . . ." She shook her head and waved her hand in dismissal. "Never mind, Trinidad didn't get his name and she never saw him. I don't have a clue how to find him." She pressed her back to the chair and took a deep breath. "Tell me about you? What's your background? Why were you available to take on a pro bono case?"

He gave her a quick smile. "You don't pull punches, do you?" He leaned back and said, "I'm a native Californian. After serving in Iraq, I came home, got my Boalt Law School degree and—"

"Clark," the security guard called from the doorway. "Your client's ready."

They both rose and gathered their belongings. The guard took them down a labyrinth of hallways to a bank of elevators, where he waived his ID card over a small screen to open another set of doors. Without speaking, he led them to drab room with a metal table and three chairs.

"Wait here," he said. "They're bringing Owens up." He shut the door behind him as he left.

Clark looked at her and said, "Johanna, if you would excuse yourself after introducing me, I'll call you back in once I establish a basic understanding with Ms. Owens."

"Of course."

There was a tap on the door, and Trinidad entered, her hands in cuffs in front of her. Her usual jaunty air was missing. The day before, her long dark hair had been worn in a heavy braid and wrapped on the crown of her head. Now, it hung in a loose bedraggled ponytail, and her beautiful blue dress showed evidence of underarm perspiration. She looked defeated.

"You can remove the handcuffs, officer," Clark said. "My client is not a flight risk, and I doubt seriously she could overcome you after breaking out of a locked exit."

The deputy sheriff nodded in agreement. Trinidad rubbed her wrists when the cuffs were taken off.

"I will be right outside," the officer said, closing the door with a click.

Trinidad went over to Johanna and sat down beside her. Johanna wanted to give the woman a hug, but Trinidad stiffened and Johanna dropped her arms to her side.

Nolan Clark introduced himself, adding, "Mrs. Hudson has asked me to consider representing you in the murder of Eloise Manley."

Johanna didn't think it possible, but Trinidad stiffened further.

"If Johanna choose you, then okay with me." She took a deep breath. "I will need your deterred payment plan."

"She means 'deferred'," Johanna interjected.

"Yes, I figured it out," Clark said without taking his eyes off of Trinidad. "I'm wondering, Mrs. Hudson, if you wouldn't mind leaving for a few minutes so I can talk in private with Ms. Owens?"

"No," Trinidad protested. "No, Johanna must stay. She needs to hear everything."

Clark smiled, understanding. "Yes, she will hear everything, but you and I need to talk in private. I must know what you are going to say, first."

"No," Trinidad insisted. "My story is no going to change. Why should I say twice? She here now."

"Trinidad," Johanna soothed. "Mr. Clark is your lawyer. He needs to hear your story in your own words. You can tell him anything, and he can't tell anyone else."

Trinidad crossed her arms.

"No. There is nothing I say to him I not say to you."

Clark raised his hands in acceptance.

"All right, Ms. Owens, Mrs. Hudson can stay. Why don't you tell me about your background?" Clark folded his hands on the table. "Tell me, how did you come to this country?"

Trinidad shrugged. "I come many years ago with my mother. Her name Trinidad, too. She go back home, and I stay here and become citizen. It not important to story." She leaned forward and tapped the desk with her forefinger. "What *is* important, I not kill Ellie."

Johanna snuck a side glance at Clark's face. He appeared unfazed by his client's attitude.

He pursed his lips. "Okay, then, tell me what you know about the day Eloise Manley was killed." He turned to a clean page in his notebook. "Tell me about that morning, what were you doing?"

Trinidad looked down at her hands. She had regained her composure, but Johanna noticed there was still a hesitancy about her that left the impression she was holding back or preparing to lie.

"Ellie called me to come over. She want me to bring Bible for Johanna. She in hurry because her boyfriend was coming over, and she didn't want Johanna to stay." She took a breath. "I don't like boyfriend. Ellie not see the way he look at her. I did. He was not good man. I could tell, but she not listen."

Knowing she was risking Clark's ire; Johanna raised her pen. "What was the boyfriend's name?"

Trinidad shook her head. "I don't know. She never introduced me. But, one day I come to visit, and I hear her on phone. I knew it was him. She call him 'Chad.'"

"Getting back to the day of the murder," Clark prodded, with a reproachful glance to Johanna. "You went to Eloise's house and . . . ."

"I live close. I told her I would be there before I go to store and then go to work. And I did. I went over, and she looked so pretty. Pretty for him. It made me angry because he bad for her. She want to be . . . loved. But he was no good, and I told her."

"And . . . ?"

Trinidad looked to Johanna for understanding. "I may have told her a little loud." She sighed. "I think I yell, then she yell, then no one listen. She tell me to leave, and I slam door."

"The police found her blood on your fingerprints," Clark said. "When did you return?"

Trinidad's eyes glistened.

"I . . . I go to store, but I see I still have Bible. We argue, but I have Bible for you. I think I will drop off Bible before I go to work." She faced Johanna. "I should take Bible to work and give to you. But . . ."

Clark did not let up, and pressed, "Ms. Owens, what happened? What did you see in Eloise Manley's motor home?"

"I . . . I look in her window to the bedroom, the curtain was pulled back, and I see her." Trinidad's voice dropped almost to a whisper. "She in same pretty dress, looking so pretty, but . . . but her . . . her . . . her head . . . her yellow hair was red with so much blood. I want to scream, but I go to her inside room. She on bed . . . I reach out to touch her hair . . . but the door is stopped . . . I push door hard, but only open little more. This was the last time I tried to touch her . . . but she was . . . was gone."

Johanna relived the scene through Trinidad's description. It was as she found it, as well. "Trinidad," she said. "Why didn't you call the police?"

Clark shot Johanna another warning look. She sat back and looked contrite.

"Ms. Owens, is there some reason why you didn't feel comfortable calling the police?" he asked.

"I . . .I knew Johanna would come soon, she would see Ellie. I saw blood on my fingers. I . . . I not think the police will believe me. I . . . I . . ." she let the sentence drift.

"Why wouldn't the police believe you?" Clark urged.

"Because this is not first time, they think I kill someone," Trinidad responded.

CHAPTER TWELVE

JOHANNA AND CLARK EXCHANGED LOOKS OF SURPRISE.

They sat mesmerized as Trinidad narrated another murder. Her story was not a long one.

Trinidad looked down at her hands, and spoke in a soft tone.

"I lived on island with my family. Nevin and I are only two left at home. Others—the other two, my sisters, they move away with own families. Nevin and I are very close. He is two years older, but not in head. In head, he is much younger. Kids tease him bad, and my mother say we go to America to live with her sister, and get help for Nevin. But in America it worse for him than on island. My mother must return to the island to take care of rest of family. She take Nevin to live with a family in Hayward who will get money to take care of him. She leave me with her cousin. I want to visit Nevin, but they don't want me to. It make Nevin too sad. I can be on my own but not enough to take care of Nevin, too. I don't have money."

Trinidad stopped speaking. Johanna was wide-eyed but said nothing and waited for the woman to continue.

"They found his body on beach near Vallejo. The family says he was trying to go home to Trinidad. It was not first time he go to water. But it was first time gang man find him, kill him and mark him with his sign."

She took a sip from her glass of water. "A month later they find man's body."

Trinidad leaned back in her chair and upturned her chin to look Clark in the eyes.

Clark raised his eyebrows and cleared his throat. "Ms. Owens, how old were you when your brother . . . ah . . . died?"

"Twelve."

Johanna noticed he did not ask if Trinidad had committed the murder. Probably because it entailed some legal responsibility he didn't want to assume. But then it came to her.

"Trinidad, is that why it is so important that I find the inheritance for Ruby? To make sure she gets money to have the best care?"

"Yes, Johanna." The woman nodded with tears in her eyes. "You must hurry and find Ellie's father and get money for Ruby."

CHAPTER THIRTEEN

JOHANNA DROVE IN SILENCE, and made her way onto the Bayshore Freeway heading for the Shade of the Pines Funeral Home in Colma. As if on a continuous loop, Trinidad's reveal during their meeting with Clark ran through Johanna's head.

Was Trinidad a murderer?

Two questions kept coming to the forefront of her thinking: first, who was Eloise's boyfriend? And second, was she too accepting of Trinidad's explanation about discovering Eloise's body? She could tell Clark was asking himself the same question.

A couple of hours later, she turned into the parking lot of an unassuming building no bigger than a fast-food drive-up, which it closely resembled. Shade of the Pines was situated in the midst of several nearby mortuaries and graveyards, without a pine tree in sight. Johanna knew most of Colma's land was dedicated to cemeteries, so the population of the dead outnumbered the living by a thousand to one. Curious, she did some research and discovered that San Francisco had outlawed cemeteries within its city limits after the San Francisco quake in the early 1900s. Colma was chosen as the location for the relocation of all graveyards. Eventually, over the years, Colma became known as "the City of the Silent."

It seemed deadly silent now. Only a few cars drove past on the roadway, and gravel crunched under her feet as she made her way to the front door. A soft bell chimed when she entered.

"Good afternoon."

Johanna jumped. The voice had come from a corner doorway, across and to the left of the door. It belonged to a tall, balding man with thin strands of black hair slicked back to a high gloss. He wore charcoal grey slacks, a maroon sweater and white shirt with a maroon striped tie. She realized she hadn't seen him at first because he blended in with the maroon-flowered wallpaper surrounding a crackling fake fire in a faux stone fireplace. Then there was the smell of a carnation scented air freshener. He so exactly fit her stereotype of a mortician that she smothered a chuckle.

"I didn't mean to startle you," he said. He had a friendly smile as he reached out his hand. "George Mason, I'm the administrator. How can I help you?"

She shook his hand and accepted the chair where he directed. He settled himself behind a desk, and waited for her response.

"I'm not here for . . . for services," she began. "I'm trying to locate family members of someone whose memorial service was provided by you some years ago, a Denise Sutton."

A slight wrinkle appeared on his forehead. "How long ago?"

"It's been about fifteen years," she said.

"Hmm . . . our records do go back that far." He raised an eyebrow. "And you are?"

"I'm sorry, I should introduce myself." Johanna smiled. "My name is Johanna Hudson. I'm a genealogist representing a friend of the family."

"I see. Do you have a death certificate?"

"No, but I have your notice." Johanna reached inside her purse for the memorial announcement.

She didn't realize how grimy it looked until he held it in his pristine hands. Holding it with only his thumb and forefinger, he looked around the room as if trying to spot the hand sanitizer.

"Hmm, yes, it is one of ours. We, of course, have updated our brand and service offerings since then." He handed it back. "Good thing it's a slow day. I can go to the office, review the database records, and see what I can tell you." He stood. "If you would wait here, please."

Johanna used the time to review emails on her phone. She had gotten as much information as she could off the standard genealogical websites. Eloise's mother, Jeanette, had one older sibling, Denise, who had predeceased her. According to the memorial pamphlet, the never-married Denise appeared to have lived at home with their parents. It was that address Johanna sought.

She returned her phone to her purse. There was an urgent message from Howard Ackerman to return his call—a call she had no intention of returning. She would deal with Ackerman on her own terms.

"Here, you go," Mason said, holding out a sheet of paper. "This is all the information we have on the funeral of Denise Marie Sutton. I was new to Shade of the Pines back then, so I don't remember Ms. Sutton's service, but you can see it was a very small one—just her mother, sister, a cousin, and a few friends. It was our basic Earth Angel Package."

While Johanna glanced at the page, the door chimed, and two young men assisting an older woman came through the door. Mason gave her a look that said: *excuse me, but these are paying customers.*

She gathered her things. "Thank you. You have been so generous with your time."

He gave a quick bow. "You're very welcome." He smiled at his new visitors. "It is our goal to provide personal attention to every detail."

Johanna nodded and moved with haste past the new arrivals, shutting the door behind her.

Sitting in her car in the parking lot, Johanna's curiosity couldn't wait for the commute back to her office. She opened the program notice.

Eloise's grandmother's name was Olivia Fields. She must have remarried at some point after Eloise's mother, Jeanette, was incarcerated, which was why Johanna had hit a wall looking for the Sutton name. The memorial brochure included a picture of Denise, who completed the set of beautiful Sutton women, same blonde hair and sea green eyes. She was twenty-five when she died of congestive heart failure.

No addresses were provided, just a reference that Fields was a resident of northern California. The final entry at the bottom of a newspaper notice was the name of Jeanette's cousin, Therese Bertrand, a teacher at Homewood School and a resident of Oakland.

She'd found the needle in the haystack.

CHAPTER FOURTEEN

"YOU FOUND 'A' NEEDLE IN THE HAYSTACK,'" Ava insisted. "You're a little closer, but there are a lot more needles out there, and the clock to find Eloise's father is ticking. If he's dying, you don't have a lot of time. "

Johanna had pulled over to the curb when Ava's call came through from Australia. She was surprised how clear the connection sounded. Ava said she would be wrapping things up in the next couple of days and would not need Johanna to pick her up from the airport. She would Uber home. Johanna had taken this opportunity to bring her up to date on their latest client's status.

"Considering how much it took to get me this far, even a little closer feels like an accomplishment," she said. "Besides, there's another 'needle'—the boyfriend. I need Trinidad to describe him for me. If I could locate him—"

"Hey, hey," Ava interrupted. "I thought you were trying to find the father and Ruby, not Eloise's killer."

"True enough," Johanna acknowledged. "I need to stay focused. But I'm pretty sure they are linked."

Johanna ended the call with a promise to keep her partner up to date.

It didn't make sense that Eloise's grandmother was searching for Eloise to cause her ill. Jeanette's mother couldn't collect an inheritance. With her daughter dead, she needed Eloise to prove she was in line for her father's estate. To complicate things further, now, with Eloise dead, it wasn't just a matter of showing a link to her biological father, Johanna had to find Eloise's daughter, Ruby, and show her connection as well.

Johanna made a call and headed back to the East Bay. She looked at the time. She had an appointment to keep.

THERESE BERTRAND LIVED OFF OF TRESTLE GLEN AVENUE in Oakland's Grand Lake District. Johanna circled the block for a second time, trying to find a parking space along the narrow street. The majority of the original homes had been built in the 1920's, when one car per family was considered the height of prosperity. The neighborhood was still sought after, and pride of ownership was evident with manicured lawns, well-trimmed shrubs and leafy shade trees.

At last, she spotted a mother hurrying her young ones into a car. As they pulled out, a space was released, and Johanna slid into it. Granted, it was three blocks away, but she was grateful to find anything within a mile of her destination.

"I should have told you to park in the driveway," Therese Bertrand said after hearing Johanna's parking tale. She led her into a formal living room with ornate moldings and vaulted ceiling. "Can I offer you a cup of coffee or tea?"

Johanna shook her head. "No, nothing for me, thank you. I know you said on the phone you had to pick your grandchildren up from soccer. I have a few questions I'm hoping you can answer."

Therese Bertrand did not inherit her Sutton cousins' beauty gene. Looking to be in her forties or fifties, she was not unattractive, but her unremarkable features and thin brunette hair underscored her average looks. She resembled a nervous sparrow as she perched on the arm of an overstuffed chair.

"I'm not sure why we had to meet. I told you everything I knew about Jeanette on the phone. You know more about this Manley woman than I do," Bertrand said, twisting and untwisting a pull on her terry top. "I only agreed to talk to you because you said someone killed a young girl, and you wanted to know if she was Jeanette's daughter."

"Of course." Johanna smiled, trying to ease the tense atmosphere. "I know it must feel strange to talk to someone who calls you out of the blue to ask about your family's past. For that reason, I thought meeting me would give you an opportunity to know who I am. Like I told you, I was given your name from the funeral director who buried your cousin, Denise Sutton, Jeanette's sister."

"I know who she is," Bertrand snapped. "Well, you're here now. You want to know if I know this Manley person?" She blinked several times, and her hands shook. "That is, if . . . if she's Jeanette's daughter?"

"Yes, that's right," Johanna spoke slowly in hopes of calming her down. "Even though she's dead, I still feel obligated to follow through with our contract."

"What do the police think?"

"I don't know," Johanna said. "They keep waving me away when I try to explain. They don't see what I'm trying to accomplish as anything directly to do with the murder."

Bertrand nodded in seeming agreement. She crossed her arms and rubbed her elbows.

"I was older by a few years," she said. "When we were growing up, Jeanette was always determined to do things her way. She was so headstrong, which was what got her into trouble." Bertrand fidgeted with the padding on the chair's arm rest while she spoke. "She went ahead and had a child, even though we all told her she was making a mistake. Jeanette didn't listen and paid the price later."

"Did you know her child's father?"

"No, no." Bertrand shook her head with emphasis. "Jeanette knew how to keep a secret. When she went to prison and everything—you said you knew she went to prison—she had to place the child with a foster family."

It took all the force of will Johanna had not to shake her head in amazement at the lack of feeling about family that placement revealed.

"I know what you're thinking," Bertrand said, as if reading her mind. "But the family was so upset with the murder and everything, a foster family was the best place to ensure the child's happiness. We meant it to be only temporary, but time went by so fast," Her voice faded into silence.

Again, Johanna resisted showing any reaction to Bertrand's words. "Yes, I heard the story from Eloise. That's the main reason I got involved," she said, "Eloise was trying to find her father. She knew about her mother, Jeanette, but nothing of her father. She thought if I could locate her rela tives . . . ." Johanna let the rest of the sentence drift. She stopped short of explaining more, and she said nothing about Ruby. She didn't know who was friend, or foe, in this drama.

Bertrand nodded, her face pale. "After Jeanette killed Eugene, Aunt Olivia couldn't handle the stress and shame. Jeanette admitted the little girl wasn't her husband's. You can imagine we were all upset."

Johanna again ignored the woman's insensitivity that there had been a child who'd lost her mother and her father and been sent away to live with strangers rather than her remaining family.

"Yes," she said. "It is unfortunate Jeanette went to prison. But I was hoping you could tell me something about the man with whom she had the affair. Were you and Jeanette close?"

Therese Bertrand looked off as if to the past. "It was like standing next to the sun. She was so beautiful and warm."

Johanna raised her eyebrows at the change in the woman's tone. "You mean Jeanette Sutton?"

"What? Yes, I mean no, no we weren't close. Well, maybe Denise and Jeanette were. After a while the entire family kind of went their own way, and by the time Jeanette and Eugene broke up the first time, we all hadn't gotten together in years. In fact, the last time was at Denise's funeral."

"Do you think you could give me the address of your Aunt Olivia? Or, maybe her phone number?"

Bertrand ran her hand through her hair. "I don't know it. She moved when she remarried, and we didn't stay in touch."

She was lying about something. Bertrand avoided Johanna's eyes. This clan may have put the "d" in family dysfunction and deception.

Johanna squinted, not sure what she believed. She tried one more time. "Did you ever hear the name of Jeanette's child's father?"

"No."

She answered so quickly, it sounded like a lie.

Johanna decided to try one more time. "Were you and Denise close?"

Bertrand blinked as if processing the change in topic. "Yes," she said, warily. "Yes, Denise had this heart condition and wasn't physically strong, not like Jeanette, and she went like that." She snapped her fingers. "Imagine a heart attack so young — funny how life is. Denise was my best friend as well as my cousin. She should have been the one to marry next, not Jeanette."

The prom king married the prom queen.

"It must have been a troubled marriage. Did Jeanette ever mention—?"

"Look, I don't know what these things have to do with looking up ancestors. You don't even know for sure if this Eloise was Jeanette's child."

Yeah, right.

Bertrand's brows bumped together in a scowl. "It's getting late, and I have to pick up the kids."

She stood and Johanna rose from her chair.

"Well, I won't take up any more of your time, here's my business card." Bertrand pocketed it and headed to the door.

"I do have one more question," Johanna said. She continued when the woman stopped walking and turned to face her. "I found some photos among Jeanette's things. They appear to be taken in the Lake Tahoe area. There was a little boy in one of them. Do you think you could take a look and tell me if you recognize anyone?"

Therese Bertrand's pale face lost its remaining color.

"You have photos?" Bertrand said. "That's . . . that's good. Do you have them with you, now? I still have a few minutes; I could take a look at them and see if I recognize anyone. "

The woman stepped forward. Johanna took a step back, her warning radar going off.

"No, they're in my office," she said. "My schedule is a little crazy. How about I check back with you and we can set up a time for tomorrow, or the next day?"

"Sure," Bertrand said. "Text me, and we can arrange to meet." She looked over her shoulder at a clock on the mantel. "I really need to get going." She motioned with her head toward the door.

JOHANNA TURNED ON THE LIGHTS IN THE OFFICE. She had learned at least two things today: the Manleys were Eloise's salvation, and Therese Bertrand was a lousy liar.

She would arrange to meet Bertrand with the photos after her visit with Trinidad. She knew her news that progress was being made would be the salve that kept the woman sane. Clark had left a message that Trinidad's arraignment was set for the day after tomorrow, and if Johanna had any luck at all she would have made progress locating Ruby.

Johanna finished going through messages and email. Ava's message on voicemail brought her first heartfelt smile for the day.

"Ta da . . . I'm done here and on the next flight out of Dodge. I wrapped things up sooner than I thought. See you soon."

It would be good to have her partner back in town. After these past few days, she wasn't sure anymore if having Australia as a field office was such a good idea.

Her smile dimmed when she moved some papers and a business card fluttered to the floor—Ackerman.

It was not yet five o'clock. Dean Cameron should still be in his office. He didn't seem surprised to hear from her.

"Nolan told me what happened to your friend. If anyone can help her, he's your guy," he said, his chair squeaking as he rocked.

Johanna ran her fingers through her hair. "He seems all right, but I'm calling for a different reason, to tell you of a conversation I had with Harold Ackerman and—"

"What! You know you shouldn't be talking with him. You're being sued for a lot of money and—"

"Whoa, buddy, I didn't call him. He contacted me."

She took the next few minutes to go over her conversation with Ackerman.

Cameron was silent.

Johanna cleared her throat. "Are you thinking my husband might have been a crook and left me holding the bag?"

"What do you think?"

Her shoulders slumped. "I don't know. I started going through his possessions, but I couldn't find anything," she said. "But, I'm not giving up."

Now, there was silence on both ends. Johanna realized her growing sense of dread was forming a knot in her stomach.

"It's getting late," Cameron said. "Email me the address where your husband worked and a couple of contact numbers, and I'll try to get a read on things." He took a long pause. "Ackerman's suit is no basis for extortion. If he had a case against your husband, he would have filed a complaint with the police. So, it's clear he wants money. I've got a busy day tomorrow, but I'll make sure we have time to meet. Will you be okay with that?"

"Yes, of course," she said. "I'm going to Trinidad's hearing in the morning if you could make it in the afternoon that would be good."

"Done."

Johanna was tired and ready to go home, but she took out the Manley file and flipped through the photos, wondering if the males in the Sutton family were as attractive as the females. In one Tahoe picture, Eugene Dawes appeared to grip his wife by her upper arm. The half-smile, half-wince on Jeanette's face seemed to broadcast a wish to be somewhere else. Why did she choose this picture to give her daughter? Johanna spread them out on her desk. Why any of these photos? And, who was the young grinning boy? He didn't seem to fit into the story line she knew so far.

Sighing, she returned all the photos to the envelope and slid it under her desk pad. The file she returned to the drawer. Johanna considered herself a good researcher, because she knew the most important thing was to ask the right questions.

CHAPTER FIFTEEN

WHEN HER PHONE CHIMED, Johanna fumbled with the bed sheets and struggled to regain her presence of mind after a fitful sleep.

"Hello," she said, squinting to see the time.

Almost four o'clock in the morning.

"Mrs. Hudson," a young female voice said. "This is Officer Leone with the Hayward PD. Do you know an Ava Lowell?"

Johanna sat up and turned on her side lamp.

"Yes, I do. What's wrong?"

"It appears she was the victim of a robbery. She was taken to Hayward Hospital and asked us to call you."

"What?" Johanna exclaimed. "Is she okay? Where did it happen? When?"

Sounds of flipping paper ensued. "She sustained head and facial wounds, and she might have a sprained ankle," Leone said. "You should speak to the doctor about the extent of her injuries. I can tell you the robbery took place in your offices. Don't worry, we secured them. We'll get somebody out later this morning to take prints."

"Thank you for calling, officer," Johanna said her mind now wide awake and racing with implications. "When did you say this took place? I was just there this evening."

"Hmm, you were at the scene. If you can come in before seven, I can take your statement. I was the assigned officer at the site. Your office was pretty badly tossed. We think it occurred sometime around midnight. One of the maintenance crew heard loud noises and got curious."

Johanna was dressed and on the freeway within the hour. She'd explained to Leone that she wanted to see Ava first and would be along after.

BUT WHEN SHE CALLED THE HOSPITAL, it turned out they would not allow visitors until regular hours.

Frustrated, she went straight to the police department. Johanna couldn't believe she was back at the Maricopa County Sherriff Department. But it wasn't Leone who greeted her. Detective Dominic Quinn was leaning against the reception counter going through paperwork.

"Mrs. Hudson, Officer Leone had some paperwork to finish up before she went off shift," he said, giving her an acknowledging smile. "I came on duty and saw your name on the incident sheet and asked to be assigned to the case. In case there's a link to the Manley murder."

Quinn looked tired. Today, he wore loafers, a tweed sports jacket, blue shirt, and navy tie. His wavy dark hair was smoothed into obedience with a modicum amount of gel. Clean-shaven, except for the world-weary eyes, he would have passed for a history schoolteacher.

"I came to give a statement," Johanna said, still half dazed.

"Yes, I've got a room set up for you," he said. "I hope your partner is okay. Let's do this so you can get on with your day."

She followed him to a small office behind a set of double doors. He pointed to the recorder at the end of the table and spoke into the mic, announcing their names and the purpose of their meeting.

"What time did you leave the office for home?" Quinn asked.

"It was late, around seven, seven-thirty," she said. "I'd had a busy day, and I'd come back to clear my desk and get ready for Trinidad Owen's arraignment later this morning."

"Were you expecting Ms. Lowell this evening?"

Johanna gave a slight frown. She had to think the police had played back her message tape. They knew the answer already.

"Yes and no. She was supposed to be back from her trip by the end of the week. But she left a message yesterday . . . I mean the day before, saying she was coming home on the next flight." She rubbed her forehead.

Quinn looked at her and then smiled. "I know you must be tired. I won't be much longer." He picked up a pad of paper and turned to the next sheet. "Would you agree it's unlikely Ms. Lowell was the intended victim?"

"Ava?" Johanna scowled. "The intended victim? No, of course not. No one knew she was coming home but me."

"That's my way of thinking, too." He leaned back in his chair. "Is there any reason why someone would break into your office? Do you have anything of value?"

Johanna said, "Not at all. Remember, we're just a small service business. There's nothing of value anyone would risk prison for."

She didn't like holding back information from Quinn but she wasn't going to risk sharing what she had learned until she knew its impact on Joel and Amber. Just as the thought entered her mind, she shook her head—not Amber, she meant Ruby.

"You said you do family trees. Seems harmless," Quinn said. "Okay, why don't you return to your office and check things out? See if anything is missing. Give me a call and let me know." He handed her a business card. "If I don't answer, leave a message."

IN HER CAR, JOHANNA MADE A QUICK PHONE CALL to the hospital and was told Ava was still under the influence of a sleeping medication given to stabilize her vital signs. Visitors would be allowed in the afternoon. Johanna clicked off her phone. Even without the visit to the hospital, she didn't have time to go to the office *and* make Trinidad's hearing. She opted for the hearing.

There were a few clusters of individuals scattered throughout the courtroom. Johanna was quick to spot Nolan Clark, who motioned her to come forward.

"The judge is running a little late. And they won't bring Trinidad up until he's seated," he said, stepping from behind the defendant's desk to sit next to her in the viewing section. "I'm going to try to get bail, but I've dealt with Kaminsky before. He's a tough prosecutor. He'll fight tooth and nail to keep her inside."

He peered at Johanna. "What's wrong? You look like the end of a hard day, instead of at the beginning of one."

"Someone broke into our office and attacked my partner."

"What?"

Johanna took him through the events of the early morning.

Clark was silent in thought for a few moments after she finished speaking. He looked at the time then down at the hands in his lap. "I know Leone and Quinn. They are a couple of the good ones, and very sharp. If there's any evidence leading to a suspect, they'll find it." He ran his hands over his slacks. "What do you think the burglar wanted?"

"I think –"

"All rise," the bailiff announced in a flat voice. "Department Five, Criminal Court of the County of Alameda is now in session, the Honorable Judge Michael Romero presiding. Please silence all cell phones."

Clark left her side and went to sit at the defendant's post.

"Please bring in the prisoner," Romero called out.

The door opened from the left side of the courtroom, and Trinidad appeared. Clark must have gone to her residence and gotten her clothes to wear. Johanna smiled when the woman, wearing a royal purple dress with bright yellow birds scattered on its skirt, entered and stood next to her attorney. Trinidad's colorful dress looked as if she were going to a family gathering.

She wore no makeup, and appeared vulnerable and young. Clark smiled approvingly at her and patted her shoulder. Trinidad gave him a lackluster smile, at the same time she looked behind her and sought Johanna's eyes.

They exchanged concerned looks.

The proceedings went quickly. Clark argued bail should be awarded since Trinidad was a long-time law-abiding resident and had worked at the same job for almost seven years. Kaminsky appeared to be a young man who never looked up from his papers and never at the defendant. He argued they had yet to determine Ms. Owens official immigration status, and she was considered a flight risk since she had inherited an unknown amount of money from the victim's estate.

Johanna raised her eyebrows, but Clark seemed unimpressed. Trinidad straightened her shoulders and leaned over to the attorney.

"Don't worry. I not do," she said in a loud whisper.

Moments later, after reviewing the file in in front of him, the judge ruled.

"Bail denied. The prisoner shall be retained in custody until. . . ." Pausing, he looked down at his calendar. "Mr. Clark and Mr. Kaminsky, there's a holiday coming up. I shall hear all motions a week from this Friday on the 16th, and the trial date will be set in six weeks, on the first Monday of the month."

Clark stood. "Your honor, if you would be willing to re-consider bail at the motions hearing, I think we will be able to show at that time there are several other potential suspects."

The judge looked over at Trinidad, who was sitting with her hands in a dramatic prayerful pose of pleading. Johanna thought she saw a faint but fleeting smile cross his face.

"Very well, I'll re-consider." He closed the file and handed it to the hovering court clerk. "Next case."

"Trinidad," Johanna called out as a female deputy sheriff led the stoic-looking woman to the side door. "I'll see you this afternoon, we can talk then."

Trinidad glanced at her and turned away without speaking.

Clark came up to Johanna. "I need to speak a few minutes with Miss Owens," he said. "Can you wait for me in the lobby? I won't be too long. I need to talk with you about Trinidad's gift from Eloise Manley."

"Sure."

He followed Trinidad through the door.

Johanna waited thirty minutes, but when he did not reappear, she texted him a note saying she had to go to her office and see what damage was done, and she wanted to visit Ava. She would get back to him before the end of the day.

JOHANNA THOUGHT SHE WOULD FIND YELLOW CRIME SCENE TAPE across the entrance to their office, but other than a fine gray dust that looked like dirt smudges on the door handle, the outside appeared normal until she entered. She gasped.

The two tall bookshelves along the far wall were now leaning backwards, with books everywhere but on a shelf. The two visitor chairs had been overturned; their undersides sliced neat with a knife. The cubicle partitions were leaning, propped up by the books, chairs and small table that covered the floor.

She groaned as she observed her desk. Drawers had been emptied and contents spilled on top. Papers were everywhere. Even the printer had been overturned. She stopped. Her eyes landed on tiny speckles of blood that covered the bottom of Ava's inverted chair. The red starkly contrasted with the white paper underneath.

Johanna put the back of her hand against her mouth in despair.

Poor Ava!

She fought back tears, with mounting anger. Who would do this? Why?

She righted her chair and began to stack papers and file folders. A large file caught her eye. She snatched it up. It was empty.

The Manley photos!

She rushed to move the drawers, books, folders, and papers from the top of her desk. Her heart beat rapid in her chest. Why hadn't she put the photos away? Why hadn't she taken copies of them?

"Ah, excuse me."

Johanna jerked up to see an older woman standing in the doorway.

"Yes, what do you want?"

"My name is Simone," she said, reaching out with her hand. "I work with Trinidad. She told me you were helping her, and I heard what happened to your friend," the woman said, shoving her hands into the pouch pockets of her green hoodie. "I got here before I have to start work. I thought maybe you could use a hand."

Simone gave a tentative smile. She was in her late fifties. Her jeans were baggy and her tan tennis shoes were scuffed. She wore her graying hair in a long braid, but it was her compassionate blue eyes that calmed Johanna.

"I . . . I, yes, I would love to have you help me." She looked around at the mess. "It's kind of hard to know where to start."

"Honey, it's always best to start at the beginning." She zipped off her jacket and tied it around her waist. And without another look in Johanna's direction, she began to stack books against an inside wall. "I'll start at the front door."

Johanna gave Simone a small smile and then remembered what she'd been looking for when the woman arrived. Clearing the last items off her desk, she lifted up the desk pad and smiled in relief: sliding out of an envelope were Eloise Manley's photos.

They were secure. She placed them in the brown folder, and then the folder into her purse.

Johanna located the large garbage bags they used to keep documents that required shredding, using it now to collect debris and unrecognizable papers. She smoothed wrinkled pages on top of Ava's desk. She replaced the printer table to an upright position.

Thank goodness they kept their laptops with them. She knew her friend well enough to know she was compulsive and would have scanned any important documents and put them on her PC.

Much of their current work was safe.

For the next hour, the two women worked in silence. It didn't take Simone long to return the bookshelves to their place along the front wall. Johanna checked the time. She needed to leave to visit Ava.

"Simone, I must go. My partner is in the hospital, and I have to see her," Johanna said, pleased how the front area was starting to resemble normalcy. "You've been a boon, and you must allow me to pay you. Perhaps you could come back tomorrow?"

"Sure, be glad to. I got nobody at home," the woman said. "I need to get goin' anyway. I'm working Trinidad's offices, too—they'll take her job if she doesn't show up. You tell her hello for me." She untied her hoodie from around her waist and slipped it on. "And, Honey, it won't take me long to get this place in order. I'll meet you here tomorrow—same time."

From her car, Johanna watched as Simone loaded a cart with cleaning supplies and trudged heavily down the walkway.

"Ms. LOWELL HAS AUTHORIZED US TO SPEAK WITH YOU," an officious nurse said, while examining Johanna's identification. She handed it back. "The doctor says she's doing fine. There was severe trauma to the head, and some facial bruising. She was pushed, and when she fell she received a minor ankle sprain. Overall, she should be able to go home day after tomorrow. You can see her now if you want."

"I want," Johanna said, grateful to hear the prognosis.

The blinds were drawn, and a ceiling fluorescent light illuminated the form in the bed. Ava lay with her back to the door.

"Ava?" Johanna said in a raised whisper.

She lifted her head. "Johanna, hi, come in, I was resting. It's easier if I'm on this side. The other side is pretty banged up."

Johanna moved to the good side, sliding a chair close to the bed and taking a seat. "When did your flight get in? What happened?" She tried not to stare at her friend's bandaged face and head.

"It was almost ten o'clock when I got to the office," Ava said, her voice strained and scratchy. "I thought I was so smart. I would drop my files off before going home." She ran her tongue over her lips. "I had jet lag, and I knew it would be hours before I could get some sleep."

Without speaking, Johanna passed her the Styrofoam cup of water from the bedside table. Ava took a deep swallow.

"Thanks, they gave me something that dries out my throat." Her voice stronger, she continued. "Anyway, I got to the office around ten. We've never had any trouble, so I wasn't concerned about my safety." She took another swallow of water. "I saw the night light we keep on for security, and the door was locked, so I went in. I was making noise because I didn't notice anything was wrong, until I got to my desk. I turned on the copy machine to start making copies of my notes and client documents."

"Of course, you would," said Johanna, smiling grimly.

Ava believed in having backup for the backup. Their files would be only half as large, if she didn't have hardcopy archives in the event the computers broke down.

"Hey, I'm in the hospital. Don't be so judgmental." Ava smiled, and then grimaced with pain. "As I was about to say, I didn't notice anything until I looked over to your desk and saw all the drawers were pulled out. Then everything happened real fast. I've been thinking the robber must have been hiding behind the door to the restroom. The police said he may have used picks to get in and locked the door behind him. Remind me to order a security camera. Anyway, as I walked over to your area I felt a presence, and when I turned around there was this guy. He had on a hoodie that covered most of his face. He couldn't have been more than two feet from me." Her voice wavered, and her hand began to shake. Pausing, she stared at it as if willing it to stop—and it did. "Oh, and he had a knife."

"Oh, Ava!" Johanna groaned. "Did you get a look at him?"

Her partner, with only one eye evident, shook her head. "Not really, he was a short little guy, wore sunglasses, and his shirt top covered his mouth. I think I could have taken him on, if it weren't for the knife. I asked him what did he want, but he didn't respond. He said nothing the whole time. He motioned with his knife for me to move toward the front. When . . . when I passed him, he . . . he hit me with something and knocked me out. The next thing I knew I woke up in the hospital."

She touched the bandage on her head and winced.

Johanna took her friend's hand. "I am so sorry this happened to you." She gave her fingers a squeeze. "Just rest and get better."

"The police said the office was trashed," Ava said. "Is it pretty bad?"

Johanna nodded. "But nothing that can't be put back together. Simone, who works with Trinidad, has agreed to help me. So it won't take long for us to be back in business."

Ava took another sip of water. "Why do you think he picked us?" she said. "I mean, Mullen's Gems is right down the hall. It's a jewelry exchange. Breaking into them I could understand. But, why us? What did he want, a family tree?"

"I don't know," Johanna murmured.

But she had an idea.

CHAPTER SIXTEEN

"**Y**OU THINK YOUR BREAK-IN has something to do with the death of Eloise Manley?" Nolan Clark said, tossing a pen onto his desk. "Help me to understand the connection."

"Hear *me* out," Johanna said. "I told Jeanette Sutton's cousin, a Therese Bertrand, I had photos."

"Who is Jeanette Sutton and what photos?"

"Jeanette Sutton Dawes was Eloise Manley's mother, and the photos—well, I don't know who they are. But Therese Bertrand—that's Jeanette's cousin, was very interested. I could tell. Maybe she told someone to break in."

She could see he was skeptical, so she explained her quest for Eloise's father's identity, and the search for her child, Ruby.

Clark frowned. "But you said the pictures weren't taken. The thief was looking for something else."

"I know," she said. "My initial theory was debunked, but nothing else makes sense. I think he just didn't find the photos. He wasn't counting on Ava showing up. The break-in has to be about Eloise Manley." Johanna chewed her bottom lip. "I do have another theory. Do you think you could locate a James Bryce?"

"Now, who is he?"

"He's the man who came to visit Eloise—to threaten her. He said he was representing her grandmother, but didn't leave a card or her grandmother's name. Eloise's maternal grandmother's name is Olivia Sutton Fields," Johanna said. "I found out she remarried and now lives in northern California, but I don't have any contact information."

Clark was taking notes, but she could tell he was getting irritated. "I'm not sure any of this is going to help Ms. Owens. It sounds more like a family dispute than murder."

"There's possibly a lot of money involved. I think people have been killed for a lot less," Johanna retorted.

He looked at her. "True enough." He picked up his phone and located a contact. "We can hire a private investigator, but it's going to cost you."

"Forget it. I can't afford an investigator," she said. "Besides I don't think I'm going to need one. This is what I do—track people down."

THE VISITORS' ROOM AT THE JAIL WAS AIR CONDITIONER COLD, and Johanna rubbed her upper arms. There were less than a dozen people huddled in muffled conversations. It had been a long day, and now, waiting for Trinidad to make her appearance, she realized she was more than tired. The door opened and Trinidad, suited in bright prisoner orange, entered with a broad smile on her face. It appeared she had mentally made peace with the outcome of the court hearing.

"Johanna, you come," she said happily. "Good to see you. Did you find Ruby?"

Johanna gave her a look of amazement. "No, I haven't found Ruby. I've been dealing with Ava being attacked, our office being burglarized, and being personally threatened. So, no, Trinidad, I haven't found Ruby . . . yet."

A silence fell between the two women.

Johanna spoke first, "I'm sorry. You're in jail, and I'm—"

"It okay, I not do murder," Trinidad reached to pat her hand, but the guard made a movement toward their table. She pulled her hand back. "Ava attacked? When?"

Johanna related the events of the past two days. Trinidad seemed to sink into her chair.

"Trinidad," Johanna said. "I've been meaning to ask you. What do you know about Eloise's boyfriend? What did he look like? What did he do for a living?"

"The police asked me same thing," she said. "His name is Chad. He work on computer in one of studios where Ellie make tapes. He not tall, he not short, he got tattoos on his arms. He look like ordinary person, nothing special."

"Do you know his last name?"

The woman pursed her lips. "I used to. Ellie maybe say, but I not remember now."

"Can you think of anything that makes him stand out?"

Trinidad smiled. "He had squeaky voice like squirrel. I thought it funny he work with sound."

Johanna scribbled on her note pad.

"Oh, Simone said to tell you she's going to do your job *and* her job--so you won't be fired."

Trinidad's shoulders slumped. "I need my job. Simone is . . . is good to fix."

"Even with your inheritance?" she said with emphasis.

"Ellie had no money, Johanna," Trinidad said, shaking her head. "She give me her trailer, that is all. It nicer than mine, but I rather have Ellie." Her voice fell.

Reproached, Johanna stopped herself from reaching for the woman's hand.

"Trinidad, do you remember anything about the man, James Bryce, who visited Eloise? Can you describe him?"

"I was not there. But I might saw him leave." She thought for a moment. "He not old, not young—in the middle. Brown hair and eyes, he look like man on TV that sells insurance for cars."

Her time was up.

Johanna watched as Trinidad was led away. She reached her car minutes later and stopped to look back at the jail. It was an austere institution, and she knew Trinidad had been putting on a brave face. Now she had a second reason to find Ruby.

CHAPTER SEVENTEEN

I T TOOK THE NEXT DAY TO GET THE OFFICE BACK IN ORDER. Simone came in the early afternoon and helped Johanna to finish up.

"Simone, I can't thank you enough for your assistance," Johanna said when it came time for Simone to leave. "Here's a check to say thank you. I know you have to start your real job now."

The woman sniffed. "Don't think anything of it. Like I told you, I got nothin' else in my life." She looked down at the check, and a smile crossed her face. "But this will come in handy. Thank you. Tell Trinidad hello for me."

She left with a wave.

Johanna opened the Manley folder, and pulled out Eloise's birth certificate. The white correction fluid, covering the name of the father, was very thick, but a college classmate had once shown her how to thin it to reveal what's underneath.

She dipped a cotton swab into a small bowl of rubbing alcohol and mild dish soap and dabbed with care at the paper. The trick was to avoid blurring the ink further. After 26 years it was noticeably fading.

The alcohol didn't work.

Johanna rubbed her forehead in thought. There wasn't enough to read. She would have to look elsewhere. Having hit a wall with Jeanette's side of the family, she would try her husband, Eugene Dawes' side. Johanna didn't expect his family to be too forthcoming, but there was a chance they knew what was going on at the time Jeanette had given birth to Eloise.

Using three genealogical databases, she was able to identify four

"Dawes" possibilities in Alameda County and three in Maricopa County. She searched through Alameda County obituaries without luck. Maricopa wasn't a large county, it had two newspapers for the past fifty years. Jeanette killed Dawes when she was in her mid-twenties. That put the date around 1999 or 2000.

She found a notice. It wasn't a large article even for Maricopa:

> Maricopa County (August 5, 1999).—The Maricopa County Sheriff identified the man shot Wednesday evening in his home at 1275 Knowland Street, as Eugene C. Dawes. Dawes was allegedly fatally shot by his wife Jeanette Dawes in what police describe as a domestic dispute. Neighbors said the family was quiet and kept to themselves. The wife was arrested and taken to County Jail. Their five-year old daughter was placed in foster care.

Johanna printed out the piece AND added it to her folder. There was no time to waste. "Hello, my name is Johanna Hudson and I'm trying to locate a relative of Eugene Dawes."

It was her third call. Earlier attempts had yielded no results. The name listed was: C. Dawes.

"Eugene? He's been dead," a woman snapped. "Who are you?"

"My name is Johanna Hudson, and I'm a genealogist. I know Mr. Dawes passed away, but I'm doing research for a client, and I was hoping to speak to a relative."

"A gen . . . genealo . . . what does that mean?"

"It means I research family trees and help people find their ancestors. Are you a relative?"

"I'm his sister, Cathy. There's nobody else in our tree. What do you want? Who did you say you're working for?"

"I'm sorry. It's confidential. I know your brother passed away but—"

"He didn't 'pass' away. That bitch killed him," her voice climbed. "She and that pinched-face mother of hers. They killed him, first with shame, then with bullets. Gene had his problems; I couldn't stand him half the time, myself. Once he missed out on getting into the pros, all he could do was drink and whine. But that *Jeanette* tore him apart and made him crazy. Gene was filled with shame."

Johanna jumped in, not wanting the flow of information to end.

"Miss Dawes, do you remember the name of Jeanette's boyfriend?"

"No, I don't." Dawes said, and then her voice lowered, "I'm sorry, I've got nothing more to say. I'm a caregiver for my mother. It's time for her lunch."

"Miss Dawes, I don't mean to bother you, but if you could tell me the name of one of Eugene's friends or maybe Jeanette's." She took a breath. "I'm trying to help their daughter."

"Their daughter?" she repeated. "Oh, yeah, that pretty little girl? She wasn't *their* daughter. She was *her* daughter. Knew it from the day she was born. Jeanette didn't admit it until later, but we all knew. She didn't look a lick like Eugene."

Johanna took another stab at it. "Did you know any of their friends?"

Dawes huffed. "There was a couple that lived down the street from them. They used to go out together. Mom and I used to babysit—I can't think of the little girl's name—when they went out. She was a good girl. But anyway, the couple got divorced and moved."

"Do you remember the wife's name?"

She was reticent to tell Cathy that Eloise was dead. But she thought there was a good chance Jeanette would have made friends with another female.

"Marilyn . . . no, not Marilyn . . . Margot. Her name was Margot, don't remember her last name but she's been in the news. I recognized her on TV the other day. That's how I remember her first name; she's in charge of some charity on the peninsula." Then, she spoke to someone over her shoulder in another room and returning to Johanna said, "I don't know any more than that, and I've got to go."

Dawes clicked off.

Johanna was drained. It had crept up on her, and now she was ready to head home. It would be nice to have someone to go home to, to eat dinner with, to watch TV, to play with—

No. She squeezed her eyes shut. She would go to bed.

There was no one to go home to.

CHAPTER EIGHTTEEN

THE NEXT MORNING, JOHANNA LAY IN BED staring at the ceiling. The edges of dawn had turned her curtained windows pale. The downward thinking spiral from the evening before was one she didn't want to repeat. She had been treated for depression after Joel and Amber had died. Pills were still in her bathroom in case . . . in case she started to slip. It had been a while since she'd felt so alone.

Her push back was activity, not medication. She threw off the covers and readied to go into the office to finish the cleanup. She turned on her phone and four messages from Howard Ackerman appeared. Johanna wanted to forward them to Dean without listening, but thought it better to hear what he had to say first.

Suppose it was about Joel.

She listened.

Message: Mrs. Hudson, I can assure you it is in your best interest to return my call.

Message: This is Howard Ackerman, please contact me as soon as possible. Your time to make things right is running out.

Message: This is Ackerman, you can try to ignore me, but in the end you are only hurting yourself.

Message: Okay, Mrs. Hudson, if I don't hear from you by ten o'clock tonight, I will have to proceed with a new legal action. I didn't tell you everything about your husband.

Johanna froze. What did he mean? It was already past his deadline. She punched in his number.

"What are you doing calling me this early? You were supposed to call last night." Ackerman whispered, evidently trying to keep his wife from hearing. "But it's a good thing you did. I don't think you realize what's at risk."

Johanna could hear him rustling out of bed, and shuffling to another room.

"Mr. Ackerman, I don't know what you think you have on my husband, but I don't like being threatened. I've already told my attorney about you and—"

"You did what!"

"Yes, I told him," she said. "Now I don't know what you think you have on my husband. Just because he may have given you investment suggestions that didn't pan out doesn't mean—"

"I can't talk now," he whispered. "I'll call you back." He clicked off.

More than a little irritated, she put the phone in her pocket and headed out the door. Any further conversation would have to wait until she found out what Ackerman had on Joel.

WITH THE OFFICE STILL IN A STATE OF UPHEAVAL, Johanna decided to work out of her townhome for the day. Her laptop on the kitchen table and a cup of coffee close by, she Googled every aspect of Joel's former employer, and followed information trails that appeared to link to activities affecting investments. She discovered several mentions to Joel Hudson, but nothing of substance.

Her phone rang. It was Ackerman.

"What do you want from me?" Johanna said into her cell phone. "First, you sue me because you say Joel directed you to a poor investment. A premise you can't prove and will not win. And now you keep alluding to some nefarious scheme that you think qualifies for blackmail. Did my name show up on a list of stupid people?"

Howard Ackerman spoke enunciating every word. "I told you, file a claim with your insurance company and keep your husband's reputation intact."

"And if I don't?"

"Your husband did business with some very rough people," he blurted. "You can imagine what they could do."

Johanna gasped.

"Did . . . did these *people* break into our office and attack my partner?" She didn't try to keep the menace from her voice. "You can tell them it had the opposite effect. I'm going to tell my lawyer not to settle, and you, and your 'people' can rot."

"We—"

She clicked off and headed to the basement.

What had Joel been doing? She'd brought out a set of files that Joel had packed into one of the smaller totes. She flipped through the first folder labeled: Correspondence 2015. It contained memos, email copies, and what appeared to be client letters. Her eyes drifted to the signature and there was no doubt it was his. Nothing jumped out at her. It all seemed routine. She stopped and squinted at the email address below his name.

She'd never seen it before.

On the laptop, she went to email and entered the address. The computer response was almost immediate.

Hello, I will be travelling and unavailable for some time. Please feel free to leave a message. I will be checking my email periodically. Thank you, Joel Hudson.

Her fingers lay frozen on the keyboard. What did he mean—unavailable for some time?

Her mind raced. It was too early to contact Dean Cameron. He'd mentioned he had a court appearance this morning.

Her phone rang and she glanced at the screen. Johanna coaxed her adrenaline to back down.

"Good morning, Mother," she said, keeping any sign of anxiousness out of her voice. "You're up early."

She and her mother were close, but not demonstrative. For Johanna, she knew her mother always had her back—whether she wanted her to or not.

"I've been worried," Elizabeth Girard replied. "I just read in the paper about Ava. Is she all right? What happened?"

Johanna took her through the event. "We had a burglar, but Ava's going to be okay. The office is already back to order."

Her mother sighed. "That's all good to hear, Johanna," she said. "However, I had to read it in the newspaper. Why didn't you call me?"

She should have, but her mother had a way of reminding Johanna of her vulnerabilities, and she needed to focus on her strengths.

"I was going to, and I have no real excuse," she said. "Can I make it up to you? How about lunch tomorrow?"

"How about lunch today?"

"Tomorrow, okay?" Johanna responded. "I'll pick you up and we'll lunch at The Yellow Cardinal."

"Promise?"

"Promise."

JOHANNA SPENT THE NEXT HOUR returning client inquires. Dean Cameron had run into delays in the court and had left a message for her to contact him in the late afternoon. She didn't mind. The delay would give her time to run down Joel's email address.

What did it mean?

She made a sandwich and ate with one eye on the computer screen as she scrolled through Oak City Bank entries. Joel hadn't many friends, at least none Johanna would call close. He would tease her that friends took time, and he wouldn't be a good friend.

Johanna knew Ackerman would be contacting her again. But unless he came up with some sort of proof, there was little she was willing to do about his threats.

She was moving on.

For now, she wanted to follow up with Cathy Dawes' partial memory about "Margot," a television lifestyle commentator. Johanna searched the internet for televised segments in the last month about charities. She located a reference dated three weeks previous by the vice-president for development at StairSteps—a Margot Beck. StairSteps wasn't a charity, it was a housing developer located in Los Gatos. It was donating its employees' time to assist with building affordable housing in low-income neighborhoods in the city. Beck had been a guest promoting the program on a daytime home improvement talk show.

Johanna ran Beck's name through a professional design member database and found her business: Beck Design. The address for her company and residence were the same: Burlingame, just south of San Francisco. This time she decided to go in person without calling ahead.

Beck Interiors was a small white cottage-y house on a side street in the retail section of Burlingame. The tinkle of a small bell sounded her arrival. There was no one in the lobby area, but the room was full of furniture. Johanna ran her fingers over attractive decorative pillows scattered and artfully placed on a sofa. She peered into a delicately formed glass vase splashed with bold colors.

"Good afternoon, may I help you?"

Johanna looked up into the warm brown eyes of Margo Beck. She recognized her from her promotion pictures on the internet.

"Yes," she said. "My name is Johanna Hudson, and I hope you're Margot Beck."

Beck looked barely five feet, and had streaked blonde and gray hair pulled back into a chignon secured with an exquisite mother of pearl barrette. Dressed in a white silk blouse and charcoal gray pants, set off with a narrow red belt—she gave off an air of confidence, class and Chanel.

Beck crossed her arms. "You found me. How can I help?"

"You have many beautiful things, but I'm not here to obtain your services," Johanna rushed. "I'm a genealogist, and I'm working for a client. I understand you might be able to tell me something of Jeanette Sutton, or you may have known her as Dawes."

"Jeanette, of course I remember her. It's been over twenty years, but we were good friends before . . . ." Beck stopped, and motioned with her head. "Would you like a cup of coffee or tea? We can talk in my office. The only reason you caught me here today is because I'm expecting a delivery of area rugs. I open to appointments only."

"Then thank you for seeing me. Coffee will be fine."

Johanna followed her into what must have been a bedroom in the store's previous life. It was now a bright and sunny office in muted rose, gray and yellows, serene and welcoming. They sat at a small table crowded with binders of samples. Beck moved them to a chair, and assembled cups and a small pot on a black lacquer tray and set it between them.

"Okay, now tell me," she said. "Who's your client? I'm sure you know Jeanette is dead."

"Mrs. Beck—"

"Call me, Margot, please."

Johanna nodded and took her through her agreement with Eloise and the search for her grandmother.

"Eloise," Margot murmured. "She was such a beautiful little girl, just like her mother. Jeanette named her after the character in *Eloise at the Plaza*." She paused to see if Johanna recognized the story, but when Johanna shook her head, no, she went on. "We all met at their wedding. Eugene was a good friend of my ex-husband."

"Did you plan to live down the street from each other?"

Margot put her cup down. "How did you know that?"

"Cathy Dawes. She turned me on to you," Johanna said. "She mentioned she would watch Eloise while the four of you went out."

"Yes, we had good times, until Eugene lost his job. It was downhill from there. Before then, we would go up to Tahoe and rent a boat on the lake and spend hours enjoying good times."

Johanna sat up. "Eloise gave me some photos of two couples at Lake Tahoe, would that be you?"

"More than likely," Margot said, visibly remembering.

"Was there a child who went with you?" Johanna asked. "There's a photo of a young boy standing at the entrance to Kings Beach."

"A boy? No, we never went up to the lake with any children," she mused. "But tell me, how is Eloise? She should be in her mid-twenties."

"Margot, Eloise is dead. She was murdered a week ago."

"Oh, no," Margot cried. "Not that beautiful girl. Who did it?"

"They haven't caught him . . . or her, yet. But before she died, I promised Eloise I'd find her daughter and biological father." Johanna leaned forward. She was taking a chance sharing Eloise's story, but she needed to trust someone. "I need to find Eloise's grandmother—Jeanette's mother."

Margot raised her eyebrows. "I'm not sure I can be of any help," she said. "Jeanette and her mother stopped speaking when Jeanette went to prison. I would visit her, but I may have been the only one who did. Jeanette's sister was the lone person from that side of the family who stayed in touch, and then she had a heart attack, so sad."

Johanna thought about her next question. "Ah, were you friends with Jeanette when she . . . she killed her husband?"

Margot nodded. "I will never forget it. She came to our house that night, with Eloise in her arms." She put her hand to her eyes. "Eugene was a pig. He never got over being a high school big shot—homecoming king and queen, what a joke. But that was the highpoint of his life, and it was downhill for him after graduation."

Johanna wasn't surprised; she sensed that might have been the case. "She left Eloise with you?"

"Yes, we just had her the one day. The next day Social Services came and got her. Jeanette's mother didn't want to raise her. I couldn't believe the woman—her own grandchild. She was a piece of work, so Eloise was placed in foster care." She shook her head. "I tried to get David to keep her with us, but he was too selfish. That's why we never had kids." She poured another cup of coffee. "Like I said, I used to visit Jeanette in prison. It killed her to be there, especially without Eloise. She took Sutton, her maiden name back, to start over. When she got sick, she wanted the Manleys . . . gosh, I can't believe I remember their name. Anyway, she wanted them to adopt Eloise, but their religion or something wouldn't let them. What a self-righteous couple."

"Did Jeanette ever talk to you about Eloise's biological father?"

Margot turned her head away and looked out the window in thought. Johanna said nothing and waited.

"No, she spoke about him, but never mentioned his name. She implied he came from a well-to-do family, old San Francisco money. She said they met at a Bay to Breakers run."

Johanna raised her eyebrows. The Bay to Breakers is an annual footrace in San Francisco. It got its name from the fact the seven mile race started downtown, a few blocks from the bay, and finished where the breaker waves crashed onto the Pacific coast at Ocean Beach.

"I guess I never saw Jeanette as an athlete," Johanna said.

"She wasn't, not at all. She said it was a bet she lost." Margot smiled with the recall. "Jeanette said they literally ran into one another. She stumbled and he tripped over her. It was love at first sight." She stopped to take a sip of tea. "She and Eugene separated for about six months after they'd been married two years. I think it was during that time the affair . . . uh, blossomed. She never said, but I got the feeling he was married. Then Eugene asked to be given another chance, but by that time Jeanette was pregnant." Margot patted her hair. "We knew when Eloise was born Eugene could never have produced her. He knew it, too. They tried to make it work, but Eloise was proof of Eugene's failures—or he took it that way. He went back to drinking."

"And her mother?"

"Olivia Sutton?" Margot sniffed. "She was out of the picture. Like I said, she paid one visit to see the baby, and then nothing. After her sister Denise died, the only person who would visit was her cousin. Therese contacted her once in a while, but not after Jeanette was incarcerated."

Johanna noticed Margot was getting restless.

"Just a couple of questions more. Do you know where Olivia Sutton is now?"

"She came to Jeanette's funeral. I was shocked to see her. For some reason, I got the feeling she came to see if Eloise's father would show up. If he did attend, he stayed well hidden," Margot said. "To answer your question about Olivia: no. We ran into each other at a political fundraiser about seven years ago. She nodded to me, I nodded back."

"I understand she's remarried."

Margot shrugged. "We didn't speak. I didn't know her new name." She pointed out the window to a large van that had pulled up to a side entrance. "I'm sorry, my rugs are here. I've got to go."

"Thank you for the time you've taken. If you can think of anything else, will you give me a call?" Johanna handed her a card.

"Of course," Margot said, putting the card on top of her desk. "So sad about Eloise."

Johanna looked around as she buckled her seat belt. The feeling someone was looking at her was strong. There were a few people walking on the sidewalk and a couple sitting in the window of a café. While there were cars parked on the street in either direction, none had anyone sitting in them. But the feeling would not go away.

Was she being followed?

JOHANNA SAT WAITING IN THE LOBBY outside Cameron's office. When she'd arrived twenty minutes before, he was harried and told her a case was blowing up. She wasn't surprised; Dean and time seemed at odds. However, she didn't mind, and was glad for the time to sort out what she was going to tell him about a Joel she didn't know.

"Johanna," Cameron had said. "I hate to keep doing this to you, so if you can't wait around, I promise to give you my complete attention tomorrow."

"No," she said. "If you don't mind, I'd rather wait."

He nodded and dashed back in his office.

Now, she used the time to make notes about her conversations with Therese Bertrand and Margot Beck. She had a picture of Jeanette Sutton and a vague sense of her mother, Olivia. She wondered if there was a record of Bay to Breaker runners over the years.

Ava might have some ideas when she was thinking better.

Johanna stared off into the room. Howard Ackerman's threats were another matter. She debated how much to tell Dean. Joel had a secret, maybe a secret life. The thought sent a feeling of dread throughout her chest. Maybe she should leave well enough alone. Wonder if Joel had committed a crime and—

"Johanna," Dean said, approaching her with an outstretched hand. "I am so sorry to keep you waiting. Come on back."

They settled in comfortable chairs in his office.

"Was Nolan able to help your friend?"

She gave him a small smile. "He's doing his best to get her off on bail, but there are no other suspects. I'll know more on Friday when she comes up for bail reconsideration."

"Well, if anyone can get her off, it will be Nolan." He handed her a bottle of water. "Okay, now tell me what's going on with Ackerman."

Over the next half-hour, Johanna went through her conversations with Howard Ackerman, including the break-in of their offices. Without comment, Dean took notes until she finished.

"If it wasn't for the burglary and his threats, I'd call his bluff," she concluded. "Joel and I had a wonderful marriage, and while I thought we told each other everything there was . . . there was something . . . he felt I . . . . Anyway, he was involved in something that he kept from me. I'm sure he thought it was for my own good. On the other hand, when I thought it through, Ackerman's warning about me not coming to you doesn't make any sense. He's the one that filed the lawsuit."

"Did he tell you why he needed the money?"

"Something about his retirement savings. I didn't believe him. Besides, did he ever give us documentation that he actually lost five hundred thousand dollars? And think about it, our business is such a poor source of easy cash. We don't have any money, even with insurance. It doesn't make sense."

"All that is true, but until he puts on the table what he has on your husband, and owns up to why he chose your business to sue, we'll have to wait him out." Dean crossed his arms over his chest. "It has been my firm belief the stupidity of people who scam and commit crimes cannot be overstated."

"I think you're right," she said. "I need to get going. I want to pay a visit to Ava at the hospital, and I need to get home." She stood.

Dean walked her to the door. "Okay, there's nothing I need do for the time being. We filed a response to the Ackerman complaint denying all their allegations of fraud conspiracy. The ball will be in their court, and from what you've told me, I bet they're going to let the ball drop."

Johanna nodded, but she wasn't as sure.

CHAPTER NINETEEN

A GRUMPY-LOOKING AVA, SITTING UP IN THE BED with her arms crossed, greeted Johanna as she tiptoed into the hospital room.

"I'm awake," Ava growled. "If they don't let me out of here soon, I'm going to take matters into my own hands and escape."

Johanna smiled. "Good evening, Ava. It's good to see you back in your old form."

Her friend's bandages had been reduced to a singular one covering a quarter of her head. The bruises on her face were exposed, and the once angry red bruise had tempered to a dark purple. They still looked sore and painful.

"I want to go home. I can take care of myself. I told the nurse to get my doctor and—"

"Here I am, Mrs. Lowell," a tall man looking down at a clipboard walked in. "I see your vitals are looking well. Let me take a look at your wounds."

Johanna stepped back to let him come forward. He took gentle care to lift her bandage and peer at the gash. Then he turned Ava's head from side to side, using a small flashlight to look into her eyes. He straightened. "Things are healing well. Any headaches?"

Ava shook her head. "When can I go home?"

"How's that foot?" he turned back the blanket without waiting for her answer. He held it lightly and moved it from side to side. "Any pain?"

"Not enough to keep me from running out of here," Ava retorted.

A small smile played on the doctor's lips, but he returned to his stern countenance. "All right, if you continue to improve, then I think you can go home tomorrow."

Ava clapped.

"Take it easy for a few days," he said. "Do you have someone who can look after you?"

"I will," Johanna interjected. "She can stay with me."

"Johanna . . ." Ava began, and then smiled. "Thank you."

He cocked his head in sympathy. "Then, under that condition, I'll leave instructions with the nurse to take with you."

He hurried out as he had come in.

"Jo, it's very kind of you to take me in." Ava smiled at Johanna. "So, tell me what's going on. I can do research while you're meeting with clients."

"The doctor said to take it easy, Ava," Johanna cautioned. "Let's start out slow. Give me your key, and I'll get your clothes and things from your house. Make a list."

She shook her head. "I'll come with you. What time can you pick me up?"

"No, you're not. Just make the list." Johanna sighed, what had she gotten herself into? "I've got lunch with my mother I cannot break if I'm to have any peace in this world. I'll see you tomorrow, how about mid-afternoon?"

"All right," Ava said, picking up a pad and pen. She scribbled the items she wanted. "Now, leave. I can't visit any more, I need to call Australia."

List in hand, Johanna closed the door behind her and grinned. Ava was going to be fine.

JOHANNA ARRIVED AT THE YELLOW CARDINAL early. Securing a booth, she used the next minutes to check her email.

A text notification caught her attention.

I think you know who I am. I'd like to speak with you as soon as possible. Respond with a time and place. James Bryce

How had he found her?

Johanna tapped out a message. She stopped mid-air over the send button, wondering if this was what foreboding felt like.

The Elephant Bar in Fremont. Thursday at one o'clock.

She hit send.

"HELLO, DARLING, YOU LOOK LIKE YOU'VE BEEN HERE AWHILE," Elizabeth Girard said, sitting down and then leaning over to kiss her daughter on the cheek. "This is a special treat."

Johanna struggled to wear a smile, the words of the text still reeling in her head. "Hi, Mom, I'm glad you insisted on lunch." She picked up a menu. "Let's order. I need to pick up Ava's things, and I have an errand to do."

Elizabeth Girard, like her daughter, was not beautiful but she was attractive. Her long thick brunette hair was pulled back into a loose ponytail. Slim, with dark brown eyes, she wore her beige line turtleneck with a tan hip-length knit topper over indigo denim jeans. Her only jewelry was a long tortoise-shell pendant that topped off the outfit. She looked chic and confident.

Her mother picked up the menu, then tossed it down. "I want a salad. I'm on a mini Mediterranean diet." She leaned across the table. "Speaking of Ava, how is she doing?"

Johanna had a question in her mind what a "mini Mediterranean" diet consisted of, but she was in no mood to hear her latest eating fad. Still, she was proud of her mother—a woman who believed in pursuing every dream.

"Ava's going to stay with me for a few days," Johanna said. "The doctor says she's doing great. But she can't take care of herself, so I invited her."

Their conversation was put on hold as the server brought their food.

"That was a kind thing to do," her mother hesitated and then said, "About the other night, I want to apologize. I didn't—"

"Mom, it's all right," Johanna interrupted. "I've been working on a client's family tree, and it's a gnarly one."

They exchanged chuckles.

"That was a terrible pun," her mother said. "Which reminds me, what day was your office broken into?"

"Tuesday, why?"

"Well, I got this call Wednesday morning from this man, who asked if he could speak with you. I told him you didn't live here anymore, and had your own place. He apologized and hung up." She took a sip of her iced tea. "Why would he think you lived with me? I thought he might be a reporter."

Johanna looked away—James Bryce.

Maybe he wanted me to know he knew how to reach the people I care about.

CHAPTER TWENTY

JOHANNA SPENT MOST OF THE EVENING and all the next morning converting her extra bedroom and bath into a guest room for Ava. After finishing touches, it was ready and she hurried to the hospital. When she arrived, Ava was in her room dressed, and sitting in a wheelchair. She was answering emails on her cellphone.

"What took you so long?" Ava asked, putting her phone away. "A date?"

A nurse appeared to push the chair to the parking lot. Johanna walked alongside.

"I have everything ready for you," she said. "So, if you don't want me to walk away and pretend I don't know you, be gracious."

"I can do gracious."

In the car, Johanna glanced at Ava, her eyes closed, her face drawn, and Johanna realized her friend, despite her protestations, was still trying to heal.

"Okay, what's the matter?" Ava said, eyes still closed. "Something is wrong, I can sense it. Is it Ackerman? You might as well use this time to catch me up to date. This traffic is at a standstill."

"All right, I'll give you the high points," Johanna conceded. "I'll start from our last conversation."

It felt good to hear herself describe the events of the last few days affecting Trinidad and Ruby. Out loud, they didn't sound as bad as when they circled in her head. She held back on mentioning James Bryce, but when she came to Ackerman, she couldn't keep her anger down.

Ava's eyes opened. "So, you think *he* had me attacked? Is there a chance Joel . . . that Joel was involved in something . . . something illicit?"

"First, Joel would never be involved in something illegal. Second, I don't think the burglar expected you to show up. I think he was looking for something specific. Something I can't tell if he got his hands on or not."

The traffic began to move slightly faster than a snail's crawl.

Ava took a swallow from a bottle of water she held in her lap. "You need to go to the police."

"That's what Dean said, and I will. But, I want to find out about . . . I mean, I wonder if it has something to do with Joel. I need to . . . before . . . before it gets out in the open or, in the press." Her voice broke.

Ava patted her arm. "Okay, I won't badger you for another day or so. And then we're calling the police. And cut the innocent bit, I know that little trick you do with your voice."

Staring straight ahead, a little smile played on Johanna's lips.

JOHANNA SLIPPED OUT BEFORE DAWN MONDAY MORNING, to visit the office and locate a few new client files to bring home. She also did not find anything that related to Ackerman or Joel, and she called the police about the burglary. She wasn't ready to suggest Ackerman until she knew about Joel's involvement. She could tell they weren't hopeful about finding the perpetrator, but they took her report, and by the time she returned home, Ava was still asleep. Johanna used the time to fix breakfast. The smell of cooking and coffee had awoken her, but after a few bites, and a half-cup of coffee, Ava had dozed off.

Johanna tiptoed down the stairs and set up the table in the kitchen as her home office. She downed her own cup of coffee and found herself staring at the laptop screen, but not seeing it. Her thoughts jumped from one to another. She decided that the Joel she married was the true Joel. She had no reason to trust Ackerman's accusations and threats. If Joel had done something unlawful, then it would come out, but she was betting there was nothing there.

Then there was Eloise Manley. Trinidad's bail hearing was in two days, and Johanna had to give her some hope she was making progress finding Ruby. She had to be getting close, there were more clues to follow. Soon she had to be successful.

Later in the afternoon, she spent two hours on the phone; make that on hold, waiting to talk with any Social Services worker who would help her about Ruby's adoption.

"I know *I* can't find out who adopted a child, but I'm hoping I can take legal action to allow me to contact the parents," she uttered for the third time to a third social worker.

"I'm sorry, I think you need to see a lawyer."

"I've got two lawyers in my life now."

"Pardon?"

"Nothing, I'll think about doing as you suggest," Johanna yielded, and ended the conversation.

She tapped the top of her notepad. It had been just over a week since Eloise Manley's murder. She refused to believe she had hit a wall. Out of the corner of her eye, she stared at Eloise's box of memories on the floor. She picked up her phone and tapped in a number.

"Detective Quinn, this is Johanna Hudson," she said. "Are you close to finding Eloise Manley's killer?"

She could tell he was splitting his attention, he sounded preoccupied.

"She's in custody."

"Trinidad Owens is not Eloise Manley's killer, but that's not why I called," she said. "Did you find Eloise's adoption papers?"

"She was adopted?"

"No, *she* wasn't adopted. She put a daughter up for adoption."

"You think the daughter killed her?"

"No, Detective, Ruby Michaels is only five years old." Johanna held onto her frustration. "I . . . I'm trying to find her because I promised Eloise to find her birth father so Ruby can inherit."

The echo of another phone ringing sounded in her ear.

"Mrs. Hudson, the department has few resources. It doesn't seem as if this adoption has anything to do with Manley's murder. Unless you have something more direct, I don't think I can help you. Have you found out anything more on Eloise's visitor?"

"No."

She still wasn't ready to share Ruby's story with the police. Eloise had kept a low profile for a reason. If her grandmother could send a man like James Bryce and found out about Ruby—Johanna was concerned that the child would be used as a pawn. She wanted to be as prepared as possible for her meeting with Bryce. If he was who she thought, she could be meeting with Eloise's killer.

Johanna cleared her throat. "I thought you might have access to an information database that could locate individuals, or maybe official documents."

"Yes, we do. It's paid for by the taxpayers, who wouldn't appreciate it if we used it for private purposes," he said. "I'm sorry, Mrs. Hudson, but I have to get back to work. If you're at the Owens' hearing on Friday, I'll see you then. Good day."

He clicked off.

CHAPTER TWENTY-ONE

THE ELEPHANT BAR WAS A CHAIN RESTAURANT with a large lounge area and a generous afternoon happy hour. Even on Thursdays, it drew large crowds, which was the main reason Johanna agreed to meet James Bryce.

Johanna was glad she hadn't mentioned meeting Bryce to Ava, who would have protested and made it difficult for her to keep the appointment. However, this morning, Ava was visibly tired and offered little resistance to Johanna's care, and none to her explanation she had a meeting to attend. She was asleep before Johanna left the house.

Johanna arrived a little early and snatched a tall table and two barstools as soon as three women rose to leave. Settling in, she assured the server she was waiting for someone and yes she could bring a white wine.

She knew it was Bryce as soon as he came through the door. Tall, dressed in a black leather jacket and pants, he looked like a hit man. She held back a chuckle—dressed to intimidate? He searched the room until his eyes caught hers and strode forward, ignoring the looks of irritation as he pushed past the other patrons.

"Johanna Hudson," he stated more than asked. "James Bryce."

"Yes," she said. "I'm curious. How did you find me?"

He waved the server away. "Not hard, your name was in the paper. You discovered Eloise Manley's body."

Johanna grimaced. Of course, there went her privacy. He took the chair across from her. She got the sense he wanted to sit facing the door, but she wasn't willing to give up her position.

"Well, you found me. What do you want?"

Bryce leaned over the table with clasped hands. "I have a client who is interested in finding her long lost family. For a number of reasons, she doesn't want her identity revealed. It's not nefarious, it's just she's fanatic about her privacy. She wants to be sure before a contact is made."

"Did she think Eloise Manley was her 'family'?"

He shrugged. "It was a good possibility. My client is very protective of her son. He became . . . involved with Jeanette Dawes, and they became close. In my research—"

"Wait a minute," Johanna said excitedly. "Are you telling me that . . . that your client thinks she might be Eloise Manley's *paternal* grandmother?"

He held up his hand. "You're jumping to conclusions," he said. "I discovered Mrs. Dawes had a child, but the paternity is in question. I visited Miss Manley, but . . . but I was not given any new information, and it was inconclusive."

"Since she's dead now—*murdered*," Johanna emphasized. "How can I help?"

He peered at her. "I didn't kill her, Mrs. Hudson."

Johanna didn't try to hide her skepticism and ignored his assertion. "You said you were representing a client. Are you an attorney? A private detective?"

"Neither, I used the word loosely. I'm a friend of the family, in this case, a go-between."

"Then I'll ask my question again," Johanna insisted. "What do you want from me?"

He reached inside his jacket, and taking out a picture, placed it between them. "Do you know who this is?"

Looking down, to keep her expression hidden, she picked up the photo. It was Jeanette Sutton looking pensive on a bench in a park. It was taken at a distance, but Johanna had no doubts.

"No," she said, looking into his eyes. "Who is she?"

She could tell he didn't believe her. Bryce put the picture back into his pocket.

"Mrs. Hudson, may I call you Johanna?" He didn't wait for her answer. "Johanna, I think you know more than you are willing to tell me. I need proof Eloise Manley was Jeanette Sutton's daughter. There is quite a bit of money involved, and my client is willing to pay you for your efforts."

"I don't understand," Johanna said. "She could pay for professional help. Why bother with me?"

This time Bryce avoided her eyes. "You appear to have developed an acquaintance with a Trinidad Owens. We think Eloise may have given Ms. Owens a . . . a token which was given to her by her mother, Jeanette. My client's son gave it to Jeanette as a keepsake, and she would like it back in order to keep it in the family."

None of it made any sense. He knew, she knew, he was lying.

"This token, what is it?" she asked.

Bryce grinned. "Johanna, you must understand that unless you tell me you're willing to work with us, I am not inclined to share anything else with you."

"All right then, am I to understand you want me to convince Trinidad to give up this *token* in return for . . . how much?"

"One thousand dollars for Ms. Owens and five hundred dollars for you as a . . . facilitator."

Johanna was silent and then crossed her arms over her chest. "Is there a reason why you couldn't make your generous offer directly to Ms. Owens?"

He grimaced. "I'll be honest with you, it was unfortunate but I did not make a good first impression with Eloise Manley, and now it appears Ms. Owens is incarcerated and may feel the same about me."

Johanna chuckled. She could imagine what Trinidad's response would be to the abrupt and intimidating James Bryce. The monies offered were a modest payoff, but she had no intention of bargaining for a greater amount. She didn't like him. But what gave her pause was the existence of a token.

"Mr. Bryce, I'm not going to be able to help you . . . or your client—"

"I'm authorized to offer more money, and—"

Johanna waved her hand. "It's not the money," she said. "I'm a friend of Trinidad's, and my focus is to get her out of jail and off the suspect list for Eloise Manley's killing. I don't know anything about a token, but I will let her know of your offer. Do you have a number where I can reach you?"

Bryce's face became rigid. His jaw was tight, and his eyes squinted. "I don't think you understand. Time is critical, without Manley there is only the token."

"You're right, Mr. Bryce, I don't understand. You said your client wanted the token returned as a remembrance. Why is time a concern?"

If he were a dog, he would have growled.

"Johanna, I thought we could have a conversation," he said, standing. "Talk with Ms. Owens. She may be in need of money and may not appreciate your intervention." He tore off a corner of the paper placemat and scribbled. "Here is my number. I hope to hear from you, soon."

AVA WAS STILL ASLEEP WHEN JOHANNA PEEKED IN and closed the door to the hallway. Her head was swirling from the conversation with Bryce, and her determination was even stronger to push past him. It was her life experience when money was involved, and here it sounded like it could be a lot of money, truth was fleeting and motivation was high.

The thought of money drew her thoughts her husband's paperwork in the basement—Ackerman's words in her ears. Joel had handled all their money, and she'd been happy to have him do it. They weren't extravagant spenders, but had had to set aside savings for vacations and a new car. Johanna knew her delay and avoidance of going through Joel's things had nothing to do with money. It was fear of making a threatening situation worse.

She opened the door and started down the stairs.

Enough.

CHAPTER TWENTY-TWO

JOHANNA HAD NOT SLEPT WELL. Her sleep was trampled with dreams of Joel and boxes. When the alarm went off, she dragged herself out of bed, took a cool shower and dressed. As she gathered her keys and purse, she heard Ava mumble, "Good luck."

This morning, the courtroom was packed. It was as if everyone wanted their case heard so they could get on with their lives, including the judge who hurried every matter along at a rapid pace.

"Matter of Trinidad Owens vs. Maricopa County," the bailiff announced, handing the judge the court file at the same time.

The judge looked down at the paperwork, then at Trinidad who was already seated. If anyone could look fetching in bright prison garb orange, it was Trinidad. When the woman turned around to look over the chamber, Johanna smiled encouragement. Trinidad returned her smile with a tenuous one.

"Miss Owens, I have read your attorney's brief requesting bail, and I have read the prosecution's request for denial," the judge stated, flipping through papers. "I understand your immigration status has been verified, and you are in this county on a legitimate green card."

"Your honor, my client," Nolan Clark pronounced, "has already proven she will follow the law and make a contribution to society, without being a burden. I have a letter her from her employer. He—"

His opponent jumped up. "Your honor, this was a cold-blooded murder. You—"

"Save it for trial, counselors. This is going to be a very long day," the judge said, cutting off the argument and clasping his hands. "Miss

Owens, I don't think you pose a significant flight risk, but this is a murder offense, and I am going to award bail in the amount of one million dollars."

The smile that had flashed on Trinidad's face quickly disappeared. She clung to Clark's jacket sleeve.

He jumped up. "Your honor, my client is a cleaner and makes a minimum wage. She cannot come up with such an amount."

The bailiff was already approaching Trinidad to place her in the waiting arms of two sheriff deputies at the side door.

"Mr. Clark, you asked for bail, and now you have it," the judge replied. "Next case."

They sat in a small interview room down the hall from the courtroom. Johanna held Trinidad's hand. They were waiting for Clark to get off his cell phone.

"Johanna, where I get million dollars?" Trinidad said, shaking her head. "I maybe have four hundred dollars in bank."

Johanna squeezed her hand. "You don't have to come up with a million dollars, only ten percent, just one hundred thousand."

At that, they looked at each other and broke out into laughter.

"Please," Nolan Clark said, putting his phone in his pocket. "Share the joke with me."

Johanna explained, and he smiled.

"I admit, it's a lot of money, and I know you don't have it, Trinidad," he said. "However, I may know someone who can help you. I made an appointment to meet with him. I need to leave now if I'm going to make it before he leaves for a flight."

"Then you must go," Trinidad said, rising from her chair. "Don't worry, I wait here for you."

She and Johanna once more exchanged chuckles.

"You two must be punchy," he said.

"Just tired," Johanna replied. "Go. Go work your magic."

The guard allowed Trinidad to stay a little longer to speak with Johanna.

"How are you doing finding Ruby?" Trinidad asked.

Johanna, exhaled a breath, and summarized the situation. She had wanted to hold off as long as possible before she had to give Trinidad the news that California is a "closed adoption" state. Meaning adoption records are sealed once an adoption is finalized. While this protects the privacy of families, it makes it difficult for blood relatives to contact one another, let alone non-family members.

Johanna had worked with adoptees who were trying to work out their family tree. It was a tedious and time-consuming effort, but for them, worth it.

"Trinidad, you need to prepare yourself," Johanna stated. "I don't think we're going to have much luck finding Ruby in the system, at least, not in enough time for her to obtain her inheritance. Without Eloise, we don't have any rights."

"Then you must find Ruby out of system."

IT TOOK NOLAN CLARK AN HOUR to confirm a bail source for his client.

"The founder of an organization with a charter to help new immigrants agreed to front Trinidad's bail for six months," he said, calling from his car. "Then they'll have to be repaid. I'm on my way back to the court to wrap this up. Can you wait with Trinidad?"

"That's great news," Johanna said. "Yes, I'll wait."

She gave him a grateful smile when he arrived, but she wouldn't have been surprised to learn Nolan Clark had come up with the funds himself. He looked too matter-of-fact.

"Okay, Trinidad," Clark said. "All the paperwork is completed for the bail deposit. You're free to go. Johanna, you can give her a lift home."

Trinidad grabbed his hands to pull him close and wouldn't let go. Clark looked over her head at Johana, who gave him a thumb up.

THE AFTERNOON DRIVE LEAVING THE COUNTY JAIL was heavy with fog that padded the air like cotton stuffing. Visibility was low, and Johanna kept her eyes on the roadway ahead, but from time to time snuck glances at the woman next to her.

"Trinidad, you're so quiet," she said. "I know you must be happy to be out of there."

"Yes."

Trinidad was wearing the same blue dress she wore when they arrested her. Now, it was wrinkled and stained, adding to what felt to be an aura of despair enveloping her.

Johanna tried again. "It will be good to be back in your own home with your own things." She cleared her throat. "I can tell your thoughts are weighing heavy on you. Do you want to talk?"

"It will be good to be home," she said. "But . . . I am tired of talking. Johanna, I lost my best friend, and I owe this man so much money I never see in my life, and . . . and I gave my word to find Ruby, and we not find her."

Johanna pulled up into the driveway of the mobile home park. The yellow crime scene tape had been taken down from Eloise's motor home. She drove past the site of the murder to a parking space next to Trinidad's modest coach.

"I'm getting close, Trinidad. I'm getting close."

"I know." The woman nodded and gestured to her home. "I go inside now. I want to be alone. But, don't worry, I okay now," the woman said, patting Johanna's hand. "I need to take bath, comb hair, and think about things before I go to work tomorrow."

Trinidad walked to the door, and then turned back. "Thank you, Johanna, for being my friend."

CHAPTER TWENTY-THREE

T HE NEXT MORNING JOHANNA AROSE EARLY, checked on Ava and
assured her she would brief her on her return home. But for now,
she wanted to follow up with Frances Lynch, the woman who helped get
Eloise off the street, and who saved her family Bible.

For a weekend morning, the Life Passage Center was bustling with
patrons guided by a scattering of assigned volunteer workers. Johanna
had never been to a homeless shelter, and she realized her pre-con-
ceived notions of a soup kitchen with mats on the floor and unruly
street people were not present here. While there was a slight cleaning
fluid smell, it wasn't overpowering.

The shelter's glass front doors opened onto a space that must have
been some sort of community center. The room was bright with light
pouring in from large ceiling-high windows that kept the occupants
from being seen from the street. Along one wall were three cubicles, each
with large signs: Social Security, Housing and Welcome. Each contained
a worker behind a desk who was speaking to a resident, with two or
three people waiting in line. The room was noisy with voices raised in
conversation. At the front of the shelter, tables were set up cafeteria-style
facing steam containers now emptied of food. At the rear were rows of
mailboxes against a wall, which also held signage pointing to restrooms,
childcare information and the dormitory.

It was then Johanna realized the residents and community helpers
were almost all women.

"Can I assist you?"

A stocky, smiling black man, wearing a security uniform, approached her.

Johanna returned the smile. "Yes, I hope so. I'm looking for Frances Lynch. I have an appointment to see her. She said this would be a good time."

"She's here," he said. "If that's what she told you, then she's ready for you." He directed her to a side door leading off from the kitchen. "That's the entrance to the administrative section. Her office is the first one on the left."

Johanna passed through the rows of tables, nodding to the women who were setting up for the next meal and others who sat quietly observing. She peered into an opened door with Lynch's name overhead.

"Mrs. Hudson," she heard. "I'm Frances Lynch. Sit."

Johanna took the only seat in the small bright room, a well-worn but comfortable, brown leather chair. Frances Lynch was a youthful looking woman probably in her fifties, thin, with blue eyes and brown hair pulled back into a mid-back ponytail. She gave off vibes of boundless energy.

"Thank you for seeing me on such short notice, Mrs. Lynch, but—"

"Frances, please, and you're right, I wanted to see you because you said you were helping Eloise Manley, and I have an interest in knowing how she is doing. It's been years since I've heard from her. I have an impromptu inspection this afternoon, and I can only give you a few minutes."

Johanna gestured with an open hand. "Impromptu?"

Frances laughed. "Yes, well, for us knowing the day and time doesn't make a difference. It can get real crazy around here. And our assigned social workers want to make sure their time is well spent. Now, tell me. How is Eloise doing?"

Johanna wrinkled her brow. "I'm sorry to tell you, but Eloise is dead."

Frances gasped. "No. What happened? When?" Tears brimmed in her eyes, and she reached for a tissue.

Johanna summarized the details of Eloise's murder.

"I had so hoped she would have a happy life," Frances said. "She was so beautiful and with so much potential. Did she tell you how I found her?"

Johanna nodded. "She said you saved her life."

"That's a bit dramatic; she was a strong young woman. She was making her own way back to life. And the baby . . . ." Her head shot up. "The baby, what happened to Ruby?"

Johanna moistened her lips. "That's why I'm here. I'm trying to locate the family that adopted Ruby. I promised Eloise to—"

"Why would Eloise want to find . . . . I'm sorry, finish what you were saying."

She waved off the apology. "I'm going to trust you, because Eloise did." Johanna said, and took a deep breath. "Eloise's biological father may have some wealth, and she wanted to make sure Ruby was given her share. Before she . . . she died, Eloise made it clear since she was unable to give Ruby anything, she wanted to give her an inheritance."

"I kept trying to tell her," Frances sighed. "She did give her daughter something—she gave her life and a chance with a good family. I told her many children have much less." She dabbed her eyes. "Ruby must be about five now. It was a closed adoption, of course. Eloise didn't want to see the family or Ruby. She refused to leave her contact information and indicated on the form she did not want to be contacted. However, I did meet them. I held little Ruby in my arms. She was a week old, and I handed her to the social worker. That was the last I saw or heard about her."

"Frances, please tell me you remember the name of the family."

"It will never leave my mind," Frances replied. "It was Lionel and Candace Michaels."

"Thank you," Johanna said, overjoyed. "This is what I came to find out. Knowing the family's name will go a long way toward me locating Ruby."

Frances stood.

"I'm sorry, but I must go. And I promised my family to come straight home so we could pack and leave early for a short trip starting tomorrow."

"No worries," Johanna said. "By any chance do you recall where the Michaels lived?"

"That's why I remember them," Frances said. "It took forever to clear the paperwork, and Eloise had given up all parental rights. But they wanted to locate her because they were moving to British Columbia and taking Ruby to live out of the country."

Canada.

"I'm glad I could help you," Frances said. "Say, why don't you come back on Saturday and give us a couple of hours?"

"I'll try."

"Hmm, we lose a lot of help to 'trying,'" Frances said.

"I can give some time now," Johanna interjected.

"Good girl," Frances patted her arm as she walked past.

Johanna stayed an additional hour to help serve a long line of women and children that had formed while she and Frances were meeting. Being a server made her feel she was contributing to a good cause, and she promised the supervisor she would consider returning.

"We don't need you to consider it, honey," the stern-looking woman responded. "We need you to *do* it." Her face broke out a smile. "Come back when you can. We can always use your help."

Johanna nodded. "I'll return."

IN HER OFFICE, JOHANNA SEARCHED THROUGH three ancestor databases, including the Library and Archives Canada, the official archives of Canada. Frances had said the Michaels moved to Canada, so there was a chance they lived in the United States, first.

However three hours later, her eyes tired from squinting at census records, she was ready to call it a day. She had promised Ava they would have take-out pizza, and she would pick it up on the way home.

Her phone buzzed. She glanced at the caller ID.

"Detective Quinn, hello. Have you found anything new about Eloise's death?"

"Interesting you should ask, Mrs. Hudson," he said. "I'm calling to ask you the same thing."

"I don't know what you mean."

"Twice in the last two days, we have interviewed people who said you had already spoken with them," Quinn's voice was stern. "We can't have you interfering in an ongoing investigation. You want to explain?"

Johanna grimaced. She didn't want to detail her search for Ruby to the police. They had clearly shown they weren't interested in her family tree pursuits.

"Which two?" she asked.

"What do you mean which two? How many have you talked with? What are you up to?"

She chose her words with caution. "I'm a genealogist. I have no investigative purposes or training. My client is trying to locate someone whom Eloise also knew. Their paths are crossing, that's all. I'm not looking for Eloise's killer. I'm looking forward to the day when you call to tell me who did it."

"Humph," Quinn said with skepticism. "If in your family tree search you come across hard information that might point to a motive, I want to hear it first."

"Absolutely," she said.

She had to admit she didn't have hard information.

He clicked off.

CHAPTER TWENTY-FOUR

With Trinidad back at home, Johanna decided she would finish tackling the last of Joel's boxes in the basement. She didn't like chores hanging over her head, and she had avoided this one for a number of reasons, all starting with "A" for Ackerman.

Upstairs, Ava was clicking away on her laptop and had announced, when Johanna went to check on her, she would take a nap when she got tired.

"Go, do what you have to do," she said. "I'm feeling better every day. I don't need a babysitter for company."

Boxes later, Johanna faced a foot high pile of papers on her worktable. She re-sorted the stack into business and personal documents. She went through each one, choking back her tears. It seemed as if she could feel Joel's touch as he must have packed each item.

Batches of photos, warranties for purchases, product reference information and what seemed like endless miscellaneous papers filled box after box. After picking through it all, she ended with one container for shredding and one for keepsake memorabilia. The rest was destined to be discarded.

It was done.

She'd saved a final plastic tote for last. It contained the papers from his home office. Joel had been an investment banker and a very good one. In addition to his anal obsession with never throwing out papers, he had an orderly mind and approach to problems. If he had given any recommendations to Howard Ackerman, the notes would be among his papers. His work office would have official records, but she was betting he would keep some sort of client file backup.

After skimming through all his papers, Johanna had a good idea of her husband's sense of order, or at least she understood it. She knew there had to be a file, and after a short while she located the Ackerman file.

She grinned.

There weren't a lot of pages, so she was able to scan through them rapidly. She compiled a contact sheet with dates and subject matter on the left side of a file folder and copies of signed forms on the right. Sitting back, looking at her work, the first entry caught her eye and she ran up the stairs with the file under her arm.

"Ava," she said, entering the guest room to find her friend noshing on a sandwich in one hand while looking at her phone held in the other. "How did we get Ackerman as a client?"

"Ah, let me think," Ava said. "My brain is still a little scrambled." She closed her eyes as if going back in time, and then shook her head. "I don't know, Jo. I mean, I don't remember. Why?"

"Was it Brandon Reed who referred him?"

"Reed? Maybe, but why?"

Johanna sat on the edge of the bed. "Because I've been going through Joel's files. I had a hunch that Ackerman wasn't lying about everything. He may have spoken to Joel about the Elan Star Annuity. And, if he spoke with Joel at all, Joel would have taken notes."

Ava pointed with her phone. "Are those the notes in your hand?"

Johanna nodded. "In March 2017, Joel met with Ackerman, who wanted to open an account and had a few buys he wanted to run by Joel. Joel made a note to thank B.R. for the referral. At their next meeting, Joel reported back that most of the items Ackerman had shown him were too speculative and he couldn't recommend any. He wrote: 'Ackerman was concerned because B.R. was a friend who had made the suggestions. Suggested he engage a genealogist to help him qualify'. "

"What? Is that how you think he got to us?"

Johanna chewed on her lip. "Joel may have off-handedly said, 'you know, my wife's company does family trees, and she's a genealogist' or something like that, and Ackerman looked us up. Or, if B.R. is Brandon Reed, he may have turned him on to us. I never mentioned my client names to Joel, or he to me. I would sometimes relate the anecdotes of my research, but I treat our clients as confidential."

"Jo, you started working with Reed in the last six months," Ava said. "I started work on the Ackerman tree before that time. As I think about it, I don't see how Reed could have referred Ackerman. Unless it was the other way around."

"I know." She nodded. "That's a missing piece I haven't figured out. Brandon was consumed with raising his ancestor profile to gain standing with his prospective in-laws. I got the sense he wasn't beyond stretching the truth or discarding it."

"Hmm, that's not good," Ava mused. "But I can go through my Ackerman notes to see if he ever mentioned how he found us."

"Great. If you could, it would tie up a loose end. I know in my gut that Ackerman is using Joel as a scapegoat. If I can show a connection between Reed and Ackerman, and the likelihood Reed suggested Elan, and not Joel, then the lawsuit should be dismissed."

There was little else Johanna could do until the next day. Going through Joel's papers had brought him back. She could hear him, smell him and . . . almost see him. She would no longer minimize his border-line, anal-compulsive behavior; he had come through again for her.

IT WASN'T THAT SHE DIDN'T THINK TO CONTACT DEAN with her findings about Ackerman; it was more she didn't think their budget would stretch to cover his lawyer fees to do the needed background work.

"Brandon," she said, her cellphone on record, "hello, this is Johanna Hudson, I was following up with our ancestor work for your family. How did everything turn out?"

"Fine," Brandon Reed responded, dragging out the word.

"Good, good." She grimaced. He wasn't going to make this easy. "So your fiancée was satisfied with the distant Beethoven connection?"

There was silence.

"Yes, it all worked out," he said at last.

"Good, good." She cleared her throat. "Say, I was speaking with a client you might know, a Howard Ackerman?"

Again silence.

"I don't think so," he said.

"Yeah, Ackerman was involved with an annuity—Elan Star," Johanna said. "Investors must have ancestors from old Europe. I remember seeing the name when I put your chart together. Didn't your mother partici-pate? I thought you might know the Ackermans."

"My mother's interest in Elan Star has nothing to do with invest-ments. Her first husband was from Switzerland."

So I discovered.

"Yes," she said. "Is that why you made the recommendation to Howard Ackerman?"

He chuckled. "I didn't say I did. I don't think I even know the Ackermans."

Right.

"By the way, you said your fiancée could trace her line to the DAR. Would it be possible for me to speak with her? We're trying to expand our database of family lines, and a verified tree like hers would be invaluable." She paused, and then added, "She might be interested in seeing how we came up with your tree. When's the wedding?"

This time the silence was extended.

"Are you threatening me?" he said.

"Why would that be a threat? Unless . . . ."

This time he didn't allow for an extended silence.

"Johanna, I've got things to do, and I'm not big on talking on the phone. My parents are still in Europe," he said. "Tell you what, let's sit down, and I can tell you what I know about Elan Star. Maybe I'll remember those Ackerman persons."

"You mean, now?"

"If you could," he replied. "Linda and I are going away for a few days to finish planning the wedding. You and I can lunch at a local restaurant. I don't have access to a car; it's in the shop until tomorrow. Perhaps you can pick me up?"

She winced. A drive to Berkeley was not what she had planned for the day, but if it meant putting an end to Ackerman's claims, she was more than willing. On her way back, she would stop by to see how Trinidad was doing with her borrowed freedom.

Traffic was not a problem. This time, she parked in the Reeds' driveway and called the house on her cell phone.

"Brandon," she said. "This is Johanna. Come on down. I'm waiting in your driveway."

"You made good time," he said. I wasn't expecting you so soon, I'm not quite ready. Come on up. It's too cold for you to sit in the car. You remember the elevator. Go to the right of the parking pad to the overgrown holly bush. The elevator is to the rear of the shrub. I'll push the button on the intercom." He hung up.

He was right, the Bay Area winter chill went to the bone. The fog had moved in, and combined with the clouds dipping to touch the tops of the Berkeley hills, it gave more than enough incentive for her to lock the car doors and scuttle for the anticipated warmth.

He wasn't alone.

"Johanna, this is my fiancée, Linda." Reed couldn't keep the smug smile off his face. "She came over to visit, and I told her about you. Take a seat."

At one time, she would have been taken off-guard, but few things surprised her anymore. She headed for a straight-backed chair near the front door.

The slim young woman sitting on the sofa in front of the large fire burning in the fireplace stood and held out her hand.

"Hi."

"Hello," Johanna responded. "Brandon has told me about your vacation plans." She looked over her shoulder at Reed who, with arms folded, seemed to be holding court.

Linda was about five-foot seven and pretty, in a high maintenance sort of way. She looked to be in her early twenties, or maybe late teens. She had blue eyes, red lips and wore heavy black mascara. Her blonde hair, parted on the side, hung long around her face.

"Yes, he would," Linda said in a breathy voice. "He is ready to be married, but I'm not in a hurry."

"Babe, let's not share our private lives with Johanna." He walked to sit next to Linda and held her hand. "However, I see no reason to go out since we're already here."

Johanna could feel her face flush.

"I feel unprepared," she said, trying to keep her voice calm. "I thought we would be talking in a . . . a—"

"A public place," Reed supplied. "Neutral territory so to speak."

Johanna said nothing.

"What did you want to talk about?" Linda asked.

From the angle of her face as the daylight from the windows hit her expression, Linda was a lot older than Johanna had thought. Tiny wrinkles at the corners of her eyes and around her mouth belied her expert makeup.

Johanna was holding onto her temper—barely. She didn't quite know the rules of this game, but for now she didn't feel in danger.

"I wanted to talk to Brandon, about an investment he suggested to a client of mine, Howard Ackerman."

"Linda and I have no secrets." Reed slipped his arm around his fiancée's shoulders. "I told you, I don't know Howard Ackerman."

"But you do know about Elan Star," Johanna said. "And not just through your mother, so don't bother to deny it. I went on the internet and discovered you used to be a director of its parent company. And even though you shut the corporation down over a year ago, you're still listed as a former director."

"I was a manager, not an owner."

"At the end, you're probably right," she said. "The owners have all disappeared. "I couldn't figure out why Howard went to my husband if he had you to help him, but you had to keep an arm's distance from any transaction, else face insider trading charges, as well. So, between Ackerman's greed and your greater greed—well, what a couple of miscreants."

"You can't—" Reed started to protest.

"Look, Johanna," Linda interrupted, stretching out the syllables in her name. "What do you want?"

"I want Ackerman to drop his lawsuit. And don't tell me you don't know him. That sofa you're sitting on came from his store."

Johanna bent over and lifted the half-tucked white tag from the underside of the seating. It read: Ackerman Furnishings—Model 33458.

Reed was silent, perhaps trying to come up with a new story. Linda pursed her lips and swiped at her right eyebrow.

"Brandon, was it you who turned the Ackermans on to the Elan Star Annuity?" Johanna asked.

He took a deep breath. "It's not a crime. He begged me to let him sign on. I told him he'd have to show proof of ancestry qualifications." Reed shrugged. "I guess he found you. Ackerman told me that you did his chart, and I remembered your name when I needed a chart done." He shot a quick glance to Linda. "Anyway, things were working out okay, even though your husband trashed my recommendation. Then things went belly up; Howard came running back to me. I assured him a decent return was still forthcoming—but maybe a little further out than we thought. And it would have been, had not the European Union adopted new financial investment guidelines."

"You don't seem to be panicking like Ackerman," Johanna said. "Did things work out for you?"

Reed grimaced. "I stayed away from it," he said. "Howard was determined to make fast money any way he could, that's all I know."

"Do you know about his suit against us?" Johanna asked.

Reed slapped the coffee table with his hand, and Linda jumped.

"I'm not saying anything else, except I think you should leave."

"For business reasons, I don't want your dirty laundry and family tree tampering to come out in association with our company," Johanna said. "Talk to Ackerman and get him to see the error of his thinking."

Linda gave her an indulgent smile. "And if we don't?"

"I think Brandon knows what will happen."

"I don't like you, Johanna," Linda said. "You don't seem to know who we are."

Johanna chuckled. "Oh, I know who you're *not*, Linda. We researched you, too. My partner has a friend who's a member of The Daughters of the American Revolution. Your name isn't in the directory. They never heard of you."

DRIVING BACK TO HER OFFICE, Johanna could not keep the grin off her face. She recalled when Ava discovered the "discrepancy."

"I can't think of two people who deserve each other more," Ava had said.

Johanna agreed.

Reed had stared wide-eyed at Linda while she raced through explanations of her attempted DAR appeal, or maybe a possible lawsuit. On his part, Reed gave Johanna an accusatory look as he admitted to his bride-to-be, that he'd lied about being the fifth great-grandson of Ludwig Beethoven because he didn't want her to think she was marrying down.

At the end, as if to spite her, instead of leading Johanna to the elevator, Brandon Reed held open the front door. Although breathless after the steep steps, Johanna got into her car humming a tune and looking forward to her next conversation with Howard Ackerman.

CHAPTER TWENTY-FIVE

W HEN JOHANNA ARRIVED AT DEAN CAMERON's office, straight after leaving Reed and his fiancée, she had to wait while he finished up a client meeting. She had no appointment, but couldn't contain the news the Ackerman lawsuit would soon be over. In less than fifteen minutes, Cameron appeared in the lobby with a welcoming smile. The client must have left by another exit.

"Johanna," he said. "I got your text with the falling confetti. What's up?" He led her back to a small conference room.

She briefed him on her search through Joel's things, Ava's findings and her morning with Reed.

Dean threw his pen on top of his pad of paper.

"Ackerman is done." He nodded. "I'll get in touch with his lawyer and ask for a dismissal."

"Go ahead, but I want to be the one who tells Howard Ackerman to his face," Johanna said, remembering his smugness about Joel. "There's one small loose end I have to make sure of before this is completely over."

An hour later, Johanna sat on a bench looking out over the grounds of a small pocket park adjacent to her office building. The scent from the grove of eucalyptus trees enveloped her in their fragrance. She took a deep breath. There was a family enjoying an evening picnic not too far away, and a pair of bicyclists rested next to a water fountain. The epitome of normalcy—everything belying the purpose of the meeting that was about to take place.

"You got here early," Howard Ackerman said, as he sat at the opposite end of the bench. "I hope this means you have good news for me."

"Oh, I have good news, but not for you." She smiled. "I had a long conversation with Brandon Reed. Can you guess what he told me?"

Seeing his face turn a deathly pale made her last few days of stress and anxiety worthwhile.

"What did he tell you?"

"Let's say, his statements made it clear you have no case against us." She leaned forward. "I'm not sure he'll be able to tell you himself. I understand he was arrested earlier today for felony investment advisor fraud. He's agreed to speak with our attorney. Speaking of attorneys, we're asking for our lawyer fees."

Ackerman had turned from pale to red. "Reed is totally unreliable," he persisted. "I'm telling you your husband was involved. He . . . he knew what was going on. This isn't over."

"No, let's be clear," she said. "It is definitely over."

She stood and walked toward her building.

In her office, grinning with satisfaction, she clicked off from Dean Cameron. He shared her pleasure at hearing Ackerman's takedown.

"You're right this is over," Dean announced. "I've already contacted Brandon Reed. In exchange for not releasing his family's name, he'll sign an affidavit saying he recommended Elan Star to Ackerman. And don't worry, we'll ask for the judge to award my fees. You and Ava shouldn't have to pay. Courts don't like frivolous lawsuits."

Her last worry lifted, Johanna finished organizing her file cabinets and shelves. She smiled at her desktop; they were ready to re-open for business.

CHAPTER TWENTY-SIX

T HE NEXT MORNING, GRASPING A HOT CUP OF COFFEE, she sat staring out onto the patio. The events of the day before still brought
reflections.

Her cellphone vibrated. It was Dean.

"Boy, you call early," she said.

"Johanna, would it be possible for you to come to my office today,
before lunch?" Dean asked.

"Sure," she said. "Is something wrong with Ackerman?"

"No, not directly. I came in ahead of time to get the papers ready for
filing." He cleared his throat. "I would rather we meet than talk over the
phone."

Not directly?

"I can be there at eleven o'clock. Will that work?"

"See you then."

Ava took things in stride as Johanna went over her findings and
conversation with Ackerman and the call from Dean. If she had qualms
about Johanna's attitude or approach, she kept them to herself.

"I'm going home to my own bed the end of next week, Jo," she said.
"And I'm ready to get back to work. I need to do some field research for
our new Australian clients I signed."

Back at the office, all was quiet. Johanna screened calls and did preliminary research on two new clients. Her phone buzzed; it was Trinidad.
Johanna let it go to voicemail, but listened in.

"Johanna, where are you? I must go see Mr. Clark, and I want you
with me," she swallowed hard enough to be heard. "Johanna, I'm worried.

I think someone follows me. I come by your office this afternoon before I work. Thank you."

Johanna felt guilty for not picking up the call when she saw Trinidad's name on the screen, and now she felt worse. Not only had she put the quest for little Ruby to the back of her mind, but Trinidad's plight had also been pushed to the side. She glanced at the clock. There was still time to visit Dean and make it back to her office by afternoon.

Dean, for once, was waiting in his firm's lobby when Johanna got off the elevator. He waved her forward.

"Good to see you," he said, directing her to his office. "I've got news for you, and I wanted to tell you in person."

He sat next to her.

"Well then tell me," she urged.

"You may have to hold onto those boxes you had in your basement a little longer." He said. "The police, along with a woman from the FBI, came to see me this morning. They wanted my statement, and they'll be here in a few minutes to take yours."

"A statement from me, why?" She asked with a frown.

"Your husband was a civilian operative for the FBI."

"What!"

Dean nodded. "I know. It's a little much to hear, but Joel Hudson agreed to help the feds nail Ackerman, who is spilling his guts. They've already used him to bring down a whole gang of crooks."

Johanna wondered if she looked as astounded as she felt. She leaned back in her chair. "Joel was helping the FBI," she murmured. "But he never said a word. He didn't say anything about the boxes in the basement."

There was a tap on the door, and it opened to the receptionist who ushered in a man and a woman both in dark suits. As soon as they were in, she shut the door behind her.

"Hello, I'm Agent John Dyson," the man said. "And this is Agent Angela Shay. I assume Mr. Cameron has informed you why we are here."

They took seats at the table across from Dean and Johanna.

"He was starting to explain," she said. "I have to admit I'm in a little bit of shock. Joel never said . . . he never even hinted."

"We're sorry for your loss." Agent Shay appeared genuinely sympathetic. "He was a good citizen to work with us. As soon as he realized Ackerman deserved monitoring, he contacted us."

"The thing I don't understand is how he helped." she said. "Did he have a direct email address to you?"

The two agents exchanged glances.

"Mrs. Hudson, we can't go into that level of detail," Agent Dyson said. "We're here because we need your statement before we close our files. We were close to picking up Ackerman a year ago, but we couldn't get anything solid against him."

"What happened?" Johanna asked, and then she realized why that hadn't worked out. "Joel was . . . he was . . . ." She couldn't finish. There was a lump in her throat, and the air seemed to have left the room.

"Mrs. Hudson, Howard Ackerman has been involved in running international Ponzi schemes," Agent Shay said. "Your husband had the proof. He was going to deliver it to us the day after he was killed in the car accident."

Johanna had anticipated the agent's announcement. Somehow, she'd known what was coming. Still, her words hung in the conference room like little points of pain striking her heart.

She fainted.

When she came to a couple of minutes later, Dean looked on as one of the agents held a cup of water to her lips. She blinked her eyes back into focus.

"Are you all right?" Shay asked. "We're sorry to have caused you more grief."

Johanna waved at them. "I'm okay. It's . . . it's just the pieces are now coming together." She took another sip of water. "I knew in my heart, Joel was a good husband. He wouldn't want me to worry. I know he would have told me everything after it was over, but he . . . he didn't get the chance. He—"

She stopped suddenly.

"It was an accident wasn't it?" Johanna said.

Dyson nodded. "Yes, we confirmed it was an unfortunate accident. "Now, could you tell us what you do know?"

Johanna took another deep swallow of water. "According to our records, Howard Ackerman contacted our office late last year. My partner . . . ."

She continued on for thirty minutes telling the events of the past months and days until she came to a quiet close.

"After Joel and Amber . . . I . . . I didn't grasp anything . . . nothing registered. But thanks to Joel keeping such good records, I was able to link Brandon Reed to Howard Ackerman, and avoid a huge lawsuit. He . . . ." She couldn't finish, and took a deep breath. "They were crooks. Both of them used the research we did on their family trees for illegal transactions."

"Not anymore, Mrs. Hudson," Shay said. "Not anymore."

CHAPTER TWENTY-SEVEN

JOHANNA WAS SURPRISED AT THE RELIEF SHE FELT returning to the office. She pulled back the drapes to let sunlight into the dark space. Simone had done a good job returning things to order. Gradually the office was returning to normal. Once Ava was back full-time, it would be as if this was just a story to share over dinner. Their mailbox was full of envelopes and brochures. Smiling, she gathered the bundle and dumped it on her desk.

It was over. The cloud she didn't know had been hanging over her head was gone. Johanna logged onto her computer and was greeted by rows of unanswered emails. Keeping busy was good. She didn't want to think too much about Joel's secret.

"Johanna, can I talk back at you?" Trinidad said, poking her head into the room.

She looked up. "Of course you can," she said, pulling out a chair in front of her desk. "I didn't hear the door open. How are things going?"

Today Trinidad wore a bright pink and yellow smock over matching cropped pants. Her hair was pulled back into a ponytail with a yellow scarf weaved into the braid.

Johanna almost smiled.

"What is the matter, Johanna?" Trinidad asked. "You are sad. I see you with my heart."

The woman's telling words almost brought tears to her eyes again, and she took a breath.

"It's been a little crazy around here, but I'm fine. And it's so good to see you outside of jail," Johanna said. "I told you that we had a . . . a burglar last week. Simone helped me to put things in order."

"Burglar? Why would a burglar steal from you?" Trinidad puckered her brow, and peered at Johanna. "Simone is good woman. She save my job. But, the boss says I no leave work again, or he find someone else. I not go back to jail."

"No worrying, you'll never go back," she said. "Now listen, so I can tell you everything I've done to find Ruby."

It took the next minutes for Johanna to go over the results of her search. She held nothing back about her visit from Bryce, or the contact she'd made with Frances Lynch. Trinidad did not interrupt and, except for one grunt when she repeated James Bryce's comments, said nothing.

"I've got a lot of leads," Johanna said. "I'm going through Canadian records to track down the Michaels. If I find them, we've found Ruby."

Trinidad nodded. "You did good, Johanna. But you not find Ruby, now. You talk about what you are 'going to do.'" She held up her hand. "But is okay, I know you try—I guess." She crossed her arms. "Now, what is 'token'? What does that mean?"

Johanna explained. "Does that sound at all familiar to you? Did Eloise say something about a token? Or have you kept anything else for her?"

Trinidad shook her head. "No, everything was in box she gave you. You have Bible, the pictures—you have everything."

"Then I will work with what I have," Johanna said. "Let's meet again at the end of the week, and I can let you know what I've found out."

"That is fine," Trinidad said, moving toward the door. Then she hesitated. "Johanna, sometime I think someone is watching me. I get feeling."

"That is not good," Johanna said. "Sometimes I think I'm being followed, too. I would not put it past James Bryce to track where we go. We both need to be careful."

"I think same. I be careful." She hesitated. "Johanna, you be careful more. Bryce knows you find Ellie's body."

After Trinidad left to return to work, Johanna wrote down all the leads, persons, and connections she'd collected affecting Eloise and Ruby. It would help her to stand back and see what stood out. When she finished, she almost laughed. It looked less like a tree and more like spaghetti.

According to Ancestry.com, Lionel and Candace Michaels were married in 1999 in Sunnyvale, California. Johanna requested an expedited copy of the marriage certificate from the county and was told she could pick it up after noon the next day. She took down the couple's Sunnyvale addresses, but didn't think they would lead to much, since both Michaels had moved to Canada. They were both in their thirties when they married, so that put them in their early forties when they adopted Ruby.

It was getting late, and the day had slipped by. Johanna leaned back in her chair. She couldn't wait to tell Ava her field trip to Australia had yielded not one, but, based on the emails Johanna opened, three new clients for the business. Their signed contracts had been scanned and received. She, too, had brought in a new client who wanted to meet as soon as possible in order to make the family tree a gift to their father. Things were looking up.

She was about ready to lock up the office when her phone rang.

"Mrs. Hudson?"

"Yes."

"Terrible thing about your partner. Stop looking."

He clicked off.

Johanna hadn't realized she was shaking until she put the office phone in its cradle. She was pretty sure it was a man's voice, but it had been disguised. She had convinced Ava they should keep some sort of defensive non-weapon in the office. Ava had disagreed, so the compromise was a can of Aqua Net hair spray. Its fumes and caustic chemicals, when applied with a direct hit, almost guaranteed temporary blindness and breathing discomfort. She reached for the travel-sized can at the bottom of her drawer and put it in her purse.

Of course, there was the assumption the can would be handy when needed.

The sun was making its way down in the sky so there was little light. The parking lot was less than half full, and few employees were heading to their vehicles. She looked around her but saw nothing suspicious. When she reached her car, she let out a low groan. She had two flat tires. Looking around again, she still saw nothing suspicious and took out her phone to call road service.

It was the crack in her driver-side window that caused her to drop her phone. A good sized rock had shattered the glass into a fine-lined web.

Road service advised, since it was commute time, it would be a little wait before they could reach her, but she could monitor their progress on her phone. Her hands still shaking, she called Ava to tell her she would be late getting home, but not why. Then she reached Detective Quinn.

He was as disturbed.

"It's clear whoever called and damaged your car, either committed or ordered the assault on Ava Lowell," he said in clipped tones. "But it doesn't have to mean Miss Owens is off the hook. I don't make the leap you did that this must be about Eloise Manley's death. According to your own admission, this Ackerman client of yours appeared capable of scare tactics."

"I know," Johanna said, sitting in her locked car. "I thought it was him for a while, but now I'm not so sure. Ackerman's fate is sealed, and the FBI has him in custody for federal charges including wire and mail fraud. He'd have no reason to make an intimidating call. Whoever did this, let the air out of my tires so he could threaten me through my car, and I wouldn't be able to identify him."

Detective Quinn covered the phone with his hand to speak to someone in the background.

"Mrs. Hudson, look, I've got to go. You may be right," he said. "I'll send an officer around to get details from you about the work you're doing regarding Eloise Manley. But don't count on it making a difference to the Trinidad Owens case."

"Never crossed my mind."

ROAD SERVICE SHOWED UP WITHIN THE HOUR, and Johanna was home before too late. While Ava lay on the sofa, Johanna sat at her feet describing the day's happenings.

After Johanna finished the telling, Ava displayed a roller coaster of emotions: happy about the new clients, furious about the tires, ecstatic about Ackerman's arrest, and thoughtful about the threatening call.

"You should start carrying a gun," she advised. "Using hair spray will just irritate an attacker."

"Ava, I don't know how to shoot," Johanna pushed back. "Besides, by the time I found where I hid a gun, someone would have taken me out."

She chuckled, but Ava wasn't smiling.

"I have two .22 caliber pistols. I'll lend you one," Ava said. "When I get better, I'll teach you how to shoot."

"Ava—"

She held up her hand. "This is not a discussion." Ava pulled the book she was reading up to her face and then looked over it. "We need to be smart about this. Whoever is behind these goings-on is not afraid to hurt people. I don't like being a victim."

Johanna exhaled and nodded. "All right."

"You'll be the feet, and I'll be the fingers," Ava said. "Between the two of us, we should be able to find Ruby in no time." She had her laptop propped up on a cushion.

"Ava, that's an excellent idea," Johanna said.

"I'm glad you agree," Ava said. "Now, let me tell you what I found out with my research." She held out a sheet of paper. "Candace and Lionel Michaels divorced in 2015 when Ruby was two. On paper it appears to be an amicable break-up. They share joint custody."

"That's great news," Johanna said. "Please, tell me you have an address for one of them."

"I do." Ava grinned. "Well, I have a county for one of them. Candace Michaels was granted a divorce in Multnomah County—that's in Oregon, maybe Portland. She listed an address there."

Johanna mused. "Did you—"

"Yes, I checked for her in Portland, but she's no longer at the address. That's as far as I got."

Johanna had pulled her shoes off so she could flex her feet.

"That's a lot of work I don't have to do. Thank you," she said. "Tomorrow I'll start looking for a Ruby Michaels in Portland in all the children source databases. Candace didn't have her daughter's name changed. I'll also start on picking up Lionel Michaels' tracks. But for now, I'm going to make a sandwich and go to bed."

"Not so fast, buttercup." Ava smiled. "I saved the best for last. You got a call from a Dominic Quinn."

"Oh, he's the detective working Eloise's murder." Johanna refused to raise her eyes to Ava's. "He called on the landline?"

"Ah huh. He said to tell you he didn't mean to brush you off the other day. But now he'd like for you to call him back."

"Er, good, I'll give him a call. Maybe he's found some evidence that clears Trinidad."

Ava laughed. "No, I got the distinct impression it was an off-duty call. He asked that you call him when you could." She held out a piece of paper with the number.

Johanna could feel a flush creeping up her chest and neck. It had been a long time since she had connected with the opposite sex. Her memory of Dominic Quinn's dark brown eyes made her smile, but she caught herself when Ava teased.

"Ah, ha."

"There's no 'ah, ha'. I barely spoke to the man."

"Right. You may want to make the call from your bedroom, so I won't be tempted to eavesdrop."

"Very funny," Johanna said.

She self-talked herself to eat first before returning Quinn's call. She didn't know why it mattered so much, but she didn't want him to think she would rush.

"Detective Quinn, I'm returning your call."

"Thanks for calling me back," he said. "I'm not contacting you on official business."

Johanna laughed. "That's not necessary. I'll take your word for it."

"Good and call me Nick. I want to know if you'd be interested in going out for dinner?"

She froze.

"Well, this is awkward," he said. "You can say you're busy for the next year, or you have a husband or boyfriend with a six-pack."

"No, uh, I'm sorry. It's just that I haven't been on a date in some time. I mean . . . I haven't thought of dating . . . since my husband. . . . I realized I don't remember how to . . . I mean . . . how to act."

He chuckled. "Whew, is that it? Thank you for leaving my ego intact. How long have you been divorced?"

"Divorced? No, not divorced," she said, eyes focused on her napkin. "My husband and daughter were killed in an auto accident a little over a year ago.

"Johanna, I am so sorry. I didn't know. Please accept my apology for blundering on."

She was glad he couldn't see her face. The pain was a little less, but the recent reveal events concerning Joel, had left her numb—and tears were close by.

"Detect . . . er . . . Nick, please, it's all right." She took a breath. "Thank you for your invitation, would it . . . could we just make it lunch?"

"Lunch it is. I know a great place on the water," he said. "And I promise to take a foot-in-mouth vaccine before we meet."

CHAPTER TWENTY-EIGHT

SITTING IN THE OFFICE THE NEXT MORNING, Johanna continued to replay the phone call with Dominic Quinn over and over, kicking herself for being so clueless. As it was, he selected a lunch spot in Palo Alto called Echoes, a Silicon Valley hangout. And, as alumni, she could visit Stanford's library to do some research afterwards.

Ava reproached her. "You are too practical," she said. "You don't have to squeeze having a good time into your workday."

But Johanna resisted. She knew these were the terms she could handle, and Ava nodded in understanding.

By late morning Johanna had visited most of the online public information sites searching for a lead to Ruby Michaels—without luck. But she caught a break when she found a clue that pointed to Ruby's adopted father. Lionel, at least up until two years before, still lived in British Columbia. At that time, he returned to his hometown of Danville, California, less than an hour from Johanna's office.

At last.

With the knowledge of his location, she located him on LinkedIn and on the Contra Costa County Chamber of Commerce members listing.

As a large networking site, LinkedIn provided a way for professionals to connect with other professionals and was useful for exchanging knowledge, ideas, and employment opportunities. Hudson and Lowell had joined and already received four referrals from its membership. The site was also proving to be a solid resource in locating persons, as in this case with Lionel Michaels. He had registered as a fabrication business owner. His photograph showed a smiling man with sandy brown hair, a modest mustache and clipped beard.

However, when she called the number shown, it had been disconnected. The business had closed. The two steps forward, one step back process was frustrating.

Another dead end.

She turned to the Bible Trinidad had passed on. It was heavy with an ornate cover and gold edged pages. It smelled of cinnamon, which probably indicated one of its storage locations. According to the last entry on the "Notes" page, the book had been handed down to Jeanette Sutton Dawes on her wedding day.

Johanna turned to the back pages. Photos had been pasted with care into black corner photo tabs. Looking to have originated in the 1800s, pictures were provided with Sutton names underneath. Several pages were full of the last of the pictures taken circa the 1980s. There was nothing else. She was returning the book to the box when a slip of paper fluttered to the ground.

It was a phone number, followed by the letter "B." Johanna realized she'd seen the handwriting before. And then it came to her. She scrambled in the box and pulled out the birthday card with the less than cheerful greeting. It was the same "B."

The phone rang several times before it was picked up.

"Maricopa County Family Services."

Johanna hesitated. She hadn't counted on the number belonging to a government office. She spoke up, "Hello, I'm calling to speak to a social worker about an old file."

"What does that mean?" A woman said, sighing. It was clear she realized this was not going to be a quick transfer call.

Johanna tried again, "I'm representing a client who wants to track parties in a former foster case. I was hoping to speak to a social worker. The person I'm representing may have a claim to an inheritance."

"Are you an attorney?" She asked. "If you're an attorney, that's a different office."

"No, I'm not."

"Okay, well, I guess you can start with the social worker on call duty today. Her name is Gina Hart."

Johanna listened to a medley of pastoral music.

"This is Mrs. Hart. May I help you?

Johanna hastily introduced herself and as succinct as she could, described the purpose of her call.

"Let me understand," Hart said. "You want to know if we have a file on a foster family that took in a young child, who's now an adult. She's trying to find her birth father. Do I have it correct?"

"It's a little more complicated than that, but in short, yes. That's why I'm contacting your offices," she said. "I would like an appointment to come in and discuss the situation with you in person."

"I'm sympathetic to your quest, but there's not much we can discuss with a private party," Hart said. "You may need a court order to see our records."

"I understand," Johanna rushed. "If, I could meet with you to explain my unique circumstances."

"Circumstances involving families are not often unique." Papers rustled. "All right, Mrs. Hudson. I can see you this afternoon at one o'clock."

Johanna groaned and agreed. This was not a good day. She had client mail and phone messages to tend to, and she'd hoped to catch up on paperwork today. She didn't notice someone was in front of her desk until she heard a throat clear. She looked up.

"Trinidad," she said. "I didn't hear you come in. I was on the phone with the foster family agency that settled Eloise. They might be able to give me the name of Eloise's father."

The woman had dressed casually in lime green pants and a floral top. Her long ponytail was braided into a crown on the top of her head.

"I heard groan, Johanna. You must tell me what is wrong. I can take it."

Johanna smiled. "Oh, it's nothing to do with you. I have so much office work and phone calls to respond to. Usually Ava would cover it, but she won't be back until next week, and then only part-time."

"Then I do it," Trinidad offered.

"What?" Johanna said, "Do what?"

"I will answer phones and do paperwork until Ava comes back."

"Trinidad, that is so generous of you to suggest," Johanna said. "But, you don't know our business, and you have your own job to do."

"Hmmph, you not have business if you not here, that I know. And, besides I work for you before I clean the offices. I come at noon and work until four. I answer phones and put paper in stacks." She leaned over the desk. "I will do for free. This is part payment I owe you for finding Ruby."

Johanna wrinkled her brow. She couldn't believe she was contemplating taking Trinidad up on her offer.

"Maybe this afternoon," she said. "I could use your help."

Trinidad grinned.

Johanna looked through her rear-view mirror at the window to her office. It had taken just a few minutes for Trinidad to grasp how to answer the phone and to sort the mail. She displayed a surprising ease with the assignment, and other than her unique way of speaking, she should be able to handle their clientele.

The Maricopa County Department of Health and Family Services, or PCDHF as it was listed on all but one signage board, was tucked in the midst of several austere looking administration buildings in the county complex. Its own façade was welcoming with abundant and fragrant star jasmine lining a curving pathway to automatic double glass doors.

Johanna checked in with the receptionist and was told to wait in an area that held assorted colored plastic chairs. She didn't have to wait long.

"Mrs. Hudson?"

Johanna stood and held out her hand. "Yes, thank you for seeing me."

Gina Hart looked like a stereotype of a social worker. Wearing one pair of glasses around her neck, as well as another pair on her graying brunette hair, her kind face was lit by a generous smile. She wore practical laced shoes, muted green plaid slacks and a beige cardigan.

"Come on back." Hart indicated a door off from the lobby that opened with a click, when she passed her badge over the lock. "This place can be pretty chaotic sometimes, but today it's quiet."

They entered a small meeting room furnished with two bottles of water. Johanna took a seat and gladly accepted the water.

"Ah, I see my secretary is giving us the VIP treatment. Not everyone gets a bottle of water," Hart said chuckling. Then like a light switch, she turned serious. "Now how can I help you?"

"My client, Eloise Manley, was recently murdered," Johanna said, not taking her eyes from Hart's. "She hired me to locate her biological father because she'd been approached by a man indicating he may have passed away, and his estate was searching for possible claimants. She never knew her father, but he was wealthy and my client had wanted to make a claim on the behalf of her daughter."

"But your client is dead," Hart said. "I would think the point is moot."

"I gave my word to search for the whereabouts of her daughter."

Johanna explained about the Manleys and how, now, she was also seeking Ruby.

"Interesting, an adopted child of a foster child." Gina Hart shook her head. "Makes you believe in social patterns." She paused. "There is something else. Did you say a man approached your client about her birth father?"

"Yes. It's my understanding the man had a letter from my client's grandmother, who was trying to ascertain if she could be verified as an heir to her son's estate. Why?"

Hart raised her hand. "I'll be right back."

She hurried out the door and Johanna didn't try to keep the puzzled look off her face. Hart returned with a thin file.

"The name Manley triggered something in my head," she said, opening the file. "It's not my case, but there's an office 'alert' on the matter. Is the man with the letter named James Bryce?"

Johanna felt a chill run up her arms.

"Yes, has he been here?"

"Oh, yes, Mr. Bryce has been here twice." Gina Hart closed the file. "However, as you can imagine, there is a limited amount of information that is considered public. Our records are protected by the courts in the event of child abuse or other domestic violence. And more than that, other than being an interested party, he has no standing."

"What did he say he was going to do?"

"He said he was going to take legal action, and I advised him that would be the only way he was going to get access to a family file. You can understand, can't you?"

Johanna nodded absently, her thinking jumping in different directions. Of course she understood— she understood their time was running out.

"Uh, Gina, would it be at all possible to see the Manley file and obtain the name of Eloise's biological father since her placement in a foster family had nothing at all to do with abuse?"

A look of dismay crossed the woman's face. "I'm sorry, but there was domestic violence. Didn't her mother murder her husband?"

Johanna stopped short of taking a loud deep breath into her chair. "Yes, she did."

"Then we're going to need a court order."

JOHANNA WAS TAKING A CHANCE DROPPING IN ON DEAN, but since the Ackermans' case was resolved, or at least over, she felt there might be room for another favor. Waiting in the lobby and noticing the time, she called to make sure all had gone well with Trinidad before the woman left to start her cleaning job.

Trinidad picked up after the second ring. "You had some calls, and before you ask, I took names like you told me. Then business slow down and I made copies."

Johanna curious, said, "Copies of what?"

"Oh, Ava call to talk at you, but I told her I in charge. She say 'good' and told me to make copies of papers on her desk and give you to bring home."

Johanna could imagine Ava's expression when Trinidad told her she was in charge.

She looked up; the receptionist was waving her forward. Dean was ready to see her in his office. Johanna said a grateful goodbye to Trinidad.

"Dean," she said, as she walked in and took the seat in front of his desk. "Thank you for seeing me under such short notice."

"You said urgent in your message, so here we are." He was surrounded by stacks of law books and yellow legal pads of paper on the top of his desk. "What's up?"

"I need a court order to open a family court file to obtain the name of Eloise Manley's biological father."

He folded his hands in the small bare space on top of his desk. "And why is it urgent?"

Johanna spent the next minutes catching him up on the latest events. "So there's Bryce who is representing Eloise's grandmother, who as far as I can tell, wants the estate for herself, or maybe even hide Eloise's existence. And there's little Ruby who has a legitimate claim but could be a major problem for her greedy great-grandmother."

Dean had already started to take notes.

"You don't live a boring life do you?" He smiled. "Okay, let's take it from the top. In what county does Ruby's grandfather live?"

Johanna grimaced. "That's just it, Dean. I don't know anything about him. I don't know his name, and I don't know his county of residence. That's why I need the court order."

"Okay, okay, I'm getting it," he said. "Let me talk you through the process, and we can talk about the obstacles." He cleared his throat. "First, we will need to contact the court clerk of the county where he has residency and obtain their procedure for reviewing estate files. Procedures vary by county. You'll need information about the deceased—the deceased's legal name and the date of death if you have it, so the court clerk can locate the estate paperwork. We ask the clerk to view the estate records. You'll need to make a copy of the final estate accounting. The executor or administrator of the estate must file a final account to settle the estate and receive a release from the court. Write down the name and address of the executor or estate's attorney. Contact the estate's attorney or executor if you want to inquire about the estate's settlement status. Identify Ruby's relationship to the deceased. Tell the attorney you want to reopen the estate, and why."

"But what if I don't know all those details?" she said. "And, I don't."

He nodded, and held up his hand to continue, "Once an estate has been administered and closed, it stays that way. However, there are times when an estate must be reopened. For example in your case, when there is a newly discovered heir. Courts can be a little suspicious when previous unknown heirs come out of the woodwork when someone passes away. If a new heir steps forward, the administrator will have to analyze whether to reopen the estate. In general, the heir should be mentioned in the will. If there was no will, then the heir could inherit under the state's intestacy laws, which apply in the absence of a will. Once an estate has been closed, you'll need to submit an 'Application for Petition to Reopen' with the probate court to reopen the estate. However, not anyone can file this petition, only "interested parties" can file. An interested party is someone with a property right or financial interest at stake, such as an heir or creditor. I need to check on this, but interested parties may need to get the personal representative's permission to reopen the estate.

"Oh, that should be fun."

Dean shrugged. "Even so, depending on your court, you may still need to serve a copy of the petition on all heirs who were listed in the original probate petition. Then it's a matter of getting a court date."

"This all sounds a little overwhelming and not very fast-tracked."

He scribbled another note. "Once you file your petition and everyone's on notice, the clock is slowed."

She sighed. "Okay, what's our first step?"

He tapped his pad. "We need a court order to see the Manley foster family file to hopefully uncover Eloise's birth father's name."

CHAPTER TWENTY-NINE

A T HOME, JOHANNA FELT THE WEIGHT OF THE DAY and the search for Ruby bearing down on her. Ava was waiting at the kitchen table and pointed to a glass of white wine.

"Sit," she said, crossing her arms on the table. "I hope you can imagine my surprise when I was going to leave a message on your office phone and Trinidad picked up."

"Ava I—"

"No, no, it was okay. She was pretty good. I did have to tell her we don't actually give clients real trees. But she took it in stride."

They both laughed.

Ava broke off. "No offense, but you look terrible," she said. "Why don't you tell me what's going on."

Johanna took her through her meetings with Gina Hart and Dean Cameron. "The bottom line is, according to Hart, the only way I'm going to find out Eloise's father's identity is with a court order." She kicked off her shoes. "Dean is going to file a petition tomorrow."

Ava sat up. "That's great news, how long will it take you to hear?"

"According to Dean, with the vagaries of the family court calendar, we could get a hearing next week."

"Something's wrong, I can tell by the look on your face."

"Ava, James Bryce appears to be one step, maybe even two ahead of me. He's already tried to see Eloise's foster care file." She took a sip of wine. "It's ironic isn't it? I have Eloise's information, and I'm trying to find her father, Bryce has her father's information but he doesn't have Eloise's birth information. Nor does he know Ruby exists," she said, considering.

"Do you think he had something to do with Eloise Manley's death?"

Ava nodded. "I think there's a good chance. You better be careful. There's that whole nightmare with your car. It looks like someone is ramping up the stakes. They weren't looking for it to be me when I was assaulted, they thought I was you. What do the police say?"

"They're investigating, but they don't sound hopeful. Without a name or description, there's not much to go on."

Ava appeared to ponder. "This Bryce person is clearly in the Sutton's employ. But it doesn't seem like he's the same guy who's throwing out threats."

"That's my thought, different styles," Johanna said. "At first, I thought Bryce was working for Eloise's maternal grandmother, but that didn't make sense after Eloise was killed. She was the link to a legitimate claim. Then, after talking with him, I realized he was representing Eloise's *paternal* grandmother—a claimant against the estate who didn't want to share."

"Now that makes sense," Ava said. "Greed knows no bounds. But now, they must be wondering why you are still looking around for Eloise's father. Because, make no mistake, they know you're still looking. They just don't know about Ruby."

Technically, Johanna went to bed early. But she spent the next hours with papers spread out on top of the covers reviewing her research and an approach to get ahead of Bryce. She assumed he knew Eloise was dead, if he didn't do the killing himself. If he and Eloise's grandmother were trying to keep control of her son's estate, then it was imperative the existence of Ruby stay hidden until Johanna could find Eloise's father. She had no doubt Ruby's life and maybe her own could be in danger, if, Eloise's father was dead, or dying.

In the morning, she beat Ava to the kitchen and had a pot brewing when she came downstairs.

"You're spoiling me for the last time," Ava said, holding out her cup for a pour. "I'm staying in my own bed tonight, and I'll be in the office tomorrow."

"Understood. I'm not going to try to change your mind," Johanna said, raising her hands in surrender. "I'm glad you were here for a few days. I'm going to miss you. But Ava, just work half-a day in the office and then gradually work up to a full day."

"I plan to, but we don't move concrete, you know. I think I can handle sitting at a desk, researching on the internet and making a few phone calls."

Johanna toasted her friend with an acknowledging cup of coffee and headed out the door. She had an idea about finding Ruby. While she was waiting for a court order she could canvas the neighborhood where, according to LinkedIn, Lionel Michaels once had his business. Maybe he shared his plans with his commercial neighbors. She would print out his picture from LinkedIn and take it to the Chamber of Commerce, and if nothing came of that, she'd walk it around.

"WELL, HE'S NOT A CURRENT MEMBER," a young woman wearing a bright name tag with the Chamber logo under "Emily" said, clicking through a file on her computer. "I'm going to have to go back each year until I find him. You must be pretty impressed if you want to hire him after doing all this. Are you sure he was ever a member?"

Johanna wasn't sure of anything, but she wasn't ready to admit it. "By any chance do you have a database by owner or maybe business name?"

"Hmmm, not here, but maybe the company that does our mailing might. They keep files by year. I could call them and find out," she mused, and then perked up. "Once I have the year then I could locate the name and referral address."

"Yes," Johanna said. "Could you check please?"

Johanna was willing to sit and wait in front of the reception desk, but Emily appeared to be less disposed.

"I'll give them a call after I open the morning mail. I've got to get it out of the way," she said, pointing at the few envelopes in front of her. "Call back in about an hour. I should know something by then."

Johanna sat in her car trying to decide how to get through the next hour. It was too far to her office and while she was tempted to buy something new for her "lunch" with Dominic Quinn, she wasn't in the mood for shopping therapy.

Her phone rang.

"Good news," Dean said. "I finished hand-carrying the filing through. I knew the clerk and she gave us a spot on Monday in family court. Can you meet me there?"

"That's great! Don't worry, I'll be there." Johanna replied, taking down the details.

Finally, she might be making headway.

An hour later, she placed a call to Emily.

"I'm glad you called," the receptionist said. "I found him. He was a member three years ago. His company's name was Michaels Fabrication and Design, and it was located on Lonetree Blvd."

Johanna bit her bottom lip. All this she already knew. "Do you have a phone number for him, or maybe an email address?"

"There's a home phone number, but of course I can't give it out without his permission," Emily responded with authority.

"Is there anything else you *can* tell me?"

"There's a note his partner kept the Chamber membership when Mr. Michaels sold the business. He's paid up through next year, you might try him."

Johanna smiled. "That's perfect, Emily. What's his name and business number?"

"His last name is Michaels, too," she said. "Hey, maybe they're related. But the location is different." She tapped on her keyboard, and a moment later, gave Johanna the address.

Johanna didn't catch the girl's last words because in the rear view mirror her eyes had locked onto a pair belonging to a man talking on his phone while he was watching her. She turned her head to get a better look. He was gone.

Don Michaels' fabrication business was located a few blocks from where Lionel had once operated. Johanna didn't know what she expected, but the open space warehouse with a generous sitting area and art on the walls, was not it. The room was divided by what looked to be a floor-to-ceiling plexi-glass wall, with a plexi-glass double door. Workers on the other side could be seen bent over equipment, but the sound was muffled.

"Johanna Hudson?" A middle-aged man with a youthful face but balding hairline approached from a side office door. "Karen, our receptionist, said you wanted to see me about my brother."

"Yes, Mr. Michaels, I—"

"Call me Don, please," he said. "Come on back to my office."

He led her to a moderate sized office that could have been situated in a bank instead of a warehouse. It too, had nice art pieces on the wall.

"Now, what about my brother?"

Johanna had taken a seat in front of his desk. She leaned forward. "I am representing a client who is interested in locating Lionel Michaels, or his ex-wife. I can't tell you the subject matter of the inquiry, but I was hoping you could let your brother know I would like to speak with him."

She handed him a business card. It was more of a calling card with

the name of the firm. From time to time she and Ava found it more useful to maintain confidentiality when following up on leads—as she was
doing now.

"What does Hudson and Lowell do?" Don asked, turning the card
over and back.

"Mostly social research. We're a small office."

"Well, that's pretty vague. Does my brother owe your client money?"

Johanna shook her head. "No, not at all. I have a few questions for
him, nothing more."

"Then why do you want to talk to Candace?"

"It's a personal matter. Either one will do," Johanna said. "Do you
know where I can reach them?"

He was silent, and a frown appeared on his face.

"I haven't spoken to my brother in about a year. We had a bad business breakup," Don said. He offered Johanna a bottle of water, but she
shook her head. "Last I heard, Candace and the kids were—wait, I guess
I shouldn't say, until I talk to her and ask her if it's okay to tell you."

Kids.

Johanna's heart was beating a rapid staccato in her chest. He knew
where Ruby was.

"Don, I can't tell you how much I would appreciate you contacting
Candace Michaels as soon as you can," Johanna said, trying to keep her
voice normal. "Please ask her to get in touch with me. It is very important."

"I thought you said it had to do with a social research project," he
said. "Do you still want to talk to my brother?"

"If I talk with Candace, I won't need to speak with your brother. If her
answers are what I anticipate, she will be very gratified," Johanna urged.
"How soon do you think you can call her?"

"Uh, I can try to reach her this afternoon," he said, looking at his calendar on an I-Phone. "I'll ask her to call you, but I can't make promises."

"No, of course not, but tell her that she will be glad she did."

Candace Michaels did not call.

Johanna returned to her office after meeting with Don Michaels hoping that maybe he would try to reach his ex-sister-in-law right after she
left. If he had, he must not have been successful, or . . . and this was the
'or' she didn't like—Candace Michaels could not be convinced to speak
with her.

She was so close to finding Ruby.

The house was quiet when she closed the front door behind her. Ava never made much noise, but it was obvious from the energy of the house she was no longer there. She kept looking at her phone to make sure she had enough battery and then to make sure the volume was up when she took her shower.

Still no call from Candace Michaels.

Lying on the sofa and half-reading a book, Johanna decided she would call Don in the morning to get his feedback, and to put pressure on him to promote her case.

Her phone rang. It was close to nine o'clock.

"This is Candace Michaels," the woman said. "I understand you're trying to reach me. I'm sorry to be calling so late, but the kids had a soccer dinner and this is my first chance to check messages."

Johanna sat up, letting her book drop to the floor.

"Mrs. Michaels, I'm Johanna Hudson. I'm so glad you called. I have so much to talk with you about. Can we meet tomorrow?"

"Call me, Candace," she said. "Can I ask what this is all about?" Her voice held more than a little suspicion. "Why don't you tell me now?"

A low alarm went off in Johanna's head. Recent events and sightings had caused her to be even more guarded than her normal cautious instincts.

"Candace, I would rather talk with you face-to-face," she insisted. "And I don't want to be . . . difficult, but could you bring picture identification with you?"

"It is very inconvenient. I'm taking a chance on you, too, you know. But all right, I can meet at eleven-thirty," Candace said, miffed. "Let's make it the Bayside Grill in Burlingame, and you bring identification, too."

"I'll be there."

CHAPTER THIRTY

JOHANNA WASN'T ABLE TO SLEEP after she spoke with Candace Michaels. When she gave up trying, she went into the office—it was just after six am. Ava arrived two hours later and listened to how Johanna had finished one client's tree and started another. After the time needed to deal with the Ackerman lawsuit, she had fallen behind. Maybe they could stay in business after all.

"I don't believe it," Ava said, dumping her purse and oversized tote on her desk. "You must be anxious to have beaten me here. And, is that coffee I smell? Is this my 'welcome back'?"

Johanna stood and gave her a hug. "You bet it is."

She poured them both a cup and went over her efforts from the day before.

Ava pulled out the bottom drawer of her desk and put up her feet. "I never would have thought of asking her for ID; good thinking. So, how are you going to present your story?"

Johanna sat on the edge of her desk. "I've given this a lot of thought. First, I'm going to talk about Eloise's life since she gave up Ruby, and then of course, her murder. I'll talk about my role in all of this, and then I'll bring in James Bryce and the search for Ruby."

"You know, I realized you could be in the same position as Eloise," Ava said. "Could you just run through this family tree for me one time?"

"Okay, in summary, Jeanette Sutton married Eugene Dawes. It was an abusive marriage and while they were separated she had a child, Eloise. After a failed reconciliation, Jeanette killed Dawes and was sentenced to prison. Because Jeanette's mother, Olivia Sutton, didn't want the burden of child rearing, Eloise was sent to live with the Manley's, a foster family; as it turns out, for the rest of her growing years. An adult, Eloise had a child out of wedlock, Ruby." Johanna paused and reached for a sip of bottled water. "Now, the only reason anyone cares about Ruby is the money she's eligible to inherit from her wealthy San Francisco father—who no one knows his name. This is where we came in."

"So, how does Therese Bertrand fit in?"

"She's Jeanette's disgruntled first cousin. She says she doesn't know where her aunt Olivia Sutton lives, but I know she's lying. She's real high-strung and I don't trust her."

"What's to prevent Candace from contacting Ruby's father direct?"

"She could, and Ava, you know what, that would be okay. Ruby would get her inheritance. That's all Eloise, or I, would want."

Ava understood.

"Just one thing, a heads up, Johanna," she said. "I don't feel good about meeting with strangers when there's a lot of money involved. What about the guy who was following you?"

"I don't *know* he was following me, and I haven't seen him since," she said. "Besides, I won't have any direct contact with Ruby. So, following me around is going to be pretty inconclusive to anyone looking in from the outside."

"Hmm, maybe."

Ava shifted the conversation to giving more details about her Australian connections and networking potential. It was almost an hour later when Johanna collected her purse and jacket to leave.

"Good luck," Ava called out.

THE DRIVE TO BURLINGAME AT THAT TIME OF DAY was uneventful. Johanna pulled into the parking lot of Bayside Grill almost a half-hour early. There were a couple of patrons heading for the entrance and she took the moments to slow her thoughts. The vista was pleasant. Burlingame was located south of the San Francisco airport, and planes provided a steady flow of takeoff and landing activity. She checked for her notebook, and patted her pocket for her phone. As she got out of the car, she looked over her shoulder. She didn't see anything that made her nervous.

Inside, there was bench along the wall, in front of the hostess stand. There were people murmuring and laughing from the bar off to the side of the entry. A little dark and reserved, it was not a formal lounge but was intended for business clients and not the family crowd. A woman sitting at the far end of the padded bench in the entry was bent over her phone, and glanced up and back, and then up again.

"Johanna?"

Johanna nodded and Candace stood. They were almost the same height except Johanna noticed Candace wore boots with two-inch heels as opposed to her ballerina flats. With burnished brown hair with blueberry blue eyes, Candace Michaels was trying hard to look younger than her fifty years, and, except for persistent crow's feet and a lip enhancement, seemed to be succeeding.

"Yes," Johanna handed her a card. "Here's my identification. I appreciate your meeting with me, and as promised I won't take a lot of your time."

"I'm anxious to hear what you have to say." Candace settled into her seat. "And here's my identification." She pulled out her drivers' license.

The hostess sat them in a corner booth facing out onto the water. They both ordered salads, and the server, after leaving water and iced tea, left them avoiding the other's eyes.

Johanna cleared her throat. "I have a story to tell, I hope you will provide the finish," she said. "It starts with your daughter, Ruby."

"Ruby?" Candace's hand went to her throat. "You know Ruby?"

"I don't know Ruby at all. I knew Eloise Manley."

"Eloise Manley," she repeated, sinking back in her chair. "I haven't thought of her for a long time. But you said 'knew.' Has something happened?"

Johanna took a breath. "Let me start from the beginning."

It took longer than Johanna thought it would. Candace Michaels listened in silence raising her eyebrows in disbelief when Johanna described finding Eloise's body. Johanna finished with her discovery of Candace's brother-in-law.

Neither spoke for a long moment.

Candace put her fork down without tasting her salad. She spoke in a low voice, "We'd tried for years to have a child and then Ruby came into our lives. Eloise didn't want to see her when she was born, but we were there in the delivery room. Eloise signed over all her rights, except we had to call her Ruby," she said, amused. "I didn't like the name at all, but you know what? It suits her. She's a charming, loving person—a jewel."

Johanna felt like yelling at the top of her lungs. She'd found Ruby.

"Did I hear you say 'kids'? Do you have other children?"

The woman sighed a smile. "Yes, after we received Ruby, we had two of our own biologically—both girls. All the girls are all about a year and a half apart. We were a happy family until Lionel . . . about a year ago he left us to live with another woman. But we're hanging in there. And, I'm okay now. I've moved on." She straightened her shoulders as if to reassure herself.

"Candace, if things go the way I hope they will. Ruby will come into quite a bit of money. But—"

The woman tilted her head with interest. "There's always a 'but.'"

"True." Johanna nodded in agreement. "But I have to find her biological grandfather. As I told you, Eloise never knew the identity of her father. I've started a search, but it would go much faster if you could fill in my gaps of information."

Candace wrinkled her forehead. "We wanted backgrounds on both of Ruby's parents, but the agency gave us only the mother's health. Ruby's father wasn't listed. However, they did disclose Jeanette Sutton Dawes's . . . ah, incarceration, as background," she said. "You know, the social worker said Eloise came from an old San Francisco family. I don't know how she would know that, unless the Manley's had informed the agency and it was in Eloise's file."

"I'm trying to get a court order to see that file," Johanna said. "I need to find Ruby's grandfather."

Falling into silence, they both retreated to their own thoughts and finished their meal.

"Well, this has been quite a meeting," Candace said. "You have done a lot of work to help Ruby." She took a sip of water. "Would you like to see a picture of her?"

Johanna looked at her in amazement and nodded. "Nothing would please me more."

Candace smiled and took out her phone, scrolling through her photos until she settled on one. She handed the device to Johanna who stared.

"She's a gorgeous child," Johanna murmured. "Ruby looks exactly like her mother, Eloise, who was also quite beautiful."

Candace beamed. "Yes, she is quite pretty. My own daughters are cute, and I couldn't love them more, but next to Ruby they pale in comparison."

She scrolled to a group photo. Three grinning, darling looking girls, but only one drew the eye.

Johanna sought the time. "Candace, I have to get back to the office.

If you could text me your contact information, oh, and Ruby's picture, I will keep you informed on my progress," she said. "By the way, Ruby may need to undergo DNA testing."

"I take it Eloise's father's family would contest more heirs—a newly found granddaughter?"

"That would be a 'yes,'" Johanna said. "In fact, while I don't think there's any . . . concern, I wouldn't say anything to anyone about this. And, if you are approached, I would appreciate it if you said nothing and let me know first."

"All right, I think I understand. How long do you think this will all take?"

"Not long, the clock is ticking."

The San Mateo Bridge was a crawl back to the office. A truck had run into a barrier and traffic was backed up to the entrance of the toll plaza. Johanna didn't mind, she couldn't contain herself. She couldn't wait to see Trinidad's face when she told her she'd found Ruby.

Yes!

She pulled into the office parking lot next to Ava's car. They both were using Saturday to catch up on new client requests. She gathered her things from her car and out of the corner of her eye, she caught a figure hurrying to a dark sedan parked two rows behind her. She didn't turn her head, but she had seen the North Face jacket before. She opened the door to the back seat and slipped her phone out of her purse, and attempted to take a picture over her shoulder. A couple of clicks, again, without looking back and she hurried up the stairs.

"You photobombed him?" Ava asked, standing behind Johanna as she peered through the side of the window blinds. "Why don't you call the police?"

Johanna turned to face the women. "First, he's gone, and second, I don't know for sure he's the same guy I saw yesterday. But I'll know if I see him again."

She reached for her phone. The picture was not a good one; the trunk had blocked all but the very top of the license plate. Johanna settled in her desk chair.

"Ava, put that guy aside for a minute. I have great news," she said. "I found Ruby."

Ava's eyes widened as she, too, sat down. "Tell me everything."

"Can I say it one time? I texted Trinidad and told her to meet us. She's going to be so happy."

Ava made phone calls, and Johanna handled correspondence, but they both knew they were biding time until Trinidad appeared. They couldn't wait to see her expression.

A tap on the door ended their wait.

"Johanna, you text me to come," Trinidad said, entering the room with uncertainty.

Today she was garbed in deep purple cropped pants and a soft yellow tunic.

"Come in, Trinidad." Johanna waved her in. "We have news, great news."

Trinidad looked from one to the other and cautiously took the chair in front of Johanna's desk.

"Great news? What is it?"

"I found Ruby."

Trinidad's expression froze on her face. Then, after again looking from one to the other, tears glistened in her eyes. She immediately wiped them away.

"When I see her?"

Johanna and Ava exchanged looks.

"You can't," Johanna said, and then seeing Trinidad's dismay, hurried. "I mean, not now. We—"

"Johanna, what you not tell me? What is happening?"

Ava reached over and patted Trinidad's hand. "Hear her out, Trini."

Trinidad nodded and took a breath. "I wait long time to hear words from you, Johanna, I waited like Ellie," she said. "You good woman, and I am impatient. Please, thank you. Now tell me, what news about Ruby?"

"I discovered Ruby's adopted mother, Candace Michaels," Johanna replied. "She seems to be a very nice person. She divorced Ruby's adopted father after they had two girls on their own. So the three girls live with their mother." She looked at Trinidad to see how she was handling the information, and went on, "I told her about the inheritance, and I told her I had no idea who Ruby's is. And I asked her to stay silent until I did confirm his identity. It is also likely Ruby will have to undergo a DNA test."

Ava chewed her bottom lip. "Well, finding Ruby was half the battle. What's your plan for finding her grandad?"

Trinidad looked up to hear the answer.

"Well, Dean is filing a petition with the court," Johanna said. "If granted, we'll be allowed to see Eloise's foster family placement file."

"Ellie's father and Ruby's grandfather's name is there?" Trinidad asked.

"We don't know for sure, but I'm checking everywhere," Johanna said.

Ava and Trinidad nodded in agreement, though both had dubious looks.

"Hey, perk up," Johanna said. "We found Ruby, and that's a big deal. We'll see what the court says, but until then I won't stop looking."

"What about your shadow?" Ava tossed out.

Trinidad looked at Johanna, puzzled. "What is shadow?"

Johanna averted her eyes. "There is a man who may be following me—like a shadow. It's not James Bryce, but . . ."

"I see him, too," Trinidad said, alarmed. "You think he wants Ruby?"

Johanna nodded. "Maybe. But he doesn't strike me as a pro. I was able to spot him a couple of times."

"Still," Ava said. "I think we should put a security alarm in the office." She raised her hand when Johanna opened her mouth to protest. "I'll back off on the alarm if you promise to inform the police."

"Deal."

"Johanna, do you have ideas if court order idea not work?" Trinidad asked. "When can I see Ruby?"

Johanna smiled. "Yes, I do have one or two other ideas. And you can see Ruby right now."

She pulled out her phone and scrolled through her photos. She handed the phone to Trinidad.

"*Sainte mère de Dieu*," the woman exclaimed, covering her mouth with her hand. "She . . . she look so much like Ellie." Tears once more filled her eyes. "I will never forget this, Johanna, I will always owe you."

Johanna shook her head. "You owe me nothing. I want to do this. I'm supposed to meet Dean in court on Monday morning."

"You call us," Ava said. "And let us know what happens."

Trinidad stood. "Now, I go. If I here I get too nervous."

CHAPTER THIRTY-ONE

IT WAS EVIDENT FROM THE ALMOST EMPTY COURTROOM that the Manley matter should not take a long time to be called. When Johanna entered, Dean gave her an acknowledging nod and waved her forward to sit next to him at the table. The judge glanced up to view the courtroom, then went back to discussing the upcoming calendar with the court clerk. After a few minutes he reshuffled the papers on the bench and picked up a file.

The bailiff called out the case and case number.

"Mr. Cameron," the judge said, waving him forward. "Go ahead and address the court."

Dean stood and spoke from his table. "Your honor, I'm here representing Mrs. Hudson who has filed a petition to open a foster placement file from 1998. Mrs. Hudson was retained by Eloise Manley, the subject of the foster placement, to locate her biological father. Subsequently, Miss Manley was murdered."

"Did you say murdered, Counselor?" The judge looked over his glasses and down at the petition.

"Yes, your honor, the police are still trying to locate the killer," Dean said. "Miss Manley had been approached by an individual indicating her biological father, who was very wealthy but had remained unknown to her and she to him, had passed away. This individual stated Miss Manley, if proven she was his daughter, would be entitled to a large inheritance. He, of course, wanted a 'finders' fee. Miss Manley was wary of being approached by a stranger and decided to locate her father on her own."

"Mr. Cameron it's going to be a long day. Could you cut to the chase," the judge said, peering at Johanna.

"Of course, your honor. As I said, Miss Manley hired Mrs. Hudson, who's here with me today. At that time, Miss Manley indicated she had no interest in pursuing any monies for herself, but she wanted to ensure her daughter's future. Your honor, Miss Manley had a daughter whom she put up for adoption at the time of her birth. It was a good placement, and as far as we know the daughter is doing well and lives in a stable home. Mrs. Hudson would use the foster placement file to gain information as to the identity of the child's grandfather which would allow the legal process to proceed with the child's parent filing a claim against his estate for the child's benefit."

"That ought to be interesting," the judge murmured. He gave Johanna a long look and nodded. "Petition granted. Good luck, Mrs. Hudson."

Johanna grinned and gave Dean a hug. "How soon can I see the file?" she said.

"I'll get the order from the court clerk before I leave today. Can you come by my office in about an hour and pick it up?"

"An hour should be fine. I've got a . . . a meeting with someone later on today who may help me locate Eloise's father."

Dean gave her a curious look and said, "Look why don't you meet me in the clerk's office in about a half-hour. Then you can take the order with you."

JOHANNA DIDN'T KNOW IF SHE WAS MORE EXCITED about the court order in her brief case, or her upcoming date with Dominic Quinn. She was able to reach Gina Hart before she left her office for the day, and arranged for a meeting.

"Boy, you work fast," Hart said. "But I'm glad things worked out for you. I hope the little girl will find her biological family and maybe an inheritance. See you in the morning."

At home, staring at her closet, Johanna settled on changing her top to something less puritan looking, and opted for a flowy maroon topper over a simple white silk tank top. She was glad they had agreed to meet for lunch. It was a neutral commitment. She wasn't ready for a man to pick her up at her front door. The parking lot had a scattering of cars. Johanna had arrived a few minutes early so she could enter a few minutes late. She didn't want to be the first one there. She looked in the visor mirror to check her lipstick.

She jumped at the tap on her window.

"Johanna?"

Nick stood next to the window wearing a teasing grin. He pointed to the lipstick. "Is that for me?"

She could feel the blush rising from her chest. He backed up as she stepped out of the car.

"A gentleman would play it off and leave me with a little pride."

"Oh, yeah, I guess one would." He shrugged. "Oh, well."

She tapped him on the arm. "Oh, well."

They both laughed and walked to the entrance.

They gave their order to the server, who offered them a complimentary appetizer.

"That's a break, I'm starving," Nick said.

Johanna played with her cocktail napkin. "I'm sorry we couldn't have dinner. I . . . I –"

"Wanted to have an out in case we didn't work out?"

She looked down at her hands with a sheepish smile. "Guilty. This is the first time I've gone out since my husband died. I was more unsure of myself than I was of you."

"Well, that's good to know," Nick said as he nodded to the server who brought their beverages. "Tell me about him."

Johanna gave him a look of surprise. She proceeded to speak of her marriage and the man she thought she'd grow old with.

"He sounds like a good guy."

"Oh, he was no saint. But, we were good for each other," she said. Then, straightening her shoulders. "What about you? Have you lost a love?"

"Yes, I did as a matter of fact," Nick replied. "She left me for another man. Just like in the movies, I came home and there they were."

"Ouch," Johanna said, twisting the stem of her wine glass. "Are you divorced?"

He nodded. "Five years."

A loud silence came between them. The server brought their food.

Johanna cleared her throat. "You know, I'm hungry. Let's eat."

Nick's eyes met hers, and a large grin crossed his face.

"So you think lunch will be okay?"

"I'm ready."

The meal was companionable. Johanna was relieved to see they shared the same quirky sense of humor and the same compassion for victims of injustice.

"Is that why you've taken on finding Ruby as a crusade?" Nick asked.

"Hmm, maybe. But it's not a crusade, I made a promise. I hate bullies and I detest people who are driven by economics and willing to trade their integrity for power or money."

He raised his eyebrows but said nothing. Johanna took a breath and another sip of lemonade.

"You know, I think we're going to get along fine," Nick said. "Tell me what you know about Ruby's grandfather."

"Not much." Johanna grimaced. "I hope to know more, tomorrow morning." She told him about the court order. "And I've done a lot of research, but it's like trying to capture fog."

"Fog, huh," he said. "Let me know how things work out. I'd like to help if I can."

Johanna hesitated and looked down at her hands.

"What's the matter?" Nick asked.

"I, uh . . . I think someone might be following me." She held up her hand to halt his response, and recapped the last couple of days. "I don't know for sure, but . . . but it's a strong feeling I get from time to time."

"Feeling?" he said. "Have you actually *seen* the guy?"

"Like I said, I'm not sure."

Nick looked past Johanna to the dining area. "Okay, tell you what. Here's my work number. I always carry my phone with me. Call me if you get into trouble." He scribbled his number on a small piece of paper and handed it to her. "But don't get into trouble."

CHAPTER THIRTY-TWO

THE MARICOPA FAMILY SERVICES' receptionist indicated Gina Hart was still on the phone, but had been informed Johanna was waiting to see her.

Waiting.

She'd been there almost twenty minutes. Ava had already called wanting to know her progress: Trinidad was camped in front of her desk.

Johanna sighed. "Tell Trinidad I have her cell number, and as soon as I hear anything, anything at all, I will call her."

Johanna could hear Ava conveying her message, and Trinidad's response in a raised voice, ". . . call with anything."

She clicked off and, taking out her laptop, began an internet search for San Francisco's top one-hundred richest men.

"Mrs. Hudson, Johanna?" Hart emerged from the corridor and moved to her. "I must apologize. I never would have kept you waiting, except it involved a foster child who I had to make sure was not at risk."

A now contrite Johanna followed the woman through the door to the same conference room where they had spoken before. "I didn't mind waiting at all. I knew you must have been tied up with something important."

"Yes, well, your case is important, too." Hart took a seat across from her. She pushed a file across the table. "Your court order allows you to have access to the Eloise Sutton placement. We, however, are not going to allow you to take, or copy, any of the papers. You may read through the file and take notes, but that is all."

"I understand," she said. "For my purposes, the information is here or it isn't."

Hart nodded and pulled out a large file of her own to go through, while Johanna read.

Johanna opened the file and gasped. In precise handwriting on unlined paper, was a letter from Jeanette Sutton to the family that would be raising her child. A chill ran down her arm.

> Hello,
>
> My name is Jeanette Sutton Dawes. If you are read-
> ing this letter you know that I will be going to prison for
> fifteen years for killing my husband. I won't try to explain
> why I did it, or justify it with excuses. I did it. I did it for
> my daughter, whose care I am entrusting to you now.
>
> I would prefer you not show Eloise this letter, but
> I know it is out of my control and I have given up my
> rights to have a say in her life for the next years. Nor do I
> want you to bring her to see me in prison. I will explain
> things to her when we are back together. I ask you to
> honor these requests.
>
> You will find Eloise to be a great kid. She is bright
> and funny, and she is determined to be an artist one day.
> When I return I plan on making sure she will be able to
> use her artistic talent. If you could give her colors and
> paper, it would mean so much to her. She's very self-reli-
> ant, but it's because she's had to learn not to count on any-
> one—including me.
>
> Eloise's real father is a good man, an honorable man.
> He does not know of Eloise's existence. His mother has
> made it clear that she has no interest in knowing me, and
> I am to have no contact with her son. I have made it clear
> with County Family Services that Eloise is not to have
> contact with her paternal grandmother in the far unlikely
> event she discovers she has a grandchild. Something I am
> determined will never happen.
>
> I would ask you to tell Eloise I love her and will always
> love her and that the years will fly by until we see each
> other again.
>
> Sincerely,
> Jeanette Sutton

Johanna put the letter down. Her thoughts raced. Jeanette would never see her daughter again. She would never know her daughter had lost her sight and would never have the chance to take advantage of her artistic ability.

She'd hoped Jeanette would have revealed Eloise's father's name or address or something. Scanning the few pages in the file, Johanna stopped.

"Gina, when Jeanette Sutton submitted Eloise to county foster care, didn't she have to complete medical forms?"

Hart looked up from her file.

"Yes." She flipped to the back of the folder and took an envelope out of a cover pocket. She opened the envelope, scanned the contents and handed it to Johanna. "It's not much, but it's something."

Johanna looked at the page and then took a pen out of her purse. As she scribbled the information, she spoke out loud:

"Name: withheld; Age: twenty-nine; Height: 6 feet, 1 inch; Weight: one hundred-sixty-five; Eyes: Green; Hair: Brown." Johanna looked up, but Hart was tapping on her phone. She continued, "He has no known physical or mental disabilities; he's allergic to cats and milkweed; no known disease in immediate family; and blood type AB."

She stared at the document for a moment, and then went through each page in the file, one at a time. The vast majority of the papers were institution forms printed in a small font with line after line of disclaimers.

One was missing

"Gina, where's Jeanette Sutton Dawes's health disclosure?" Johanna asked. "Shouldn't she have a page in here as well?"

The woman frowned. "She certainly should." She reached for the file and flipped through the pages. She looked in the back pocket and smiled. "Here's her envelope. It was at the bottom."

Johanna accepted the second brown envelope and read the contents out loud.

"Name: Jeanette Sutton Dawes; Age: twenty-eight; Height: five feet, five inches; Weight: one hundred and fifteen pounds; Eyes: Green; Hair: Blonde; No physical or mental disabilities; No allergies; No known disease in the family; and Blood Type: A."

She blew out a breath.

"What is it?" said Hart.

Johanna grinned. "She supplied an address for her nearest relative: Olivia Sutton Fields, mother."

CHAPTER THIRTY-THREE

WHEN JOHANNA RETURNED TO THE OFFICE, she was greeted by Trinidad sitting behind Ava's desk, reading a magazine.

"Ah, Johanna, any news?" she asked. "I come early to my job to find out how you are doing." She motioned toward the door with her hand. "Ava asked me to watch office. She said since I'm here anyway I can make myself useful. She said she had to go to Mormon Tunnel to do research. She'll be back in another hour."

Johanna smiled. "You mean the Mormon *Temple*." She put her purse down. "Were there any calls? Anyone come by?"

"No. I keep my eyes on the phone and door. Oh, the mailman came, but I don't count him. She indicated a small stack of mail on the edge of her desk. "Johanna, what is news? Did the court order come? Did you read about Eloise's mother?"

Johanna sat at her desk, kicked off her shoes and recounted her day's findings with Trinidad. Trinidad sat silent looking perplexed.

"How we find him, Johanna?"

Johanna noticed the "we," but made no comment. "I'm going to start with the obituaries. I'm not sure he has died, and I've got to start somewhere. It will be slow going, but I know his age, and I know he lived in San Francisco."

"I don't know what obitu . . . is, but if you do it, I know it's the right thing." Trinidad stood. "I go to work now. I cover for Simone this time. She's been very mysterious. She not tell me what her emergency." She stopped at the door. "Johanna, do you think I can meet Ruby one day? I would like to do that."

Johanna smiled. "I think so, yes."

THE SAN FRANCISCO CHRONICLE NEWSPAPER WAS pretty good about publishing, on a daily basis, the deaths of its residents and those who died in its environs—particularly anyone of wealth. However, it helped to know the last name of the deceased. Eloise's father was twenty-seven when she was put into foster care, at the age of five. That would make him around fifty-five today. If he had died sometime in the last sixty-days, Johanna could narrow the search by drawing a circle on a calendar going back two weeks prior to Eloise's death.

It was slow going.

"You know, not every family wants a mention in the Chronicle," Ava said, returning with an armload of books. "Without a last name . . . . " She didn't finish her sentence.

"Ava, you don't have to remind me. Remember I'm the one doing the searching." Johanna said, not glancing up from her laptop screen. "How do things look for our new client?"

Her partner slipped off her shoes and put her feet on top of her desk. "Do you have any idea how many Peter Joneses there are in Australia? Don't answer, I'll tell you. It's one of the most common names on the continent."

"Talk about searching," Johanna said. "I'm still going through obits for week one of last month. This way is taking more time than we have." She leaned back in her chair. "I wonder if Nick could help me."

"Nick?" Ava responded.

"Yes, Nick Quinn, I told you he's with the Sheriff's Department. They have to identify dead people every day, and they have to have a better system than this one."

"Hmm, that must have been some lunch," Ava teased.

Johanna ignored her, picked up the phone and tapped in a number. She explained her predicament, but she knew it was a long shot.

"I'm sorry, Johanna," he said. "I can't help you."

"Why not?"

"I'm in the law enforcement business, not lost and found. These are public tax dollars at work not a benevolent society.

"All right, I get it. But you said to ask if I needed any help."

He must have realized how he sounded, because he softened. "When you get a specific name, I'll run it for you."

She tried to keep the frustration out of her voice. "Thank you. That will be a big help."

Johanna had begun a list of potential names that met the age requirements of Eloise's father. By the end of the day she had almost made it through the month and had a list of fourteen names. At this rate, it would be a week before she had a complete list, and then an unknown period of time to vet the names. She tossed her chart to the side.

To break up the tedium of her search through the obituaries, she changed targets and embarked on locating Olivia Sutton Fields. Jeanette's mother had moved twice since the foster family file, and Johanna finally thought to search county property tax records for forwarding addresses. In no time, she narrowed down the pool of names, and took out her cell phone.

On to Olivia Sutton Fields.

"Mrs. Fields?" Johanna asked, her finger resting on the phone number of a potential find.

There was a pause.

"No, no there's no one here by that name," the woman said. "I'm sorry you have the wrong number."

She clicked off. Johanna didn't believe her. She tapped in the number again.

"I told you—"

"I'm sorry, for calling back, but I didn't get a chance to explain." It was her turn to pause, then, "I'm trying to locate the mother of Jeanette Sutton Dawes."

Now there was a gasp. "Why? What do you want?"

Johanna was pretty sure she had the right person, but she couldn't afford to be wrong. "I didn't mean to startle you," she said. "I have news of your granddaughter."

"Eloise?" the woman murmured.

"Yes, Eloise," Johanna said, with a note of triumph. "Mrs. Fields, it is Fields now, isn't it? I was hoping we could meet and I could talk to you in person."

"No. Well, I suppose." She hesitated. "I . . . I'm ashamed to say I have never reached out to Eloise. My daughter and I uh . . . never . . . we never really got along."

"Yes, maybe we could meet over coffee?" Johanna urged. It didn't sound as if Olivia Sutton Fields knew her granddaughter had been murdered.

"Coffee, yes, all right," Olivia said, flustered. "There's a Starbucks on the corner of Van Ness and Jackson. There's plenty of parking. I'll meet you at two o'clock. I have to go now, someone's at the door."

She clicked off.

Johanna sat back in her chair and exhaled the breath she'd been holding. Now that she'd discovered the whereabouts of Ruby, the critical answer Olivia Sutton Fields could provide was the identity of Eloise's father.

"Johanna, be careful," Ava said. "Remember, she was cold-hearted enough to leave her granddaughter to strangers . . . ." She sighed. "Just be careful."

With Ava's cautions in her ears, Johanna sat outside the coffee shop in her car.

Arriving thirty-minutes early, she had backed her car into a parking space which had a good view of the front door. This Starbucks was a busy one, even for a mid-afternoon. Distracted by a text from a client, she looked up to see a two-seater Mazda pull into the lot. An older woman stepped out of the car and throwing a light shawl over her shoulder, walked inside. Johanna caught her breath. She would recognize Olivia Sutton Fields anywhere. It was like looking into the face of her granddaughter, Eloise Manley.

Johanna hurried to the entrance. Olivia Fields had already secured two upholstered side chairs beside a small round table.

"Johanna Hudson?" she said.

"Hello, Mrs. Fields, I'm so glad you agreed to meet with me."

"Olivia, please."

Johanna offered her hand, and it was shaken tentatively. They set their coats in the seat to mark their claim as they ordered coffees from the counter. Minutes later, they sat across from one another.

Olivia took a quick sip and set her cup down. "All right, what is all this about?"

"I'm a genealogist. I research family ancestry lines and prepare family trees." Johanna took a sip of coffee. "About a month ago I met Eloise Manley for the first time. I was introduced to her by a mutual . . . friend. She wanted me to help identify and locate her birth father."

Olivia's well made-up face paled.

"Her father . . . why?"

"A week before I met her, she'd been accosted by a man who tried to intimidate her into verifying she was Jeanette's daughter. He had a letter, that he said was from her grandmother, which indicated Eloise's father was a prominent San Francisco figure, and therefore she may be eligible for a share in his estate."

Olivia frowned. "I sent no such letter."

Johanna wasn't surprised to hear her announcement; it was one of the few things James Bryce said that made sense. She'd been right to think Eloise's paternal grandmother had sent the letter.

"So, you're telling me you don't know a man named James Bryce?" Johanna insisted.

Olivia shook her head.

Olivia Fields had not approached Eloise.

Johanna rushed, "Eloise felt, excuse me for saying this, since you had not contacted her in all these years, she felt, and if not for the possible money, you wouldn't have contacted her at all. She'd decided to enlist my help and do it on her own."

"I . . . it was the . . . a bad time," Olivia's words stumbled.

Johanna raised her hand. "You don't have to explain. It's all irrelevant now," Johanna said in a lowered tone. "I'm so sorry to tell you this, but your granddaughter was murdered."

Olivia stared. Her lips parted, but only a gasp escaped. Johanna filled the silence by providing the full story.

"Eloise became blind? And now she's dead?"

Johanna nodded.

"She was such a beautiful child. I have no excuse. I am so ashamed," she said. "When Jeanette killed that awful man—a high-school never-was-been, I must confess, I was relieved. We hadn't spoken in several years. I opposed the relationship from the beginning. He had no character and only wanted Jeanette so they could complete a visual of a power couple. He didn't love her, he loved himself too much. When they separated, I was elated. She called me to ask if she could come home to get her life together. I knew how difficult it was for her to ask me, and I said yes."

Olivia used both hands to grip the cup as she took a long gulp.

She continued, "She wasn't my only child, she had a sister." Her eyes glistened with pending tears, but she dabbed them dry with her fingers.

"They were very close." She hesitated. "Anyway with Jeanette back home, we seemed to settle into semi-closeness. She told me about a man she met at the Bay to Breakers. They appeared to have hit it off but I knew something was wrong. He never came to the house, and she never mentioned his name. My gut told me he was married."

"She never mentioned his name?" Johanna couldn't hide her disappointment.

"No," Olivia said.

"I take it, you weren't happy when Eugene Dawes, came back into her life."

"I begged her not to go back to him." Olivia shook her head. "But I didn't know she was pregnant, and I bet she was thinking Dawes would make a divorce settlement, and her life, impossible. But I think the truth of it was, her mystery love was not ready to leave his wife."

"So you have no idea who he was, or what type of work he did?"

Olivia wrinkled her forehead in thought. "When Jeanette returned home, we had to get used to each other again. She was always a private person, and she would make and take her calls out on the patio. But one time, I saw her take a business card out of her purse before she made a call. From what I could see from out the kitchen window, and the way she grinned, I knew it was him."

Johanna leaned forward. "Did you ever see the card?"

Olivia looked down at her hands. "I'm embarrassed to say that when she was in the bathroom, I looked inside her purse for the card. I was so afraid she would catch me. But I had to know who she was involved with. It was a generic business card with a phone number written on the back."

Two steps forward, one step back.

"Can you remember the name of the company, or the phone number?"

"Not the number, except that it was a '415' area code for San Francisco, but I caught the name of the company." Olivia narrowed her eyes as if seeing the card in front of her. "It's been so many years. It was a commercial real estate firm, with the name of . . . Mist . . . or, Fisk . . . or, maybe Shaw? I remember thinking the card was so fancy. It was a gloss gold with embossed black print. The back was matte gold, which made it easy to write on."

Johanna raised her eyebrows. It never ceased to amaze what people found important to remember from the past. In her research, these random memories were often the key to locating a family member.

"Olivia, I promised Eloise to find her father. She wanted to leave her daughter, Ruby, your great-granddaughter, with an inheritance," she said. "There is a chance her father may have died, or maybe is dying. At any rate, time is of the essence. Is there anything else you can tell me?"

The older woman seemed to be half-listening. She looked up. "You think that this James Bryce killed Eloise?"

"I don't know."

"You say she was blind, poor child. The Manleys didn't care enough to give her treatment, how unthinkable."

Johanna bit the inside of her mouth, wondering how this well-cared for woman in front of her could ignore the hypocrisy of her own role in Eloise's neglect. She looked at the time on her phone.

"Olivia, I must be going. Thank you so much for meeting me. You've given me more information to work with."

They both stood.

"You'll let me know if there is anything to this inheritance issue, won't you? Or, if you find Eloise's father?"

"Of course."

She needed air.

Heading to her car, after waving a mutual goodbye, Johanna held back a profanity even as a tear slipped down her face. She was remembering another little girl. Johanna had no doubt why Jeanette never got along with her mother. The woman had not once asked about little Ruby.

BY THE TIME JOHANNA RETURNED TO THE OFFICE Ava had gone home early for the day. Not taking time to remove her jacket, she began searching on her laptop for the largest commercial real estate firms in San Francisco's area code. Granted a fancy business card may not mean the biggest, but it could mean it was successful. She would start there. There were eighteen such companies.

It was close to seven o'clock by the time she had visited each website to hope against hope the gold and black colors would be a part of a masthead. That search ended nowhere.

She'd copied down the names of the top management of each. Then, returning to each firm, she, when possible, eliminated names whose pictures were of men who, looked too young to be Eloise's father. But the vast majority didn't have pictures at all. Still, she was able to eliminate three companies.

After another hour, Johanna pushed back a feeling of frustration. She had to narrow her field of inquiry. There was little assurance Eloise's father's firm had not updated its brand and changed its business card, to something more—modern. She tossed her pen on the keypad. She rubbed her eyes and stared at the screen.

There was a tap at the door before it opened.

"Trinidad," Johanna said, straightening in her chair.

The woman entered after situating her cart in the corridor.

"I see your light on, and I come to talk back about how things are going."

"I'm glad you did," she said. "I was going to call you. I met with Eloise's grandmother today."

Trinidad's eyes grew wide. "Johanna, that is wonderful news. What did she say? Did you ask her why she sent that terrible man to scare Eloise?"

Johanna shrugged. "She said she didn't."

Trinidad clicked her tongue. "And you believe her?"

"I don't know. She was . . . she wasn't very compassionate . . . er . . . caring about her daughter. And, she only showed a little interest in Eloise, and none in knowing Ruby." Johanna motioned for the woman to sit down. "She said she didn't know Eloise was dead."

Trinidad pursed her lips. "Oh, this is not good. How will you ever find Eloise's father in time?"

Johanna tried to smile, but she knew it was a poor attempt. "I've still got a couple of ideas to flesh out."

"What is flesh out?"

Johanna reached over and patted the back of the woman's hand. "I've got a couple of more people I can talk with who might be able to help."

Trinidad hesitated. "I must go back to job. I hope you find the flesh soon."

"I will."

She'd spoken with more bravado than she had. She wasn't sure where to go next. She didn't know how much time she had to find Eloise's father—she seemed to be running in circles. She took out a pad of large sized post-its. She wrote the name of each person in Eloise's known circle of contacts on a separate sheet. She placed them around her desktop to see if there was a connection she'd overlooked. With Eloise's name in the center, she scribbled down in a few words what each person had told her with a line to the person it led to. In a short while, the diagram took on the shape of a spider.

It was dark outside, and she was exhausted. She'd find the "flesh" tomorrow.

CHAPTER THIRTY-FOUR

THE WALKWAY UP TO THERESE BERTRAND'S HOUSE was covered in falling cherry blossoms from a nearby tree. The woman stood in the doorway holding open the door.

"I can't imagine why it was so urgent to meet with me again," she said, standing aside as Johanna entered. "I told you everything I knew when you were here before."

Johanna chose to sit on the sofa, and Bertrand chose a stiff backed chair across from her.

"Good Morning," Johanna said. "I appreciate your time and yes, it is urgent. When I was here last I didn't tell you why I was looking for Eloise's grandmother—your aunt, or her father. There could be quite a bit of money involved as a result of a potential inheritance."

Johanna let the words hang in the air, and then realized the fixed blank expression on Bertrand's face showed little reaction, let alone surprise.

"You've talked with your aunt, haven't you?" Johanna demanded. "You know about Eloise and her child?"

The woman fidgeted with the fringe on her chair and blushed.

"She didn't have to tell me. We're working together. We know you aren't doing this out of the kindness . . . the kindness of your heart," Bertrand stammered. "How much are you getting?"

Johanna looked at her in amazement. "I don't know about the kindness of my heart. But I made a commitment and I intend on keeping it," she replied. "And for your information, I'm not receiving a dime from Eloise's estate."

"You got that right." Therese Bertrand leaned forward, her forearms folded over her thighs. "Eloise was loose, like her mother. Living like she did. I bet she never knew her child's father. That's why she was cursed with the loss of her sight," She spat out the cruel words with a small sneer playing on her lips.

Johanna was losing the battle in disguising her disgust. She stood.

"I'm sorry to have wasted your time—and mine."

Bertrand followed her to the door. "You need to butt out of this. I don't know what you think you've figured out, but we're way ahead of you."

"Do you know who Jeanette was seeing during her separation?"

"Not yet, but I can assure you that you won't be on our list to tell when we find out."

INFURIATED, JOHANNA MADE THE RETURN TRIP to her office in record time. It wasn't the threats, but the cavalier way Bertrand appeared to be handling her Cousin Eloise's murder and the possibility of an heir to a fortune.

Johanna didn't trust it.

On the other hand, if she let her feelings take over; she risked overlooking information that might lead to Eloise's father. She sat at her desk staring at her spider chart. She picked up her phone.

"Detective Quinn—"

"Ah, it's back to Detective Quinn now," he chided.

"Yes, this is business," Johanna insisted. "Hear me out. You know my partner was assaulted two nights ago while our office was being robbed. I think the person who did it is a man named James Bryce. Bryce confronted me last week about the research I was conducting on Eloise Manley. Bryce also visited Manley before her death. Trinidad Owens can attest to Eloise's meeting with him."

She waited. Quinn was silent.

"You already know about Bryce, don't you?"

"*Mrs. Hudson*, we appreciate you coming forward," he said. "In fact, yes, we are familiar with Mr. Bryce, but we hadn't connected Bryce to the break-in of your office. So, I'll look into that. Is there anything else you think I should know?"

Johanna thought about her options. Quinn had made it clear finding Ruby's grandfather held no interest for the police. They were only interested in Bryce because of his link to Eloise.

"Detective . . . Nick," she said. "If you could tell me if there was . . . if there was anything from Eloise's motor home that could point to her history. Anything at all, that related to her past."

"Johanna, I can't—"

"You said you would help me if you could. I'm not asking about any murder evidence or findings. I'll take anything you might have come across that would be classified as public information—if you could guide me in the right direction."

He exhaled a long breath. "Okay, you know the Bible you showed me?"

"Yes."

"I figured you took a picture of the family page." He continued, "You may want to go over those family names again, particularly the last one."

"Okay, I will. Can you tell me what I might find?"

Quinn cleared his throat. "Mrs. Hudson, as you so eagerly pointed out to me—you're the researcher."

She smiled.

"Thank you, Detective," she said. "Have a good day."

"The same to you, Mrs. Hudson."

CHAPTER THIRTY-FIVE

IF THE CONVERSATION WITH THERESE BERTRAND had left her frustrated and angry, her talk with Dominic Quinn had left her frustrated but hopeful. She peered down at the list of fading names from the family tree page in the Sutton Bible. The last on the list of twenty-three names was a Phillip Sutton, but there were no birth or death references. However, the entry before his had the date of death of 1935. So Phillip had been born after the depression. It was a blind lead, but she pulled out her laptop and started to search.

This was a Sutton Bible. Jeanette had given it to her daughter as it had been given to her. Phillip Sutton could be Jeanette's father, Olivia's ex-husband—and Ruby's great-grandfather.

Johanna went to her three favorite databases: Ancestry.com; Family Search and Archives.gov. She could spend weeks searching each one, but she didn't have the luxury of time. She starred again at the names, and then her eyes widened. If Dominic was trying to help her, he had guided her to Phillip Sutton because he was still alive, and they had located him.

She could do the same.

This time she would comb through county public records. Of course, she didn't have a specific county name, but the nine counties comprising the greater San Francisco Bay Area all had up-to-date online databases and efficient search technology—and they were free. By evening time, she had done a first pass through all of the counties' birth, marriage and voting record, and had a solid list of five names that could fit the age of Jeanette's father. Of course, if none panned out, she would have to expand her search for a much older or a much younger Phillip Sutton.

Loud voices and a car door slam nearby caught her attention. The workday was ending. She rubbed her eyes. As if on cue, her phone rang.

"Johanna," her mother said. "I called to see how you were doing. I got your message about Joel and those Ackerman people. I'm glad it worked out."

"Hi, Mom, yes," Johanna said, distracted. She continued to peer at her computer screen while she spoke. "I got Ackerman off our backs and onto the desks of law enforcement. That whole thing was a nightmare."

"Are you still at work?" Elizabeth Girard asked in a tone that signified her daughter's answer had better be good.

"Uh, yes, but I'm packing up to go home."

"Johanna, I worry about you. You have got to get a life. Researching other people's lives does not do a thing for developing one of your own. And—"

"I went on a date."

She mother said nothing for a moment.

"A real date? When?"

"About a week ago, and yes, it was a real date."

"How did it go?"

"It went quite well. In fact, I would have invited you to our wedding the next day, but it was a civil ceremony, and since we only had his lunch hour . . . well, there wasn't the time."

"Very funny," her mother chuckled.

"I had fun," Johanna said with seriousness. "We'll see where it goes."

"That's all I wanted to hear," Elizabeth said. "What's his name?"

"Oh, no, you're not going to get one of your friends to run him through NICS. Besides, he works for law enforcement."

NICS was the National Instant Criminal Background System, a database used to identify persons with one year or more of prison incarcerations; those involuntarily committed to a mental institution, or, persons dishonorably discharged from military service.

Elizabeth Girard had been an analyst for the State of California Bureau of Investigation, until her divorce from Johanna's father twelve years before. The break-up had been full of rancor and in the end; Elizabeth had felt it best to resign. Now, she worked as an in-house consultant for a security firm. Neither mother nor daughter spoke of those earlier times.

"Hmm, a cop," her mother said.

"Mom, don't you have a book to read or something?"

"No, actually I—"

"Good night, mother."

"Good night, sweetheart."

THE NEXT MORNING, AFTER SENDING AVA OFF to her follow-up doctor's appointment assessing her recovery, Johanna fell to whittling her list of possible Phillip Suttons down to one. And, after a few phone calls, she found him.

"This is Phillip Sutton," he said, his voice firm and no-nonsense. "What can I do for you?"

"Mr. Sutton, are you familiar with Jeanette Sutton?"

There was a long silence.

"Mr. Sutton?"

"Yes, I knew Jeanette Sutton," he said at last. "What's this about?"

Johanna chose her words carefully, "Mr. Sutton, my name is Johanna Hudson, and I'm a genealogist. I'm helping a client trace their background. There's a chance my client is related to Jeanette, and perhaps to you. I was hoping to show you some pictures and ask a few questions. Would it be possible for us to meet wherever and whenever it's convenient for you? I'd rather not have our conversation over the phone."

"Oh, that's it," he said, his tone lifting. "I didn't know what you would want with . . . Well, anyway, are you with those ancestry people?"

"No, no, I have my own service." She was beginning to feel a bit deceptive, but she had to see him. "When would be a good time to meet?"

"Oh, anytime works for me," he said. "I'm in an assisted living facility, not much to do. I'm not sure I'm going to be much help though, with those pictures. I'm blind."

In her car, driving to Morgan Hill where Phillip Sutton lived at the Valley Gardens Village, Johanna's mind whirred. Sutton was blind. Was it possible Eloise had inherited her blindness from her grandfather, and it had nothing to do with any lack of care by the Manleys? She'd brought the pictures anyway. She would describe them and perhaps they would trigger a memory.

Morgan Hill was an affluent residential community located south of Silicon Valley. Valley Gardens Village was a pleasant looking facility tucked next to a large man-made pond surrounded by leafy trees, giving Valley Gardens the feel of a small-scale resort. Johanna inhaled the scent of honeysuckle as she made her way up the curving walkway. A massive water fountain in front of the entrance trickled soothingly over large stone jugs. Five golf carts stood ready in a row off to the side of the automatic front doors.

"May I help you?" asked a young woman dressed in a navy suit and red-striped blouse.

She was seated at a massive desk adjacent to a tall counter. It all resembled a hotel, down to the piped in music, hushed conversations, the faint ding of an elevator and the opulent display of white roses with lilies in a large crystal vase on a center table.

"I'm here to visit Phillip Sutton."

The woman gave her a curious look, and tapped what must have been a call button, because within seconds another young woman, also dressed in a navy pantsuit but wearing a lime green blouse appeared. Her name badge read Melissa.

"I'll escort you to see Mr. Sutton," she said. "Please follow me."

Through double doors that opened onto a patio, Johanna could see a resident in a wheelchair looking out onto yet another water fountain. Nearby, two couples at a card table played an animated game of bridge. Melissa led Johanna past a general activities room where residents sat staring at a wide-screen television set to the tennis channel.

Melissa wasn't much of a talker and other than a cursory smile when Johanna commented on the well-planned residence, she said nothing. They went through another set of double doors which led to what appeared to be small cottages with individual pathways leading off from a meticulous and colorful groundcover expanse.

Walking up to the second cottage on the right, Melissa rang the doorbell.

The door was opened by a tall man wearing dark glasses.

"Good Morning, Melissa, can I assume this is Johanna Hudson?"

Phillip Sutton was a very handsome man. Even though it was clear Eloise got her coloring and exquisite features from her mother and grandmother, there was an essential something she had inherited from her grandfather. He wore his thick brown hair on the long side and showed a faint graying at the temples. A mischievous smile left the impression he could be a scamp.

"Mr. Sutton, thank you so very much for meeting with me," Johanna said, shaking his outstretched hand. "Please call me Johanna."

"Come in, come in, and call me Phil," he said. "Melissa, thank you for the escort. The kitchen already dropped off our lunch, so there's no need to check back."

Melissa nodded. "Okay, let the front desk know if you need anything. I'm on duty until six this evening."

If Melissa was curious about Phil Sutton's guest, she hid it well. After a quick nod to Johanna, she closed the door behind her.

They sat in a small living room area. It was an open space living room that led to an airy kitchen and dining room. A hallway to the left of the dining room likely led to the bedroom.

"I took the initiative and ordered lunch. I . . . I don't get many visitors and I thought I'd take advantage and make it an occasion," he said, a frown appeared on his forehead. "Did I overstep?"

"No, not at all," Johanna said, feeling sorry for a man who looked forward to a lunch with a perfect stranger. "Phil, how about I speak to why I'm here and then we can talk while we eat?"

He ran his hand over his balding head. "I know why you're here."

Johanna blinked. "You do?"

"The only person in my long past family who would care about my genealogy is my ex-wife. What's she trying to manipulate now? Lost treasure? Free toaster?"

Johanna put on a broad smile, glad he couldn't see the soundless chuckle.

"Oh, I made you laugh. You must have met the indomitable Olivia."

She realized he could see quite well without his sight. "Yes, I did meet your ex, but as I said on the phone, my visit relates to your daughter, Jeanette."

He sighed and looked past her. "A man has two daughters, both of them striking beauties. Both of them with good hearts and keen minds, and both die before their parents, both tragically." A tear rolled down his cheek. "It was almost more than I could bear."

His grief was palatable. Then he stiffened his back.

"What do you want?"

"Mr. Sutton, were you aware Jeanette had a daughter?"

"No," he shook his head. "No, I didn't know. Olivia and I separated not long after I walked Jeanette down the aisle to marry that Dawes fellow. Then we divorced about a year after. The girls drew back from both of us. About two years later, Olivia claimed she'd developed a stress related heart condition. I didn't want to put them in a position of choosing."

He stopped, sighed, and then continued. "No, that's a lie. I wanted my freedom from family—from Olivia, and the girls. I faded into the background and out of all their lives."

It seemed as if he had been saving up his thoughts and feelings for the first person who took the time to listen. Johanna was stunned as he poured out his life to her.

"But, I missed them—the girls, not my ex. Olivia tried to cut me off from my daughters, but they both stayed in touch. When Denise died, I thought I would never recover. Jeanette's marriage already had major cracks. They separated, got back together, then she ... she went to prison." He looked thoughtful. "So they had a baby?" He looked toward her waiting for her quiet "yes." "No surprise there. Yes, she always wanted a child, even if it came from that jerk she married. But Jeanette's child must be grown now. What's her name?"

"It's Eloise, but—"

He broke out into boisterous laughter.

"Good for her, good for Jeanette," he said chuckling. "*Eloise at the Plaza* was our story, Jeanette's and mine. Olivia hated our connection. My daughter would beg me to read it over and over, and then when the movie came out we—"

"Excuse me, Mr. Sutton, Phil, I'm so sorry to tell you this, but Eloise is dead. She was murdered two weeks ago."

It was as if a light had been switched off. Phil Sutton seemed to age before her eyes. His skin took on a gray tinge, and his jowls sagged.

"Tell me what I have missed," he said expressionless. "Tell me about ... Eloise."

He removed his dark glasses revealing vivid blue eyes, and clasped his hands in his lap.

"I'm sorry, but I only met her twice," Johanna said. "She was charming and quite beautiful. She ...."

Johanna took the next minutes to introduce this man to a granddaughter he would never know. As she spoke, Phil Sutton faced an open window looking out onto a small yard. The heady fragrance of lemons from a nearby tree drifted through a window. He listened without speaking, but, when Johanna recounted how she found Eloise's body, he flinched.

Her words came to an end. The silence that came upon them held them in place.

Phil spoke, "You met Ruby?"

"I've only seen a photograph," Johanna replied. "Like all the Sutton women, she's going to be a beauty. She has her mother, Eloise's and Jeanette's sea green eyes."

With that he broke into sobs.

She was at a loss, whether to speak or reach over and squeeze his shaking shoulders. Instead she did nothing and sat looking out onto the yard and waited. It wasn't long. Sutton wiped his eyes with the backs of his hands and put his dark glasses back on.

"I'm sorry for breaking down like that, but I was a lousy father," he said in a voice devoid of feeling. "I cheated on Olivia. Made promises to the girls I never kept. I . . . I was never there for them. I was too selfish." He stood holding onto the back of a chair, and looked down at Johanna as if he could see. "What do you want from me?"

She was ready.

"Do you remember anything, anything at all, that Jeanette could have said or implied about a man she was seeing when she and Dawes separated?"

He shook his head. "You're looking for Eloise's father?" He returned to his chair and sat. "Like I said, Olivia and I divorced after Jeanette got married. I'd been diagnosed with a form of optic atrophy for some time. Shortly before the wedding, it was clear I was losing my sight. Olivia was not made out to be a caregiver, so I was on my own, and had to make do. Jeanette stayed in touch—off and on, no thanks to me. But one time . . . one time, she called me—it was in 2000—the new century. She called for money, but she was going on and on about running in the Bay to Breakers, and how training for it made her feel like her old self. She said she had met a man who ran with Eloise's suite number. I remember her saying as if . . . as if she'd called me yesterday. She said it was a sign."

"What was the number?"

He smiled. "Why, Eloise's suite at the Plaza was '1832.'"

"No first or last name?"

He shook his head and put his hand to his forehead. "That was the last time we spoke. Oh, we would keep in touch with courtesy calls on her birthday or Father's Day, but when I think back that was the last decent call we had until the end."

"The end?"

"She called to tell me she was going back to Dawes. She needed to settle down." He gestured to Johanna. "Now, talking to you, I know she wanted a family for her baby. I guess the guy didn't want to marry her. Anyway, I acted like a fool and ranted, trying to get her to see that having no man at all in her life was better than Dawes. I said some terrible things, and she hung up on me. That was the last time we spoke."

There was a knock at the door, and Phil rose to answer.

"Would you like me to clear your dining trays, Mr. Sutton?" An older woman dressed in a navy blue jumper asked.

They had not touched the food.

"Yes, please." He stood aside.

Johanna gave a quick smile and a nod to the server, who deftly stacked the plates and trays and left as inconspicuously as she came.

Johanna stood and gathered her purse.

"Phil, I need to go," she said. "I didn't realize the hour. You have been so generous with your time and patience."

"It's I who want to thank you for the afternoon of memories," he said. "I don't get many visitors anymore. I don't want to see faces from my past. I . . . I suppose I'm a quasi-hermit now. When you said you knew about Jeanette, you brought her with you. For this past hour or so, I had her here. And now you tell me about Eloise and Ruby—Ruby, Jeanette's granddaughter, my great-granddaughter. I . . . I," his voice drifted.

"If I can, I will put you two in contact," Johanna said, patting his arm.

"That would be wonderful," he said. "I'm sorry I wasn't able to help you find Eloise's father."

"Oh, but maybe you did."

CHAPTER THIRTY-SIX

B ACK IN THE OFFICE, JOHANNA RUBBED HER EYES and stared at her computer monitor. She'd started searching for Eloise's father after leaving Phil Sutton. He'd given her the runner number, now if she could just trace it back. Her years as a genealogist had taught her one thing, there was always someone out there who kept records.

She was surprised to discover that The Bay to Breakers was a social salve to the devastating April 18, 1906 earthquake that rocked San Francisco. The subsequent fire and destruction were unimaginable. But San Franciscans, displaying their typical fortitude, began rebuilding the city and orchestrating events to lift civic morale. One of those events, the Cross City Race—now known as Bay to Breakers—was first held on January 1, 1912. Then there were 218 registrants. Johanna shook her head, last year she knew they had over 50,000 participants. She didn't want to count on the chance there was a list out there with runner numbers and names. It was too farfetched.

An hour and a half later she had a website: AthLinks. She let out a yelp that caused Ava to jump in her chair.

Ava grinned. "Okay, I'll bite. What'd you find?"

"I don't believe it." Johanna gave herself a hug. "A website with the names and bib numbers of every runner in the 2000 Bay to Breakers race."

"Hey, that is great," Ava said. "How many runners were there?"

"Almost fifty-two thousand."

This time, Johanna wasn't put off by the daunting task ahead. At least she knew that somewhere in the seemingly endless list of names, there was Eloise's father's identity. Due to the layout of the website, runners were sorted by finishing times. Bib numbers were shown beneath the runners' names along with their country identification. Johanna calculated she should be able to view eight hundred names in an hour. If that held up it would take her eight days to get through all the names. Seven days, if he didn't finish in the last batch of runners.

Arrgh!

"Johanna, I know you're hot on a trail, but don't forget you said you'd interview the Bakers. They live in Alameda," Ava called over from her cubicle. "I've taken the Pattons and the Finleys. It's your turn."

"I'm on it. I'm scheduled to meet them today at one o'clock," she said, wondering how she was going to fit in time for new clients with her Sutton research.

Ava must have been reading her thoughts.

"I'd take them on, but I'm up against a couple of promised deadlines," Ava said. "But I have an idea. Why don't you get Trinidad to help you search? She would feel much better if she was helping out, and we wouldn't have to see her hang-dog look every day."

"Ava, that's a great idea," Johanna said, thinking of all the benefits of having the participation of Ruby's greatest advocate. "I'll ask her to come by before she starts work. I'll let her know there's something she could do to help."

Of course, when Trinidad tapped on their door an hour later, Johanna was not surprised. The slightly out of breath woman, didn't want to wait to assist. She was wearing a bright turquoise-striped smock and matching pants, so startling even Ava had to blink.

"I here, Johanna, to help you and Ava," Trinidad said.

In no time, Trinidad setup a makeshift desk large enough for a laptop. She chose to sit in the corner next to one of the bookshelves where she could place a glass of water. Once Johanna had told her what was needed, she undertook her assignment.

An hour later, it was close to noon. Ava offered to get sandwiches. "I'm going to the post office, then to the library, and then back here."

Johanna gave a frustrated sigh and clicked off her monitor. "I better be on my way to see the Bakers. While the timing could be better, we need the clients," she said, packing up her tote. "Trinidad, I should be back in a couple of hours. We're not expecting any visitors, but could you answer the phone?"

"Yes, yes," the woman said not lifting her finger or her eyes from the screen of names.

Johanna was relieved the family chart requested by Claire Baker was straightforward. They were meeting at a Starbucks in downtown San Leandro.

"My mother's side of the family has been pretty good about keeping records on our ancestors," the woman said, "because they have great genes and live forever. My great grandmother is still alive at ninety-eight."

Claire Baker was in her forties, and Johanna agreed if she were an example of the aging gene, her mother's youth line was pretty strong. Solidly built with warm brown eyes, high cheek-bones, and thick brown hair worn in a low ponytail, the woman gave off an aura of health and well-being.

Johanna smiled. "Good genes go a long way, although sometimes what is getting passed down is more a tradition of a maintained lifestyle and values a family member inherits. Perhaps in your family it's a combination of both."

Claire nodded. "That's a good point. Anyway, that's my mother's side. I know little about my father."

"Did your mother trace any family history for his side?"

"I'm not sure. She refuses to talk about him. I lost my father when I was thirteen. He was . . . uh, well, he didn't die, he left us." Baker twisted the stem of her glass without looking up.

"Oh, I see," Johanna said, adding a note to her pad. "So you're looking to fill-in your chart from his side?"

Claire Baker took a sip of her coffee and put it down, once more avoiding Johanna's eyes. Seconds passed, and then she glanced up.

"I'm looking to find him."

Johanna stared at her for a moment. Was it something in the water? As of late, she appeared to be attracting clients who were looking for more than classic genealogy—requests for finding missing persons.

"You want me to find your father?"

"No, but do you do that, too?" Claire asked. "I would like you to find my nearest relatives so they can tell me where he is."

"That I can do," Johanna said with a smile. "We don't claim to locate missing persons; you'd do better with a private detective. However, you'd be surprised at the requests we get sometimes."

Johanna turned to a clean sheet of paper in her pad.

"Okay, now tell me what you know about your father. When is his birthday?"

SITTING IN HER CAR, JOHANNA WAITED in a short line of autos watching the lowering of the High Street suspension bridge that crossed the Oakland estuary from Alameda. She used the moments to go over her meeting with Claire Baker. In the years she'd been earning her living as a genealogist, it always amazed her that no request for a family tree was alike. Not only did the motivations vary widely but the life stories of those who came before held unique drama, romance, pathos, and the full range from joys to tribulations. Her gut told her it was a matter of time before she found Ruby's grandfather.

Pulling onto the freeway, Johanna glanced into her rearview mirror. She was being followed.

It was a dark sedan. The windows were tinted, but she wouldn't have been able to see inside anyway with the oncoming dusk. The car had been parked across the street from the Bakers; its gold-plate rimmed license plate holder had caught her eye.

Turning into the almost empty office parking lot, Johanna parked and reached for her phone. No need to give Ava a heads up, there were no lights on their floor at all. She debated whether to contact Quinn. But another look in her rear-view mirror showed the dark sedan was no longer there. It had been her imagination.

There was tapping on her drivers' side window and she jumped.

The first thing that caught her attention was the muzzle of a gun in one hand and Ava's scarf in the other. Both hands belonged to Therese Bertrand.

The woman was dressed in a hoodie that partially hid her face, but her voice was clear enough through the glass. "Get out of the car without trouble, or I will kill your friend," Her voice carried through the glass as she motioned with the gun.

Johanna opened the car door and stepped out as Bertrand moved back only enough to allow her to clear the door.

"Where's Ava?"

"You'll find out," Bertrand said, waving Johanna toward the building entrance. "She's in your office. I had to . . . let's say, show her the error of her ways."

To Johanna none of this made any sense. But she entered the building and elevator with Bertrand's gun in her ribs. She had to make sure Ava was okay.

"Let my partner go," Johanna pleaded. "She was attacked a couple of weeks ago, and she's not well."

"I know." Bertrand grinned. "I'm the one that paid the visit."

"You . . ." Johanna frowned, and then continued. "Of course, it was you. You never spoke. Ava would have recognized a woman's voice."

Bertrand shoved her down the hallway. The door to the office was ajar. She kicked it open with her foot and pushed Johanna forward.

Johanna bent to look around the cubicles. There was no Ava. Mixed feelings of relief and anger overtook her.

"You lied."

Bertrand shrugged. "A girl's gotta do what a girl's gotta do." She motioned for Johanna to sit. "Give me that picture."

"What picture?"

"Don't be cute." She pointed to the desk. "Get me those photos."

"Why are you so anxious to have Jeanette's pictures?"

Johanna slid to the floor, tucking her purse to the side. She sat against the cubicle wall, stretching her legs out in front of her.

"Get up," Bertrand said in an agitated voice, but she held the gun steady as she backed away from Johanna's legs. "That money should be mine, and I'll kill you before I let you ruin everything."

"Did you kill Eloise?"

"What?" Bertrand's face turned pale. "No, of course not. I didn't know who she was, let alone where she lived. I didn't know what had happened to her in that trailer park until you told me."

"How did you know she lived in a trailer park?"

"Remember, you told me."

"No, I didn't," Johanna said, shifting her shoulder to within an arm's reach of her purse on the floor next to her desk. "Did James Bryce offer to share a finder's fee with you?"

"I don't know a James Bryce. So, shut-up and get me those pictures."

"Or, maybe he tracked you down like I did, and wanted to know if Eloise could be Jeanette's daughter. He needed proof. Did he offer you money? That's why you wanted the pictures. Bryce gave you the address, and you found Eloise. We thought she was expecting a boyfriend, but it was you."

"Shut-up," Bertrand screamed.

Johanna gave a small smile. "You know you're going to have to kill me. I know it, and you know it. So, I have nothing to lose." She shifted her position. "Why did you have to murder her? You were never going to get any inheritance. You could never claim a close relationship—second cousin? Likely not. Or, did Bryce agree to split the money with you, if you came up with proof—the token."

"Stop talking, and give me those pictures," Bertrand yelled.

"Maybe you didn't mean to kill her," Johanna said. "Did you argue? Maybe Eloise was upset her family knew about her all those years, but abandoned her to a foster family. I can imagine she was upset that you finally showed up when you thought there was money to be had." Johanna spoke slowly, "She was angry, and then you discovered she was blind."

Bertrand stared at her mesmerized and wiped at her forehead with her free hand. Her voice lowered. "It was like Jeanette was right in front of me. They looked so much alike; her daughter took my breath away. But, yeah, she was angry, real angry. She jumped on me and barely missed scratching my eye out." She looked down at healing scratches still apparent on her arms. "You wouldn't know she was blind. She pushed me to the floor and then went right for a baseball bat."

"But Bryce needed pictures." Johanna sought her purse with her peripheral vision. If only she could reach her phone. She had to keep talking and make small body shifts toward her desk. "You knew Eloise looked like Jeanette's twin. He needed you to positively identify her. One of the pictures is of a little boy—maybe it was all Jeanette had of Eloise's father, a keepsake that only she would know the secret—the token."

"Stop talking."

Johanna ignored the command. "You know who fathered Eloise, don't you?"

Therese Bertrand's face was flushed and small beads of sweat appeared on her forehead. She looked around as if feeling the effects of claustrophobia—looking for air space. Johanna straightened her back and flexed her legs underneath her.

"Therese, this isn't going to work. I—"

Johanna's eyes sought a shadowy figure through the corridor window. She swallowed, and then continued with a raised voice.

"Those pictures you want must be important if you killed Eloise and intend to kill me to get them."

"It was an accident," Bertrand protested, her gun hand shaking.

Johanna caught her breath at the words. Then, the door burst open and Trinidad, wielding a mop handle, swung at Therese Bertrand's head. The contact made a loud crack. The handle broke in her hand, and Bertrand dropped her gun as she fell to the floor unconscious.

"I here," Trinidad called out.

Trinidad stood over the woman, her chest heaving. Johanna scrambled to her feet to stand next to her. She held Trinidad's shaking shoulders in a hug. They both stared for a moment as Therese Bertrand's blood seeped from beneath her head, but Johanna was relieved to see her fingers move.

"Thanks, ladies," a genial voice said from behind them. "You saved me an enormous amount of trouble."

The women whirled around to confront the voice coming from the door. Their eyes widened on James Bryce who was holding a gun pointed at them. He motioned with the firearm for them to move to the side. The women compiled. He bent down without taking his eyes off of them to check Bertrand's pulse.

"Still alive," he said. "Too bad. She's a real pain."

"What are you going to do?" Johanna asked in a wavering voice.

Her eyes searched for Bertrand's gun that had skidded when Trinidad hit her. She spotted it nearby under the leg of Ava's desk chair.

He gave her a questioning look. Placing his gun down on the counter, he slipped a phone out of his jacket pocket.

"What do you think? I'm calling the cops."

CHAPTER THIRTY-SEVEN

QUINN APPEARED MINUTES LATER. "I heard the call and recognized your address," he said.

The two women hugged each other with Bryce standing off in a corner allowing Quinn to have access to Bertrand. The paramedics arrived and examined Bertrand. They rapidly loaded her onto a gurney and hustled her out of the small office.

Johanna reached for Quinn and pointed to the retreating gurney. "She killed Eloise Manley," she said, trying to breathe evenly. "She confessed. Her name is Therese Bertrand."

They were interrupted by a burly looking uniformed officer who edged Quinn to the side.

"They said she suffered a concussion. They'll get her stable and take her to Hayward General."

"Follow behind them and stay with her," Quinn said. "We want to talk with her as soon as possible regarding the murder of Eloise Manley."

He turned to the two women. "Now, Mrs. Hudson and Miss Owens, can you tell me what went on tonight?"

"Wait." Trinidad raised her hand. "Mr. Detective, talk at me first. I go to my shift or I lose job," she pleaded.

Johanna said to Trinidad, "Don't you think you need to take some time at home? This has been pretty traumatic."

The woman shook her head. "No, Johanna, what is traumatic is when I not have money to pay rent." She gave her a smile. "Don't worry about me. I no work for two days."

"How about you answer a few questions now, Miss Owens and if we have more you can come in tomorrow?"

"That is good." Trinidad nodded.

Quinn's questions were brief, and Trinidad promised she would come in to sign her statement the next day.

Johanna stole a quick glance at Bryce, but he appeared to still be engaged in answering questions. Quinn was giving instructions to the officers, who were tagging and going over the room.

Trinidad readied to leave, then turned back to whisper to Johanna. "I almost not remember what I came to tell you. I finished numbers. Maybe I find him, Ellie's father. I put green paper where I think."

"Yes, that's good to know," she said, and gestured silence with her finger to her lips and a look to Bryce. "We'll talk tomorrow."

"Yes, yes," Trinidad said. She looked over her shoulder at the now crowded room and hurried out the door.

Quinn turned back to Johanna with a concerned smile. "Now, your turn, Mrs. Hudson. Can you take me through your version of what happened this evening?"

Johanna was only half-listening. Her eyes sought the stack of pages and the bright green post-it sticking out from its middle.

She hastily took him through the unfolding of events starting with Bertrand's attack and confession, ending with Bryce's arrival. Quinn scowled.

"An accident, maybe, but we'll find out." He peered into her eyes. "This Bryce guy, do you think he was in on it with her?"

"I don't know," she said. "If you had asked me yesterday I would have said he was the one who killed Eloise. He and Bertrand may be working together, but tonight he was the one who called the police."

She let her shoulders drop with an exhale.

"Hey, you should sit down," he said, leading her to a chair. "Do you think he was pretending to save you? I mean, he could see Bertrand was disabled, maybe he was covering his losses."

Johanna looked over her shoulder to see Bryce still in conversation with an officer. Bryce sensed her glance, and their eyes met. He turned away, and Johanna faced Quinn.

"I don't know," she said. "Maybe."

"Look, it's almost eight o'clock. Let me finish taking your statement while things are wrapping up here and you can come in and sign it tomorrow," Quinn said. "Will that work?"

She wanted them all gone, so anything that would speed things along would work fine.

Still, things did not move as fast as she would have liked, but within the hour, Quinn and his officers were ready to leave. Bryce had left fifteen minutes earlier with a thoughtful look at Johanna.

"One of my officers will take you home. Or they can follow you," Quinn offered.

Johanna looked around at the office once more in chaos. "Following me will be fine. I can drive myself." She went over to get the stack of papers on her desk, and smiled at Quinn. "This is a little homework to calm my nerves. It will put me to sleep."

"If you say so," he said. "How about you come to the station around one o'clock? That will give you some time to rest up, but not lose the details from tonight."

"Sounds like a plan."

CHAPTER THIRTY-EIGHT

H IS NAME WAS GRANT RAMSEY.
Trinidad had circled the bib number and placed the sticker next to his name. Sitting at her kitchen table, Johanna took a deep breath. At last, they knew the name of Jeanette's lover, Eloise's father and little Ruby's grandfather.

It was late, but even with the night's events, Johanna couldn't rest. She would sleep late in the morning then make the trip to the police station.

But for now, she would Google Ramsey.

He was celebrity enough to have a Wikipedia entry. It wasn't long, but it gave the highlights of his personal background and business acumen. She next ran a name profile, pulling up his company address and a phone number. Johanna leaned back in her chair, a large smile appearing on her face.

The search was over. She printed out the information and packed the papers into her tote. She'd contact Trinidad first thing in the morning and let her know they found their man.

Johanna started her shower and glanced in the mirror to see if she resembled the crazy woman, she felt like.

There was a noise. She slipped her phone in her pocket.

It sounded like someone trying to be silent. She peeked around the bathroom door.

A heavy hand smothered her scream.

Johanna forced herself to relax, allowing her body to go limp. She hoped he thought she had fainted.

He swore but didn't release his grip on her mouth.

She was being lugged down the hallway. Her limbs bumped against the legs of a side table. Her skin burned from being dragged over the carpet. She struggled not to pull his hand from her mouth. Maybe he would think she was still unconscious. But, she couldn't breathe. She grabbed at his hand.

They reached the bottom of the stairs.

"Good, you're awake. You better not yell, or I will hurt you. You hear?"

She froze, exhausted from the happenings of the last hours. Her nerves were frayed, but she knew that squeaky voice from somewhere, but where?

She nodded. He removed his hand.

"I won't open my eyes, and I didn't see you," she rushed. "Just go. Take my purse."

He gave a little laugh. "I'm no thief. I don't want your purse."

She noticed he stayed behind her out of sight.

Maybe he didn't want to kill her.

Johanna swallowed. "Then what *do* you want?"

"You tell me the dude's name and I won't have to hurt you."

She didn't believe him.

"I don't know his name, and I had a very difficult day," she said, with more bravado than she felt. "I just left the police. I'm tired and I'm going to bed. So . . . so we'll forget about all this and you leave."

She tried to twist her body, but it seemed like he had her in a hammer lock around her neck, and both her wrists were held by his one hand, like a large handcuff.

"Liar," he said. "I saw it all. I was at your office in the parking lot." He squeezed her neck. "You wouldn't stop looking. You just wouldn't stop."

He gripped her tighter. The heat from his breath covered her ears.

She remained silent and realized, if he felt he had to kill her, he didn't want to do it in her home.

"You come with me, and be quiet. In exchange, I'll leave the kid alone."

A chill ran along her arms. His promise to "leave the kid alone" left her cold and furious.

"I don't know what you're talking about. What kid?"

He snickered. "Don't bullshit me, lady—Eloise's kid. I followed you." He pulled her closer. "You're not going to win this one. You see, I have all the cards in my favor. Now, tell me."

He attempted to drag her by the neck, but again she forced herself to go limp.

"Wait," Johanna squeezed out the word in a rasp. She struggled to get one hand free, but he held it too tight. "Wait, I'll go with you without a fight, if you answer a few questions."

He laughed, it sounded like the bray of a donkey.

"This ain't TV, lady. I'm not going to give you my story, and then you stall around until the police bust in to save you."

Exactly, she thought, but why would they?

"Just two questions, Chad Thorne. You see, I know you," she squeezed out the words as his grip lessened a small amount. "I'm so tired. If you answer two questions, I will tell you what you want to know without making a scene."

He hesitated, and then stepped around to partially face her. He was near six feet tall, with dark hair and eyes. He had a craggy face with a ruddy complexion as if he worked outdoors; he was dressed in a dark navy running suit and shoes. He still gripped her by neck and hands, but she could speak without choking.

"Okay," he said, "but question and answer is over with two questions."

"I know you're Eloise's boyfriend but—"

"No, not her boyfriend, her husband."

CHAPTER THIRTY-NINE

JOHANNA'S MIND REELED WITH THE IMPLICATIONS and ultimate meaning of his words.

Eloise was married.

Assuming he wasn't lying, and her instincts told her it didn't make sense if he was—it was too easily disproved. But, what hadn't made sense was why he'd been following her—and Trinidad. Now it all clicked.

It seemed he was following the path of her thoughts.

"Yeah, we were married the day before she was killed," he said. "I cut it a little close. What a break, though, who could have thought she had a cousin, that Bertrand nut case?"

He shoved her to a stool next to the doorway where he lessened his grip on her throat but not her hands. He made her sit.

Johanna winced, remembering the beautiful, but sad Eloise, who just wanted a glimmer of joy from life.

"Eloise told you about the letter and the visit from Bryce," she said, not bothering to hide the disgust in her voice. "That's when you decided to marry her, and maybe put yourself in a position to lay claim to . . . to Ruby's money."

"Yep, you got it. You figured it all out. That makes Ruby my step-daughter, right?"

Good grief.

Johanna's mind raced with the consequences.

"So what are your questions?" he demanded. "Time to cough up his name."

"You were following me. How did you keep track?"

"I do contract work in digital sound. I watched you get in your car, and later I put a tracer on it," He spoke as if what he'd done was an achievement and not a crime. "Then after your office was broken into, I told the old lady cleaner who let me in, that I was with the phone company, and all I did was to put a mic device in your office."

So simple.

Her mind raced with who would be looking for her. She could think of no one.

"Okay, what's his name?" He tightened his hold on her neck. His breath warm and dank.

"I . . . I get one more question," she said with a rasp, trying to leverage her balance by shifting her shoulders.

"No more questions," he said, applying even more pressure to her neck. "I know you know who he is, don't you? Tell me, and I'll let you go."

Knowing that was not likely, she could barely nod, but managed a deep breath, and with a solid twist of her shoulder, she struck Thorne hard in the sternum with her elbow. The blow surprised him. He released his hand from around her neck, but he continued to grip her two hands. Johanna straightened her shoulders and braced her legs. Thorne attempted to recapture his control, but the break was all Johanna needed. She faced him and gave him a sharp knee to his groin.

Thorne groaned and doubled over as he slid to the floor, still holding onto one of her hands. He attempted to get to his feet but slipped to the floor again.

He seemed to deflate. Then, as if realizing his situation, his body tensed. His face turned an angry red, as he tried to pull himself up using Johanna as leverage.

She jerked her hand from his grip, and rubbing her neck, ran to the front door. With a glance back at the man struggling to stand, she sprinted down the hallway, yelling over her shoulder.

"I lied."

Johanna didn't go to her car. She didn't have the keys anyway. Instead she made sure Thorne wasn't close on her, ran and ducked behind the neighborhood park's playground furniture. She could see with the glow of streetlamps that he came out of the door and headed in the opposite direction. She knew soon he would give up and turn around, coming her way.

Her phone was still in her pocket, and she punched 9-1-1 and whispered to the operator.

She peeked out from behind the park slide and saw Thorne attempt to open her car door. Then, he walked with determination along the sidewalk, peering into neighbors' homes sheltered by gated fences. Soon he would find her. She tried to make herself small.

Sirens sounded in the distance. Thorne must have heard them, too. Giving one last vague look in her direction, he half-walked, half-ran into the darkness of a tree-lined side street.

Johanna slipped out of her temporary hiding place and tried to keep an eye on the retreating figure. She smiled. Two police cars cornered him without sirens and lights. They had him trapped.

CHAPTER FORTY

T HE NIGHT'S HAPPENINGS HAD TAKEN MORE OF A TOLL on Johanna than she'd grasped.

She sat in the police station with an officer's jacket over her shoulders. Therese Bertrand and Chad Thorne were now both in police custody. Johanna shivered and quiet tears wouldn't stop slipping down her cheeks. Quinn approached her. She looked up at him with a dejected smile.

He exaggerated shaking his head, and teased, "Even when I was a beat cop, I never had such an active night with the same victim as I have spent in the last twenty-four hours." He sat across from her. "Bertrand's attorney has already shown up. He's saying Manley was manslaughter, a misunderstanding, an accident."

Johanna crinkled her nose in disbelief.

Quinn continued, "Thorne confessed to attempted murder, but he's setting up for a mental incapacity plea. Doesn't matter, he'll be off the streets for a long time. They both will."

"If you need someone to attest to his state of mind, I'm your girl." Johanna stood, slipping the police jacket off her shoulders. Her legs felt weak. "And this time, I think I'll take you up on your offer to have someone drive me home."

CHAPTER FORTY-ONE

JOHANNA SLEPT IN. WHEN SHE LOOKED AT THE TIME, it was almost eleven o'clock. She rubbed her still aching neck. The red bruising she would cover with a high collar. The night before was fading into a forgettable nightmare.

She had two calls to make. She reached for her phone.

After being handed off from Grant Ramsey's secretary, who passed her to his assistant, Johanna tried to express the importance of her call without going into details.

Finally.

"Mr. Ramsey, thank you for speaking with me," Johanna said, hoping the nervousness she was feeling was not in her voice. "I'm assisting a young woman who may be—"

"So, you heard I was dying," he interrupted. "And now you're trying to get in on my money, too," His voice sounded like gravel, and his words were broken up with coughs. "How did you get this number, anyway?"

Ignoring his question, Johanna understood the assumption he was making. "Mr. Ramsey, I'm sorry to hear of your . . . your medical condition, but it's important we talk. I've met—"

He hung up.

Really.

Johanna didn't try again. She knew it would likely draw a repeat performance. She would move to Plan B—as soon as she had one. Instead, she placed her next call. It went a lot smoother. After minutes of summarizing the previous night's events, Johanna asked the pressing question.

"Nolan, how soon will it take to have the charges dropped against Trinidad?"

"If, I get going on the paperwork, by tomorrow, but I'm going to aim for today."

"Good," Johanna said. "I'll let her know, her nightmare is over."

She picked up her phone a third time.

"Quinn, I need a favor," she said. "And, before you read me the tax-payers' bill of rights, I think you owe me a favor for solving an active murder investigation."

"I'm not sure about that. What's the favor, Mrs. Hudson?"

"I need an address."

PACIFIC HEIGHTS IS SAN FRANCISCO'S MOST AFFLUENT and exclusive neighborhood, overseeing the Golden Gate Bridge, San Francisco Bay, the Palace of Fine Arts, and the Presidio. Among the conclave of mansions, Johanna remembered reading that a forty million dollar Edwardian mansion was listed as San Francisco's most expensive home. The Heights was where San Francisco's old money rubbed elbows with tech billionaires from Silicon Valley.

It was where Grant Ramsey lived.

Johanna took her time walking the small hill to lower Pacific Heights. She'd been lucky and found parking not too far away. She didn't want to arrive sweaty or looking more out of place than she already felt. She stopped in front of a large Victorian mansion encircled by an elaborate scrolled wrought iron fence. The house was a subdued gray with white trim. It had a modest but colorful front garden of impatiens and geraniums heavy with fragrance. There was a wide porch but she noted there was no seating for outdoor encounters with the neighbors.

She pushed the button on the small metal box secured to the gate. She raised her hand to push again when a woman's voice asked her business.

"I'm here to speak with Mr. Ramsey. My name is Johanna Hudson and I have a matter of some urgency to bring to his attention."

There was a long pause. "What is it about?" said the voice, lowered, not quite so strident.

She recognizes my name.

Johanna took a breath. "It's not something I would want to go into detail about out on the sidewalk. It's a very personal matter, and I don't feel comfortable talking with anyone besides Mr. Ramsey."

A bell buzzed, and the gate clicked open.

Johanna hurried up the walkway and reached the massive front door before it opened. In a moment, she was looking at a trim woman, her almost white hair was styled in a page boy. She wore black slacks with a silk pale pink over-blouse.

"I'm Grant's mother, Charlotte Ramsey," the woman said. "He's ill. You can tell me what you need him to know."

They stood on the porch facing one another. Johanna could tell from her demeanor that the odds of getting past Ramsey's mother were slim. She also had no doubt Charlotte Ramsey, with the help of James Bryce, had worked to keep Eloise's existence hidden from Grant Ramsey.

"Mrs. Ramsey, if I could see your son for no more than five minutes," Johanna said. "You can clock me."

"I have no intention of 'clocking you', Mrs. Hudson, because I have no intention of giving you any time with my son. Have your attorney write a letter and our attorney will respond."

"An attorney," Johanna said. "Why would I need an attorney? You don't know what I want to say."

The woman's face flushed red, and she moved to shut the door. Johanna jammed her foot inside to block its closure.

"How dare—"

"You have a darling great-granddaughter. She's five and she's beautiful," Johanna persisted. "Attorneys will cost a lot of money, and in the end; the result will be the same. There is a legitimate claim against your son's estate."

"Get off this property," Charlotte Ramsey called out.

Johanna stepped back in surprise, and when she did, Ramsey slammed the door.

Before leaving through the gate, Johanna turned back to the door. She knew she was being watched, and she knew Charlotte Ramsey would like nothing better than to call the police to have her removed or, better, arrested.

She made her way downhill to her car. There was a man leaning against it. She stopped a few feet away.

He was tall and dressed in a dark running suit and white Nikes. His hazel green eyes were in stark contrast to his dark hair starting to gray at the temples and he wore a salt-and-pepper beard which added to his already arresting presence. He was a very handsome older man.

"Who are you? What do you want?" she questioned.

"Don't worry," he said. "I saw you leaving the house, and something told me you were paying me a visit. I'm sorry about the way I treated you on the phone. But my mother has a tendency to monitor my calls."

His voice was deep and soothing. But then he broke into a coughing spasm.

Johanna came closer. "Are you all right? I have water in my car."

"Thank you, I'm battling COPD, and water sounds good right now."

Johanna opened her car door and reached in the back for the six-pack of bottled water she always kept with her. Chronic obstructive pulmonary disease could be deadly. She handed him a bottle, and opening it, he took a long swallow.

Johanna spoke first, "You're Grant Ramsey, aren't you?"

"That I am." He nodded. "And you are?"

"Johanna Hudson," she replied. "I tried calling you yesterday. I'm a genealogist. I do family ancestry charts, and I wanted to speak with you about Jeanette Sutton."

"Jeanette . . . ."

His jovial smile evaporated leaving behind a pained look and another expression Johanna couldn't put her finger on.

"Why don't we walk over to Lafayette Park?" he said. "It's a couple of blocks away. We can find a bench and talk."

Lafayette Park nestled on a nearby hill with open and treed green spaces. It was a picnickers-and-puppies haven, but for now there were just a few people walking dogs as they jogged. Ramsey pointed to an empty bench not far from the tennis courts. They sat at either end.

Johanna cleared her throat. "Mr. Ramsey, I came to see you about Jeanette Sutton. I'm sure you know what happened to her. She—"

"Yes, I know she went to prison." He waved his hand with dismissiveness. "She murdered her husband. My mother showed me the news article. Jeanette and I had something special, something I've never been able to find again." He gave Johanna a small smile. "And, believe me I've tried. But what about Jeanette brings you to me now? She died in prison."

There was no easy way to say it.

"Jeanette had a daughter, your daughter."

His frown deepened, and then he tilted his head as if his hearing was failing him. He stood, and without speaking, walked toward a grove of trees. She could hear him coughing—or was it sobs? Johanna leaned back on the bench and stared out onto a small pond. The last rains had created a water retreat for three ducks that seemed comfortable putting on a show for the lady on the bench. After a while, Ramsey returned and sat next to her. He appeared to have aged.

"Mr. Ramsey," Johanna said, reaching into her purse. "Do you recognize this picture?" She lifted out a photo.

He squinted and then smiled, nodding his head. "That's me when I was twelve," he said in his deep voice. "I loved Jeanette more than life itself. I gave this to her on our last night together as a token. She told me she was going back to her husband. She wanted something to remember me by, but nothing that would make him suspicious." He handed the photo back.

"Ah," said Johanna, the final puzzle piece snapping in place. She returned the photo and 'token' to her purse.

"I was ready to leave my wife for her, and Jeanette knew it. She loved me, too." His words wavered, and he took a swallow of water. "I didn't know how much until now. Where is my daughter?"

Johanna hesitated, and then said, "I'm so very sorry to tell you your daughter, Eloise Manley was . . . was killed three weeks ago. She's—"

"What!"

"Please let me explain, and it will help you to understand why I'm here."

It took Johanna almost an hour to recount the stories of the two women connected to this man's life. His eyes glistened when Johanna told him of Eloise's foster family and her blindness. He put his head in his hands when she told him how Eloise died, and about Therese Bertrand's admission of guilt.

She stopped speaking and waited for him to absorb her words. He looked up at her.

"Did you find Ruby?"

Johanna smiled and nodded. "Yes, I—"

A voice calling for Mr. Ramsey interrupted her. A young man hurried in their direction.

"Mr. Ramsey, your mother is very upset," he yelled. "She sent me to find you." He caught up to them, casting a curious look at Johanna. "I can walk home with you."

"Son, I'm old enough to walk myself home," Ramsey said. "Tell my mother I'll be there as soon as I can."

"Mr. Ramsey, she said to tell you if you don't come with me, she will go to the police and tell them you are missing, and—"

"All right, all right, enough," Grant Ramsey snapped. He began a spasm of coughing and rose from his seat. "Go back to the house. Tell her I'm on my way."

The young man hesitated, looking unsure of his survival if he returned without Ramsey.

"You'll come right now?"

"I'm right behind you. I want to say a few words to this young woman as I walk back."

"Mr. Ramsey, please, I need to have you come with me. Your mother—"

Johanna held up her hand. "Mr. Ramsey, why don't you go home and allay your mother's fears? I can return tomorrow, and we can continue our talk." She picked up her tote and grinned. "You may have to let me in, but I'll return."

"No," he said, shaking his head. "I've been manipulated enough. I will come to you. Give me your business card."

She handed him one from her wallet.

"Here's my card," she said, "but recently our office has gone through multiple unplanned renovations. Could we meet at a restaurant?"

JOANNA RETURNED TO THE OFFICE. Ava was saying goodnight to Trinidad, and the workplace was once more on its way back to normalcy.

Since it was Saturday, Trinidad was dressed in white pants and an indigo blue smock. It was one of her more conservative looks.

"I come to help," she said, stacking books on the shelf. "Ava here by herself. Maybe you help. She go to a meeting."

Ava smiled. "I'm signing a new client, making this a record month. Our name has been in the papers, and I guess publicity is publicity."

Ava still wore a tidy bandage on her temple, but she looked like her old self.

Johanna gave each a hug and pointed to her phone.

"I've got to make a call," she mouthed. "You may want to hear this."

They both looked at her with expectant curiosity.

Candace Michaels picked up the phone on the first ring.

"When I saw your number, I knew you must have something," Candace said. "Did you find him?"

"I did," Johanna said. "I found Ruby's grandfather."

The squeal from the two women next to her drowned out Candace's response.

EPILOGUE

I.

THE PAST WEEK HAD BEEN ONE OF THE MOST roller-coaster in Johanna's life. It began with picking up Candace and Ruby to meet her grandfather, Grant Ramsey. Trinidad had accompanied them. Johanna still choked up, remembering. They stood on the sidewalk outside the car, watching the little girl skip down the walkway, and Trinidad gasped.

"It Ellie," Trinidad whispered. "Ruby is like Ellie." Her tears made a slim trail down her cheeks, but she stifled them. She didn't want to scare the little girl.

After the introductions, Trinidad had held Ruby to her chest for some time without speaking. Johanna reached and tapped Trinidad on her arm.

"I sorry, little one," Trinidad said, releasing Ruby to Candace, and dabbing at her eyes.

"Why are you crying, Trinidad?" Ruby asked. "Are you going to see your grandfather, too?"

"Me?" Trinidad took a breath and eased out a smile. "No, my grandfather is away. I cry because I happy to see you."

The little girl giggled. "But you don't know me."

"Ah, but I do, little one," she said. "I know you, here." Trinidad pointed to her heart.

"Come on," Johanna said, looking at the time. "We need to get going, and I'm going to have to stop to get a box of tissue."

Grant Ramsey's introduction to Ruby was no less dramatic and poignant.

They gathered in the den of the Ramsey mansion. The curtains had been pulled back and a table of finger foods had been set up in front of the fireplace. Johanna looked on in concern as the elder man and the little girl stared at each other in the first minutes of their meeting. Candace walked her daughter forward and stood behind her. Ruby reached out to shake his hand.

"How do you do, Granddad?" she said in a coached voice.

Bending down, Grant took her small hand in his large one. "I'm doing quite well right now," he said, his eyes brimming with tears. "And you, how are you doing?"

"Fine, thank you," she said primly. Then she leaned forward with her hand covering her mouth and whispered in his ear. "But why is everybody crying? This is a happy day."

II.

Two days later, little Ruby held the hand of her great-grandfather. Phillip Sutton, wearing his dark glasses, lightly touched her face, and Ruby didn't flinch or grimace. Trinidad and Candace Michaels looked on. They were in the facility's living room; a small fireplace held an artificial flame.

"Excuse me," Ruby said to Sutton. "My mommy told me I am going to meet a lot of people who knew me when I was little." She brushed at the pleat in her plaid skirt. "I'm five now so I'll remember you. You have a dimple in your chin just like me."

Phillip Sutton smiled and placed his hand on her head and let his fingers trail her long curls. "I would very much like to think that you'll remember me." He squinted, as if seeing. "I can tell you look like your grandmother, Jeanette, when she was your age."

"Really?" Ruby bubbled. "Am I going to meet her, too?"

Candace moved to put her hand on her adopted daughter's shoulder.

"It's all right." Phillip held up his own hand. "No, no, Jeanette is gone. One day you'll hear the whole story, but I know she would want you to remember her as well."

"Another one to remember." Ruby pursed her lips and then smiled. "I know, I'll make a list."

The laughter was unanimous.

III.

A week later, Johanna looked on as if from a distance, instead of from the head of the table in Dean Cameron's law office. It was the only space big enough to hold, as he put it, all interested parties.

And they were all there—Charlotte Ramsey with her attorney, Grant Ramsey, Ava, who had come for moral support, Johanna and Candace Michaels who entered with Ruby after waiting in the lobby.

They'd been there for about an hour. Charlotte Ramsey's attorney had cited every reason why Ruby was a "pretender" as a claimant, and then when it was clear there was no argument from Ruby's representatives or Grant Ramsey to Ruby undergoing DNA testing, he punted.

"Mrs. Ramsey is a widow, and would like some assurances she will be able to maintain the lifestyle she's come to enjoy while living with her son. And, she incurred quite a bit of expense retaining Mr. Bryce —"

"This is not a settlement meeting," Dean Cameron said. "We are here to reach agreement that Miss Ruby Michaels is the granddaughter of Grant Ramsey and therefore a claimant to his estate." He turned to Ramsey.

"There is no doubt in my mind," Ramsey said. "This meeting is to satisfy my mother. I will meet later with my attorneys." He turned to Charlotte Ramsey. "And with your lawyers, Mother, to delineate the details."

He looked to Candace Michaels who had taken one of the empty seats at the end of the table.

"Perhaps you would allow Ruby to visit for a short time," he said, his eyes brimming with near tears. "I'd like to get to know her before—"

He broke into a fit of coughing. Ruby, who went to stand next to him, looked to her mother in concern. Dean retrieved a glass of water, and Ramsey drank deeply. Ruby put her hand on his shoulder and gave him light pats.

"Don't worry Granddad, I'll come and visit. I'll add you to my remember list."

IV.

AFTER SAYING GOODBYES OVER AND OVER, Johanna and Ava traveled, smiling all the way, back to their office where Trinidad waited. Within minutes, all three had their feet up on the desks in the office, as they talked over recent events.

Their property manager hadn't appreciated the building's notoriety of the past days, and told Trinidad she would have to look elsewhere for employment.

"It okay, ladies," Trinidad said. "I no like boss anyway. My cousin say okay I work for him."

"I didn't know you had family in the area," Ava said.

"He not in area. He in Fresno, and I move." She gave a weak smile. "But it okay now. Ellie is gone, and you find Ruby."

Johanna caught the glance from her partner.

"It's too bad Ellie didn't get a chance to meet her father, or her daughter, Ruby," Ava said.

"Yes, but I know Ellie is happy," Trinidad said with a calmness. "I sad in heart she not here, but so happy to see Ruby. It all weighs same at end."

Johanna and Ava exchanged looks.

"Do you mean, balances out?" Ava offered.

"Yes, yes," Trinidad nodded. "My feelings are balanced."

Today she was wearing a yellow sleeveless dress with tiny bright red butterflies. Johanna absently wondered where the woman bought her clothes.

"Trinidad, Ava and I have an idea," Johanna said, and Ava, knowing where she was headed, nodded concurrence. "We would like to offer you a position as a receptionist in our office. Would you consider working for us? It's clear we need someone to cover the office and take messages."

Trinidad's face lit up.

"Yes, yes, Johanna and Ava," she said, beaming. "I would very much like. I would be even more balanced."

THE END

R. FRANKLIN JAMES GREW UP IN THE SAN FRANCISCO BAY AREA, graduated from UC Berkeley, and flourished in a career of public policy and political advocacy. In 2013, the first book in her five- star Hollis Morgan Mystery Series, The Fallen Angels Book Club, was published by Camel Press. Her first book in the Remy Loh Bishop series, The Appraiser was published in 2019. The Inheritance, the first book in her Johanna Hudson series will be released in November 2020. James resides in northern California with her husband.